CARNIVAL

Also by Robert Antoni

Divina Trace
Blessed Is the Fruit
My Grandmother's Erotic Folktales

CARNIVAL

ROBERT ANTONI

BLACK CAT

New York

a paperback original imprint of Grove/Atlantic, Inc.

FIRST EDITION

Printed in the United States of America
Published simultaneously in Canada

Library of Congress Cataloging-in-Publication Data

Antoni, Robert, 1958–
Carnival / Robert Antoni.
p. cm.
ISBN 0-8021-7005-6
1. Triangles (Interpersonal relations)—Fiction.   2. Greenwich Village
(New York, N.Y.)—Fiction.   3. Trinidadians—United States—Fiction.
4. Trinidad and Tobago—Fiction.   5. Race relations—Fiction.   6. Rain
forests—Fiction.   7. Novelists—Fiction.   8. Carnival—Fiction.   I. Title.
PS3551.N77C37 2005
813'.6—dc22   2004054136

Black Cat
a paperback original imprint of Grove/Atlantic, Inc.
841 Broadway
New York, NY 10003

05 06 07 08 09   10 9 8 7 6 5 4 3 2 1

for Mums & Pops

and for Gabriel & Marina,
stars of my constellation

"We are all a lost tribe."

—Peter Minshall to masplayers

I

1

Laurence de Boissière was once the tennis champion of Oxford. Don't think I'm too highly impressed by that as a tennis title, but it meant something to Laurence. He loved tennis, though he did not go to Oxford to play it. In fact, until he arrived there, it had not even occurred to him that they would have a team. But in a matter of days he had all those English boys running redfaced around the court. This gave him an odd sense of inner satisfaction, which he found he grew to like, although, being extremely well-mannered, and still a little shy, he kept it hidden. And in any case for Laurence the sport was little more than a healthful distraction from his studies. He was really an excellent tennis player. More than that, he was a natural. Beautiful to watch on the court. So talented, the story goes, that his coach at Oxford promptly advised him to give up his degree and go to the States to train as a professional. This old coach had been around, he knew what he was talking about. He had connections, vision. He was an American himself, from a place called Carmel, California, where such things were imaginable. But only the sound of the name, *Carmel,* was enough to convince us. Laurence, the coach said, would be a first, and he was right. Not only would he have been the first West Indian to dream of playing on the professional tennis circuit, something which may not have occurred to the coach, in those days he would have been one of the first black men. He would have been famous. He would have been endorsing brand-name sneakers and kids' cereal. He would have made some serious money.

A few years later Laurence did come to the States, but not as a tennis player. He came as a poet. People at home, still following Laurence's story—still swooning a little over the name of a place that sounded like it wanted to be a chewy candy, a place that in their own minds already glittered like Hollywood—said the boy was crazy. "Mad like toro," they said, and it was a real shame for the rest of us, but he'd made an admirable decision. A few of us said it was the only choice that Laurence could have made. It did not prevent his climb to fame and fortune, either. It simply shifted the parameters. Soft-toned it some. I was there to watch it happen. At least the second trajectory. As a matter of fact, when he arrived in Manhattan—not fresh out of Oxford, but from London's West End where, in addition to being a prize-winning poet with three books already published, he'd also established himself as a successful playwright—though we hadn't heard from each other in a full ten years, I was the first person Laurence called. He made a point of telling me so himself. And truth is, I was flattered.

There are two secondary boys' schools at home, one Anglican and government run, the other by the Jesuits, and Laurence and I went together to the Roman Catholic college. But we'd been friends long before then. Because I happened to be one of a dozen spoiled white children literally playing on the precious clay courts back behind the British Club, on the Saturday morning Laurence made his appearance, causing a bigger commesse than he did later at Oxford. A lanky and very shy little Laventille boy holding the cheapest kind of wooden drugstore racket that looked like it had been strung with fishing-twine, wearing new and unmarked crepe-soled washykongs, baggy shorts and a stiff-collared shirt his mother had obviously sewn out herself from 12¢ cotton. A lanky and very shy yet willful little Laventille boy who, despite any auspices of his French-Creole surname, could never have made it past the club's front door.

Ann-Marie, my freckled, carrot-headed cousin, steupsed out loud. She sucked her teeth. Stomped off the court, her ribboned braids flying, the Pied Piper leading the rest of the spoiled little white children behind her. Laurence and I stood at opposite ends of the court littered by bright yellow balls. We stared at each other over the net. And I can tell you that from that moment, even at nine years of age, even before I could have possibly articulated it for myself, I knew that I adored and despised this boy even as much as I did myself.

I dug a ball out of my pocket. Bounced it with its hollow thud and the puff of detonated dust on the clay surface. Lobbed it over at him.

He swung, holding his racket by the middle of the handle, spinning halfway around, missing it altogether. Eventually he managed to swat one into the net. Then to get it over onto my side.

By now the other children had returned, accompanied by several adults, my auntie, Ann-Marie's mother, among them. It was ten in the morning and the adults, also wearing their tennis costumes, were drinking rum-cocktails out of little glasses. Sam, the club's owner, held the beaded silver shaker rattling with ice.

Suddenly my throat ached, like I'd been shouting. The sun was beating down on my head, sweat stinging my eyes. The damp clay smelled like vegetable rot.

We were a spectacle too amusing to stop. The children giggled, my auntie actually guffawed. Laurence and I kept on. Now I missed the ball as often as he did. My racket felt so heavy I could hardly hold it up. My flesh like it was melting off me, sliding from my bones in great, dripping shingles. On the other side of the net, Laurence's face appeared to have been pounded out of that same wrought-iron as the gate behind him.

So it was ironic, to say the least, that when he called to tell me he'd reserved a court for us at Hudson River Park—though our tennis date was still another two weeks off, though for years now I'd sworn myself off tennis as an exceptionally bourgeois, white people's sport—I went out immediately and bought the cheapest wooden racket strung with fishing-twine Walgreens had on offer. I was dead broke.

"Compère," I'd said into the receiver, surprised, genuinely excited to hear his voice. "Me ain't hit a ball since Bazil wearing shortpants!"

I'd felt ridiculous, embarrassed. Two minutes talking on the phone, and already I sounded like I'd never left. Like a country-bookie. Not Laurence: now he spoke like a proper Englishman.

"Fair enough," he'd told me. "Neither have I."

It was one of those perfect Saturday mornings—streetside gypsy flower vendors arranging their bunches in white plastic buckets in the bright sun, the halal butcher in his crimson turban just rolling up his galvanized curtain, sleepy bent-over Asians in front of the markets laying out vegetables on beds of crushed ice—one of those perfect, sunny, early summer mornings, when you knew you'd rather be scrunting the most precarious kind of existence in this place, than live like a prince anywhere else on earth.

All I'd found for a tennis outfit was a pair of cutoff Levis and a Despers T-shirt. But fifteen minutes later I remembered that Desperadoes was the Laventille steelband, and I decided Laurence might take it the wrong way. So waiting for the light at the corner of Broadway and West Houston I balanced my racket for a second on the rounded top of a mailbox, pulled the T-shirt up over my head and put it back on inside-out. The rubber soles of my sockless red hightops were so thin I could feel the cracks in the sidewalks. Count the glass buttons of the basement gratings beneath my feet.

There was still a trace of shyness in Laurence's smile. I wasn't sure if his polo shirt had the creases from being packed in his suitcase, or if it had actually been pressed. But hugging him I smelled the burnt-steam smell of the drycleaners' irons. Mingling with aftershave, or more likely French cologne. We held each other for a second, and I looked over his shoulder, down at the fuzzy little balls attached to his socks hanging over his heels. He looked like he'd put on a few pounds, but I could feel the hard muscles running across his back. He was still in excellent shape. The only exercise I'd done in as long as I could remember was to climb the six flights of stairs to my apartment for which, for the first time, I whispered a prayer of thanksgiving.

Laurence bent over and bounced the ball a few times, quickly, with his left hand, and I took a deep breath. Prepared myself for a royal cut-tail.

But he paused before the service.

"William," he said, "you got your Despers jersey on wrong-side-out."

I exhaled slowly. Relaxed my grip on the racket.

"Didn't want you to take it the wrong way."

"Come again?"

"I was afraid you'd feel insulted."

"Oh-ho," he said.

And with those two syllables—not just the syllables themselves but the way he pronounced them, pounding hard on the second one with the blast of air chopped off and squeezed into a high-pitched singsong—with those two syllables I felt a sudden surge of warmth inside my chest. For a second we were back on the damp clay court back behind the British Club. Though I wasn't sure if the emotion I was feeling was thrill, or dread.

Laurence bent over and bounced the ball a few more times. Then paused again.

"Compère," he said, his pursed lips loosening into a smile. "You got that one wrong-side-out, too."

2

The story we all heard was that after Oxford he'd fallen in with theater people. In the west end of London, but more precisely in the largely West Indian area of Notting Hill. He wrote a play in verse inspired by CLR James's book of the Haitian revolt, in which Toussaint L'Ouverture daubs his face with the blood of his former French master, whom he had also defended fiercely and loved like a father. The play was performed in the local theater and the *Times Sunday Supplement* named Laurence London's new rising playwright, though until that moment he'd thought of himself exclusively as a poet. A very beautiful and elegant Senegalese actress played the part of L'Ouverture's muse, taunting him in the critical scene from the heights of a crystal chandelier as L'Ouverture knelt, his reddened face shining, gazing up at her from below, and soon after the play's run was concluded we heard she married Laurence. The marriage created quite a stir in London circles, and it was even reported about in the tabloids, not because of Laurence's rising fame, but because his new wife was a model and a celebrity already famous in her own right. Her face had even appeared on the covers of several fashion magazines, including *Elle* and French *Vogue*. But as Laurence's wife she gave up her modeling career, not that she could have had many more years of it left, anyway, and both of them dedicated themselves to the theater, and within three years they had two sons.

All of this was even bigger news for us at home, as you can well imagine, and the magazines were fished out of someplace and handed around, already tattered with the covers creased up, and once again people spoke of Laurence's accomplishments with an admiration that spilled over into envy and even awe. There were two factors, however, that stuck at the back of everybody's mind, though nobody mentioned either of them aloud. These two things jarred, and they tainted Laurence's latest accomplishment in the marriage. Because although his wife had arrived in Paris an infant in her mother's arms, and her family migrated to London only a year later, where she'd been brought up and educated so that by now of course she was a perfect Englishwoman herself, the part of the story none of us could get beyond was the part about her African origins. Somehow it felt like a regression. That, and the fact that her elegant face on the covers appeared even darker than Laurence's. So no one was surprised to hear, after three years, that he had left her.

We were looking for a place to have a couple of cold beers and cool down after the tennis. Not so easy to find at ten on a Saturday morning, even in this alcoholic, insomniac city, since all the late-night bars had already shut up tight, and the chichi cafés wouldn't be opening for lunch for another hour. But we were in no hurry. Lazying our way along. Savoring a moment of quiet. Only the tight squeak of Laurence's tennis shoes against the sidewalk, flop of my own hightops. I dumped my ruined drugstore racket in the first trashcan. Laurence carried his zipped into the outside of his white leather bag, Wilson stamped in red across the pill-shaped pouch. The heat had just started rising in waves off the fresh asphalt patches along an almost empty West Side Highway. River dancing behind it, sumptuous, blue blue blue.

We cut across to Hudson St and followed it for a few blocks until it split into Bleecker, into the heart of the West Village. At one point we passed an empty lot completely paved over with pieces of jagged glass-bottle—like the choice shards we used to tie to the tails of our hexagonal, warring madbull-kites—in the hard white sun the parking lot glittered like a field of diamonds.

The tennis had started off slowly, very slowly, until Laurence came up with the brilliant idea that we swap rackets. Of course, he still had a clear advantage. But at least now I had a chance of returning the ball. Answering his serves. And after a while we even managed to get a few decent volleys going. After a while, when I'd worked up a decent sweat, I was pleased to discover that not only did a lot of it come back from oblivion, I was thoroughly enjoying myself. Sadly, by the end of the first hour, Laurence had popped three fishing-twine strands of the drugstore racket. Then, with an overambitious, grunting, two-handed backhand, the ball passed right through the racket.

Laurence held it up to the sun, incredulous, examining the strings. Broken ones poking out like guitar wires.

"The treacherous instrument is in thy hand," he said. "Unbated and envenomed."

"My line you thiefed!"

We'd performed it together in Father O'Connor's sixth-form special English—me playing Laertes to his Hamlet—but at that moment I refused to be distracted. The score was love-30, best I'd done all morning, though admittedly, the last point was gained on the pass-through backhand.

"Service," I said.

"Always thought it was a metaphor for your namesake's own uncapped ballpoint. Think about it, William."

"Stop dodging, and serve."

"Or Hamlet's own drawn, uncircumcised prick—our boy *had* been focking his bro's crazy sister."

"Serve, nuh!"

"Focked his mother too, of course. But not so well as his uncle. Why else should she protest, 'thou'rt fat and scant of breath'?"

"Listen—"

"And since sex is the twin sister of death, then metaphorically at least he focked the same uncle too; focked his bro; focked his bro's crazy sister's father. Let me tell you, plenty poison in our boy's envenomed point. Plenty work."

I let him enjoy himself.

"Only family he couldn't fock was his own father."

"Or out-fock."

"Very nice! Question is, who was more Freudian, Hamlet or Shakespeare himself?"

He dropped the racket and turned to face me.

"Or to put it more pertinently, who of the three was most West Indian?"

"Fine," I said, "we'll call this last game a draw."

"Agreed. And take back this ruined instrument. It's bent and busted. It don't work."

"Careful. That's hitting below the belt."

"Allow me to make it up with a cold one. Must be an open tavern someplace in stinking Denmark."

3

We found one around the corner from Sheridan Square, Bar None. Like a dark dank cave, lit by its yellow-blinking jukebox, smelling of sweat and stale cigarettes. We bummed a couple from the bartender and he reached over the zinc counter to light them for us. Jamaican according to his accent—neat braids with white beads at the ends that clicked together every time he moved his head—we asked for Red Stripes in his honor. Turned out he was an actor, or budding actor, he even knew of Laurence's plays, also his poetry. New York is the city of coincidences, after a while you just take it for granted. His story was he'd left Kingston as a boy, grown up in west London, last six months spent here in the city, taking acting classes and tending bar. Another one of us, I thought. Francis explained that so far he'd only managed to land a couple of TV commercials, minor part in a soap, B-movie—"You do the celluloid ting to make some bread"—but his first love was treading the boards. He tried to disguise it, but it was also obvious he was enamored with Laurence. At first sight. Laurence didn't seem bothered, either, which surprised me. He seemed to enjoy it.

We bummed a couple more cigarettes and Francis opened a couple more ice-cold Red Stripes, we drank them out of the bottles, then he insisted on pouring us each a shot of Mount Gay. Laurence went so far as to make a joke out of the name, map of Barbados on the label—an erect penis—which neither Francis nor I had noticed before. And even I had to laugh. Laurence was in good form. We insisted Francis drink the shot with us, he was about to close up anyway, then he poured all three of us another, then one more for the road, and then he refused to let us pay, for any of it.

We knocked fists with Francis and stumbled out into the sun again. Which hit me in the face like a lightning-bolt, sidewalk swimming beneath me.

I had to stop for a second and shut my eyes.

"I'm blind," I said, "take my arm."

"Not in this neighborhood."

"Then I'm going to lie down right here in this rocking pirogue and have a sleep."

"Seasick?"

"Bit queasy."

"Out of shape my friend."

"Out of sorts," I said. "Out of my league. Out of my focking mind—you realize it's not even noon?"

"Buck up, compère!"

He put his arm around my shoulders, holding his tennis bag in the other hand, leading me along the sidewalk.

"Let the neighbors peg us for a couple of bullers. Me ain't bothered."

"A-tall," I said.

It was an enjoyable feeling, the weight of his arm across my shoulders. Gesture of it.

"Where we headed?" I asked. "Anyplace in particular?"

"Didn't I say? Been given strict instructions to meet the missus and her posse. One of those shameless, imitation-French dives in SoHo—you know, the brunch business? Furthermore, I've told her the two of us are liming partners from day one, and she's keen to meet you. Made me promise to drag you along."

This hit me like another lightning-bolt. I was happy Laurence was holding me up. Though my first thought was my wallet, and the fact that all it contained was a single five dollar bill. I didn't want to have to ask him to buy me lunch. Yet I allowed Laurence to continue steering me down Seventh Ave without protest. This was news to me that he hadn't broken up with his first wife after all, or they'd gotten back together, and suddenly I was consumed by a gossipmonger's curiosity to meet the exquisite actress and former fashion model and, I assumed, their two young sons. Already I anticipated a good mauvilang when I got on the phone with my friends Shay-lee and Oony.

I have the dangerous habit of inventing scenes before I get to them—because not only do I usually get them wrong, inevitably I wind up putting a loud goatmouth on myself in the process—but this was one scene I couldn't keep from conjuring up. It belonged in SoHo: Laurence's wife looking tall and slender and appropriately *Vogue* in her boldly colored dashiki and head-tie; boys wearing matching sailorsuits, navy bandannas knotted around their necks, heads shaved like their father's beneath the cute little caps; and maybe their posse would include a spinster nurse brought back from the Mothercountry—or maybe she'd be a young, chinless au pair—but whoever the help was she was sure to be very proper, and perfectly English, and as white-skinned as Laurence's polo shirt.

Suddenly we were standing at the corner of Spring and West Broadway, and Laurence dropped his arm from my shoulders so that I could follow him between the bumpers of two parked cars. Over to a place called Café de Versailles across the street. He stopped at a crowded sidewalk table beneath the awning, but the people sitting around it were so unlike the ones I'd envisioned, that I continued into the café without him. The fact that I'd left Laurence outside only registered a second later, and that discovery was accompanied by another dizzying rush of alcohol, so just about all I could manage gracefully was to stumble a few steps more into the restroom.

I took a long pee. Suddenly caught up in a struggle between my aim and my balance as I perched on those two protruding footstands —instead of a proper toilet they'd gone so far as to import one of those porcelain plates with the hole in the middle—and let me assure you it smelled authentic too. I got down relieved in more ways than one. Splashed cold water on my face, reversed the T-shirt again, straightened myself in the mirror.

Laurence was still standing when I got back to the table, still holding his bag.

"Didn't I say my friend arrived with me? Didn't I tell you he was here at my side a moment ago?"

He put his arm around my shoulders again. Looked into my face.

"Rescue me, William. These scoundrels don't believe we've spent a strenuous morning on the courts. They accuse us of actual carousing. Consuming alcoholic drink."

"I deny it unequibbocally," I said—in truth a slur and not a joke at all—but it came off as one, good enough to make everybody laugh.

I had no idea who these people could be. The woman sitting at the table, tall and slim and attractive enough, was not the covergirl-actress of Senegalese origin. Blond and in every way fair, striking gray eyes, even behind the horn-rimmed frames of her reading-glasses. For eyebrows she had paper-thin blue-black lines painted on, curving extravagantly between the bridge of her nose and her cheekbones, making her look oddly like a blond Greek. Surrounded by an entourage of five young men—all very much with her, you could tell at a glance—all primped-up for Saturday-morning-SoHo.

Half a dozen empty espresso cups with their accompanying saucers and spoons and ripped sugar packets, an ashtray overflowing with butts, and a dozen plastic-covered catalogs strewn before them on the table.

"Allow me to present my fiancée," Laurence's voice of mock-formality. He slipped his arm from my shoulders and took hold of her hand.

"Miss Ashling Worthington. We're to return to London to be wed in a few weeks' time."

Now he looked around the table, studying the others, his smile mischievous.

"And this is Ashling's troop of lovely bridesmaids. As you can see, they've been busy all morning selecting patterns and laces for their gowns."

There was a moment of silence, but I think I was the only one embarrassed.

Laurence went on, "Truth is that Ashling's stepdad, of whom you may have heard—CEO of that small but prestigious British publishing house—Ashling's stepdad has generously given us a loft around the corner. Our much appreciated wedding present. And this is Ashling's team of interior decorators. Who, as I say, have been busy all morning selecting fixtures to fancy it up."

Two Mexican-looking waiters came running with chairs, the decorators shifting noisily around, our chairs fitted in on either side of Ashling.

For the moment the decorators did not appear overly pleased.

Ashling raised her reading-glasses to the top of her head, turned to face me. She leaned forward and I looked into her stunning gray eyes, suddenly finding it difficult to breathe.

"Quite a bit more than Laurence makes out," she was saying. "We're practically gutting and starting over. Including moving the kitchen to the front end. Which means of course all new pipes and electricals, in addition to fixtures. And all must be resolved before we leave for London."

She had on jeans and the kind of men's tank-top undershirt we call a marino at home—my father wore them religiously to stave off catching a "fresh cold"—her sedate breasts and soft chocolate areolae prominent beneath the thin, stretchy, ribbed material.

For a bizarre instant I saw her transported to my own kitchen, leaning back against my own peeling formica counter, surrounded by my own fixtures: rusted potbelly iron sink, rusted mini-fridge, rusted two-burner electric stovetop. Rusted teakettle screaming mercilessly behind her.

Now she was going politely around the table presenting her decorators, listing their various specialties as though they were surgeons, and I was attempting to look from face to face, pretending to listen.

Despite my efforts I couldn't keep from glancing back down at Ashling's breasts. Attractive, certainly, but there was something peculiar about them, her nipples, and for the life of me I couldn't figure out what it was.

Only when she'd finished introducing everybody, and she put her hand on top of Laurence's and leaned back in her chair—and I leaned forward and took another boldfaced, careful look—did I realize they were pierced with studs. Two tiny silver bits, dots of mercury, hugging each one.

We have an expression at home, country-bookie-come-to-town, it's what I felt like for a second.

Now Ashling and Laurence were discussing renovations. She shifted her glasses to her nose again, blond hair falling forward over her face. Paging through one of the catalogs searching for something. Meanwhile Laurence reached for the cigarettes in front of her, tapped one out and lit it for himself, slid them over.

Suddenly I realized, with the impact of a biblical revelation, that I knew one of the decorators. Though I had no idea from where, or under what circumstances.

I must have sat there holding the cigarette between my fingers, poised before my lips, unlit, for a full minute.

Then I remembered: a former student in an undergrad Gen English Lit class, which I'd taught as an adjunct at NYU. Almost two years back.

Name was Philip—Ashling had said it herself a few seconds ago, but I was only now hearing her—and when I looked over at him again Philip was smiling at me in an intimate sort of way, a way that did not make me feel at all comfortable.

Clearly he recognized me too.

A couple of seconds later Philip leaned discreetly towards the decorator beside him, whispered something into his ear, and now they were both smiling, both staring at me. That decorator then turned to two others, mouthed some silent message, followed by a wry wink—*one of us,* I imagined it said—and now four of them were looking intimately in my direction. In fact the only decorator not now staring at me was the one going through the catalog with Ashling and Laurence.

Now I recognized the faces of two other decorators from our class.

Now I began to feel considerably paranoid.

The class had been a fiasco. Though no fault of NYU's, the students', The Great British Masters', or anybody else. Anybody but myself. And I'd sinned twice. Broken two cardinal rules. The first instituted by me, second by the feminist contingent of the academic academy:

1) I'd gotten involved with a woman
2) I'd gotten involved with a woman who was my student

Ksegna. Yugoslavian Serb, Belgrade from its fashionable day, 6-foot-2, older—a few years older than me, twice the age of her classmates—and best friends with Philip. Philip and all of his group of friends. And just as Ashling was Aphrodite to this little group, Ksegna was Venus to hers. For a moment in the history of this city the group was even notorious on the Lower East Side. My neighborhood. Practically the whole of my undergrad Gen English Lit class.

I became a member of Ksegna's posse also, by choice, but with a difference. And not simply because I was their professor. I adored her too, instantly, and Ksegna *was* worthy of adoration. But here is not the place to go into it. Suffice to say that it was a trap I walked into with open eyes. A trap I allowed myself to be lured into, thinking—wanting to believe, perhaps—that it was actually so safe. When of course the danger was staring me in the face the whole time.

The difference between me and the rest of Ksegna's group, which I alluded to above, she picked up on straight away, pun intended. I wanted her to. Went out of my way to make it clear from the onset. And given the particular configuration of our little group, in that way I had her all to myself. Given the particular configuration of our group I had believed—I had actually convinced myself for the moment—that I could hang out with Ksegna as a kind of "boyfriend" without having to perform the prescribed duties of a boyfriend.

Ha! She had me naked in the sack the first night. And the two nights after that. Twice in my own sack across the street from our Little Fish Big Fish Bar, a third night in her sack up in Chelsea. Each night a worse hell than the one before. While kind and generous Ksegna, worthy-of-adoration Ksegna, liberated Yugoslav, 6-foot-2 Venus, Aphrodite, tried everything in her power to illicit a response. And she had an arsenal.

There are a variety of ways to deal with this predicament. A variety of excuses to be offered—following the embarrassment of course, the mumbled apologies. After all it is nothing new, this predicament, and surely every male of the species, despite his sexual orientation, must experience it sometime. The difficulty enters when the situation repeats itself. And when it repeats itself enough times, when it becomes the only possible kind of experience, difficulty degenerates to misery rather quickly. Here is not the place to go into it.

With most women I said I was drunk. And usually that was sufficient. Or I had a medical problem—once I was extremely drunk, and stoned, and instead of medical I said mechanical—like a Midas tune-up could fix it! Once, before I could say anything at all, a woman got so angry she cuffed me in the mouth and stormed out. That time was actually easiest of all.

Have you ever had somebody try to put a condom on your flaccid penis?

The thoughtful women were the problematic ones. The sensitive, speculative ones. Usually the ones I cared deeply about. All of those dreadful heart-to-hearts. And something about my "artistic" personality—something about my face, or body-language, or a combination of such things, because I wish I could tell you myself—promptly led those sensitive, speculative women such as Ksegna to the same conclusion. Always put to me as a question, delicately, as though it were an option I ought to take into consideration: maybe I was gay?

I had also learned from experience that at this particular juncture, rather than deny it—what possible difference would anything I had to say at this point make anyway?—the easiest method was to simply agree. To the speculation that is, though occasionally I even erased the interrogatory marker. Once, when I'd gotten carried away with my own fictional autobiography, when I was feeling particularly sorry for myself, particularly self-condemning, I even committed the unpardonable sin of claiming I was HIV positive.

As you can imagine it made for a quick, clean kind of closure. An easy exit. Furthermore by agreeing with the speculation, I could even make them feel better about themselves—after *their* frustrating, debilitating experience—and they could easily write it off. Put it efficiently behind them. Usually, thankfully, they even went out of their way to avoid me in future. So we wouldn't have to suffer the embarrassment of seeing each other again.

You'd be surprised how well it worked. After all, the saddest feeling in the world is to feel undesired. The second saddest feeling.

As usual, at the end of that third night with Ksegna, our third descent into Hades, I let Ksegna do the talking. Let her handle the heart-to-heart. I simply nodded my head at the appropriate moment. Shrugged my shoulders like an imbecile. I'd been weeping anyway. That was standard too.

This time it backfired. This time there was no quick, easy exit. This time Ksegna took me on as her own special project. As though she were doing charity work. Homework: Ksegna decided that she would be the one to see me out of my closet herself. She would personally supervise my own liberation.

Ksegna, as director of all her dedicated, indefatigable posse. All the boys of my undergrad Gen English Lit class.

Thinking back I can only laugh. Because let me assure you it was extremely comical. In a Vaudeville/burlesque kind of way: characters chasing each other back and forth across the stage, in various stages of undress, up and down my squeaky six flights of stairs. Up and down. After all, I lived across the street from our Little Fish Big Fish Bar.

And the more I demurred, the more strident became Ksegna's indefatigable posse.

And the lock on the door downstairs has been busted since I moved in.

And for the whole of that interminable semester I faced them every Mon-Wed-Fri.

———————

Laurence called over the maitre d'—an Italian who could only mumble a few words of English—and he asked for a couple of menus for the two of us. Ashling and her decorators had already had their brunch.

The maitre d' stared back at him blankfaced.

"Menus," Laurence repeated, "*due!*"

Then he winked at me, "And bring us a couple Bloody Marys."

I stretched my leg past Ashling and kicked him under the table. Laurence thought it was a mistake and kept on.

"B-l-o-o-d-y M-a-r-y," he shouted. "*Due!*—pomodoro, celery, VODKA!"

I kicked him again.

"Listen," I said, "just realized I got to be going."

Laurence looked at me with the same stunned face as the maitre d'.

"Terribly nice to meet you," I told Ashling—sounding, absurdly, like I was trying to imitate an Englishman—and coming off as completely false, though I meant it.

I stubbed my cigarette out in the ashtray. Exhaled a lungful of smoke over my shoulder, leaned forward and kissed her on both cheeks. Then stood up.

Now the decorators decided they were each entitled to a kiss on both cheeks themselves. Rising in unison and leaning their faces towards me, eyelashes batting.

I made the rounds.

"Walk you to your subway," Laurence said—suddenly looking a little disgusted—jumping up also, hurrying behind me.

Soon as we were out of hearing distance he leaned onto my shoulder.

"What the *fock*?"

"Long story. Not worth repeating. But I had to get away from those decorators!"

The statement made me feel like a homophobe. Which I promptly overcorrected.

"Guess I led one of them on. Inadvertently. Philip. Ended badly."

Laurence looked as incredulous as he had earlier when the ball passed through the drugstore racket.

"He want to redecorate your flat?"

I laughed. "Metaphorically speaking. And let me tell you, our boy's unbated instrument was neither bent nor busted."

"Wait a minute—"

I cut him off, enjoying Laurence's confusion, his reaction to all this. Slung my arm around his shoulders. Looked him in the face.

"As a matter of fact, compère, it was Philip and two of the other decorators sitting with us at the table."

"Stop right there, don't want to hear it." And after a second, "Can't figure it either—you had your eyes positively plastered to Ashling's tot-tots!"

I burst out with another laugh.

"Sorry."

"Don't apologize to me."

"Listen, we got some catching up to do."

"Five centuries' worth."

"At least."

We were walking up to Houston St so I could catch the F-train going across, then back down. Though I never took the F, especially from the confusion at Houston St, and it would probably be quicker if I walked. I could get off at Delancey. But today was Saturday morning, Little Italy would be packed with tourists. I could get off at Canal.

"By the by," I said, "what is it with our lovely Ashling's tot-tots? Her nipples, I mean. They appear to be pierced."

Now Laurence laughed himself.

"Rebel child," he said. "Remains of her punk days, down King's Road. Tattooed-on eyebrows, lots of other pins and needles, but those are the only two remaining. Truth to tell, of those I've grown quite fond."

"Unequibbocally."

He smiled. "Family couldn't even find her for a couple of years. Not that they looked much. Closer now for their sorrows though, specially her stepdad."

Laurence paused, "That, you can probably guess, is fortuitous on my count for a variety of reasons."

"Counting up the bread?"

"Soaked. Enough to be recklessly generous. Position at Worthington Press does me no particular harm either. Nepotism being your younger poet's rite-of-passage."

By now we'd reached my stop. Suddenly I felt relieved—this last subject was not one I wanted to discuss with Laurence. Nor did I care to answer any questions about my own publishing record, the novel I'd been peddling unsuccessfully, and rewriting, for the past five years.

We hugged. I started down the stairs.

"Listen—" I heard him say when I was halfway down.

I cringed slightly. Turned around to look back up at him.

He had his hands resting on the railing, leaning forward, muscles showing along his bent arms.

"Reminds me," he said. "Something I wanted to talk to you about. I'll give you a call, you can give me some pointers."

He was smiling down at me in a cocky sort of way, a way that I knew instinctively I didn't like.

"What's that?" I said despite myself.

"Been thinking I might try my hand at a novel."

4

Laurence went to Oxford as an island schol. The tests were sent from Cambridge, and the boy who won for his year—I don't think a girl ever won, or was even encouraged to take them—went to university on a government scholarship. One scholarship for Literature and Languages. Another for Science and Maths. These scholarships were highly competitive. For a poor Laventille boy to win was the intellectual equivalent of a Rio slum rat becoming Pelé. Or these days Ronaldo. In addition we always believed that there was a natural prejudice by the Cambridge graders against Catholic boys. That the graders always gave the government boys a ½ point or a ¼ point lagniappe, which would have been enough. Despite the fact that all the boys took the test together at the same time, locked into the same hall, and before the doors were opened all the exam papers were sealed together into the same large brown envelope, with the Education Minister's signature across the flap, to be shipped overseas. We always believed the graders knew, or they were tipped off, or they could somehow tell the difference between a Catholic boy's and a government boy's test. We even had heated arguments on the subject. When in reality of course the Cambridge graders probably could not have cared less, and those subtler sorts of differences among us probably never occurred to them, and they probably only read the first and last sentences of each boy's essay, anyway.

Everybody knew Laurence would win for his year, even before he took up his pen. As though the test itself were irrelevant. And in many ways I suppose it was. I did not bother taking the exam, not because it would have been an utter waste of time, and not because I did not want to compete with Laurence; I'd long ago decided to go to school in the States, I had my escape all planned out, and the scholarships were for universities within the Commonwealth.

On Father O'Connor's recommendation I went to a Catholic school in the Bronx, Fordham University. And just as my four years started running out, just as I started to panic, I managed to accomplish something which, in its own small way, was news enough to make the mauvilang at home. If only for a moment. Though in their version of course I'd done it purposely: on the basis of five short stories written during a Christmas holiday spent in the dorm—in reality nothing more than five vignettes, with the island setting as the same main character in all five—I'd gotten myself accepted into the MFA program for creative writing at Columbia University. Much to my own surprise, because I do not remember x-ing off that box on the application, they even awarded me financial aid in the form of a teaching assistantship. Which got me started along that road. And in that way I could make my break from my family's money too. Even sooner than I could have hoped.

Of course there was a bit of a fiasco when I arrived at Columbia and they took a look at my face. Because my being West Indian had led them to certain assumptions—which were not altogether false—though they were not true enough, either, to enable me to fulfill their prescribed quota. Not very easily. At least not in the clear-cut way they liked to envision it. But they could hardly take their acceptance and their assistantship back. And in any case I was so pleased to be living in New York City at last, that the only creative writing I got around to doing—and I stretched their two-year program into three—was to rewrite the same five stories a dozen more times. The same five stories I turned in as my thesis at the end of the program. Same five stories I'd chopped up and spliced back together into a novel, that first summer, sitting in my apartment on the Lower East Side.

But the real reason I never took the Cambridge exam, the real reason I made up my mind to escape to the States in the first place, was that my father had won an island scholarship for his year, and that was a competition I had no desire to partake in. A competition I knew I'd lost in advance. Even if, by some miracle, I could have won a scholarship. My father had gone to Oxford too, though he'd studied law. His first step to becoming QC for our branch of the Colonial Department—Queen's Counsel. Of course, like my mother, he'd come from generations of West Indian money. And although the family fortune was no longer anything compared to what it had been four or five generations back, on either side, there was still lots left. Plenty blood money: my father did not need to win that scholarship in order to make something of himself, any more than Laurence had needed to win his. For entirely different reasons. Because clearly Laurence could have gone to Oxford for his tennis—or he could have gone for at least two other sports, or he could have gone simply for his brilliance—but he went to Oxford as an island schol for the same reason my father went, for the same reason he won his tennis trophies. For the simple pleasure of winning them. Or maybe simply to deposit them on the dusty sill of his mother's parlor in Laventille.

———

When he called, as promised, a few days after our first tennis date at Hudson River Park, that was the reason. Not, I was pleased to hear, to discuss the strategies of writing a novel. And anyway I'd soon learn that was another arena in which he needed little help from me, or anybody else. Laurence had found a spare racket in one of the unpacked boxes, and he wanted to give it to me as a present. He was always extremely generous in that way. He'd also reserved a court for us for the following Saturday. We played on the two Saturdays after that, and for four Saturdays in a row we stopped by Bar None to see Francis. For four Saturdays in a row Laurence and I stumbled around the West Village, arms slung over each other's shoulders, blinded by sun and Red Stripes and Mount Gay. Until I'm sure the neighbors did begin to peg us for a couple of local bullers.

But just as quickly as our routine started it ended, because then he left with Ashling for their wedding in London. Then—"to give your decorator-pals enough time," according to Laurence—a month-long honeymoon in Bali. And by the time they returned I was juggling three adjunct teaching jobs, at three schools, meaning that most of my days were spent, not in the classroom, but riding trains, and I really did need my Saturday mornings for sleep. Pretty soon it was too cold for tennis anyway.

They had even sent me an invitation, with the gold-embossed seal of the family's coat-of-arms stamped across it. I was climbing the stairs. Exhausted after a late evening adult ed summer session of The Great Masters. Holding the envelope between my teeth to rip it open, stack of books under my arm, actually thinking it was junk mail, an announcement for the opening of some new club. In the yellow stairwell light I made out the fancy cursive. *Lady and Lord something something Worthington announce the marriage of their daughter Ashling*—I stopped my climb for a second.

So in addition to being rich, she was also royalty.

And now, by proxy, so was Laurence.

Suddenly I had to laugh out loud. I could hardly imagine what they'd have to say about this at home: a true true blue-blooded lady, soaked to her ivory-pure skin, with pierced nipples and tattooed-on eyebrows. This outdid even our carnival imagination. My friend

Shay-lee worked at the BWIA desk in the airport, had access to a WATS line. I'd have her call me for a proper mauvilang-session at the first opportunity.

My answering machine was blinking away—Shay-lee calling already, I thought, smiling to myself—but I left it alone. Dumped my books on the kitchen counter and flopped into bed. Lying on my back, looking up, studying the wedding invitation. Obviously Ashling had changed her name at some point. Or she'd had her name changed for her. She was Worthington's stepdaughter, I remembered, and in terms of titles, I wasn't sure how that worked. Depends on how the title was got in the first place, I suppose. Whether it was inherited, or purchased, or bestowed by honor of merit. But how were titles passed to succeeding generations? Did gender make a difference? I had no idea. And in any case if Ashling did have any claim to a title, she was probably surrendering it by marrying Laurence. You could marry into royalty, so I suppose you could marry out of it also? Unless Ashling kept her name?

Then I thought of something else: maybe Laurence would change his? Instead of Africanizing it, he'd aristocize it? gentrify it? Britishize it? Laurence Worthington. Even had a nice ring—solid, earnest-sounding. One of those late-nineteenth-century travel writers. A noble novelist, surveying the Empire. *Letters from the Blistering Tropics*.

It was funny to think about.

But it wasn't my friend Laurence. A-tall. And one thing they weren't giving up, either of them, was her dowry. Including the soon-to-be-done-up loft in SoHo. Another thing for sure, Laurence had done even better for himself this time. This marriage, I decided, would last for a few years.

In fact I never met Ashling again. Much to my own disappointment.

That fall I ran into him a couple of times in Grand Central. I was schlepping up to the Bronx, to my alma mater, for one of my adjuncts; he was headed over to Jersey, to Princeton. Laurence had decided to go the academic route himself. It ran in his family. (His mother was still a teacher in the Catholic elementary school in Laventille.) He'd actually given me this news on our last tennis date, before he left to be married and honeymooned. And that morning in Bar None we'd even celebrated, at Laurence's insistence, the three of us, with a bottle of Dom Perignon—Francis had to call the fancy Indian restaurant across the street and have them send the champagne over. Without any actual teaching time under his belt, Laurence had managed to land a permanent position which consisted of a 2/2 load—meaning, if he taught a couple of upper-level seminars, that he could get away going in one day a week—and even better than that, they'd promised him tenure in a year. Thankfully he never mentioned his starting salary. Of course it made perfect sense, his curriculum was stunning. With three prize-winning books of poetry already in print. Then there were the plays, his theater experience.

In the end he didn't even have to wait the year at Princeton. Because that same spring his first novel was out, and by summer it was everywhere. Published simultaneously overseas by the small but prestigious British press, and another here in New York that was just as prestigious, but the polar opposite of small. I found it in every bookstore I looked. Then I didn't even have to search anymore, because Laurence's novel started finding me. Staring at me in rows of copies out of the bookstores' display windows. *Suggested Summer Reading.*

A slavery novel, but this book went further. Beyond grievance. Beyond retribution also. Effortlessly spanning hemispheres, epochs, even prose styles. And it was written with a poet's ear, with a poet's hand for compression. Needn't even be pigeonholed as a West Indian novel either. One of those controversial, political, crossover-crossfire hits that struck at readers, and critics, and academics alike. Killed them dead. Everybody and his brother. And Princeton knew that if they didn't tenure Laurence quickly, somebody else would.

I kept telling myself we'd run into each other. Even though I wasn't doing my jaunt up to the Bronx that semester, and I knew Laurence never made it down to my neighborhood. Eventually, when I simply could not put it off any longer, I called to offer my congratulations. Tell him we needed to get together as soon as possible to toast his success. I even lied, saying I wanted to buy him a bottle of champagne, as if I could have afforded it. Laurence told me he was leaving for London first thing in the morning. I felt relieved. He was just about to hang up when I asked after Ashling.

"She went back six months ago. Thought you knew."

"What?"

"Turns out Manhattan wasn't to her liking."

"Wait a minute," I knew he hadn't changed address. "You guys broke up?"

"Not entirely. Still best of friends, just living on separate islands—remember, separation runs in both our families."

He went on, "I'm back and forth anyway, between theater people and publishers. You know how it is, those guys'll fly you cross the Atlantic for a cup of tea."

I almost said, "Know what you mean!" but I realized how absurd that statement would be.

"What about classes?" was all that came to mind.

"Sabbatical this semester. And Princeton couldn't be more pleased. Cheap publicity for them."

I paused, "Don't you miss Ashling?"

It sounded as though I was the one who was heartbroken. Maybe I was?

"Ashling simply would not hear of raising a child in New York City. And I did not attempt to convince her otherwise."

"Wait a minute!" the repetition made me feel more foolish still. I forced myself to slow down.

"You guys planning to have a kid?"

"Indeed. You're talking to the proud father of a two-month-old popo: Laurence de Boissière-Worthington. With a hyphen. Although—brushing aside the noblesse oblige—personally I'm fond of Larry Jr."

"Oh-ho," was all I could manage. To rhyme with popo.

For an absurd moment I even found myself worrying whether Ashling would be able to nurse properly. How would the child react to the taste of those tiny silver nuggets? Maybe he'd like them?

"Catch you for the toast when I get back," Laurence said.

"For what?"

"Champagne—we'll drink a bottle when I get back."

We would too, more than one. Though not to toast his novel.

"Bung-o!" I said, having no idea where that came from.

And after a pause, "Give my love to Ashling."

He'd already hung up.

———

The following afternoon I caught a vaps, and I went out to buy Ashling a congratulations card. No idea why, I hardly knew her, had only met her one morning in my life. But I went out to look for a congratulations card for her just the same. That was the afternoon I made the startling discovery that there are only two categories of infants. At least according to Hallmark: puffy cotton-white babies with tiny wings and halos, puffy charcoal-black babies with tiny horns and tridents. The world consists of but those two. Nothing in between. And neither category seemed quite right for Laurence and Ashling's son.

Then I realized I didn't have her London address anyway. And I refused—for reasons that had nothing to do with Ashling—to send it to her via Worthington Press.

Laurence and I never did manage to get together to celebrate his novel. Several weeks later he called, but it was to tell me he'd reserved a court for us for Saturday. Spring semester was already over, though I hadn't noticed the weather warming up. Almost hot already. Before I had a chance to think about it I gave him some excuse. When the truth was I had no reason at all to stay in on Saturday morning. Not even to sleep.

A couple of weeks later he called again, again I invented something.

Then he called and woke me up at five in the morning.

"Listen," he said. "On my way to JFK. Pass by your place in ten minutes—navy blue Delancy's car. Meet me downstairs with your manuscript."

I had no idea what he was talking about.

"You there?" he asked.

"Yeah, what you mean?"

"Your novel. I've decided to give it to my editor at Worthington —nepotism, remember?"

Another silence.

"You there?"

"It's not ready."

"That focking book was ready five years ago. You told me so yourself!"

Now he was angry.

"I lied. Nasty habit."

The statement made me sound like a spoilt child. Exactly what I was.

"Besides," I said, "you haven't even read it."

"Seven-hour plane ride for that, compère."

Another silence.

"Ten minutes!" he said. And hung up.

5

I floated through that summer. Starting from the moment Laurence informed me that his editor had liked my novel, enough to put it on his spring list. His news left me giddy. I couldn't concentrate. And if I didn't have much of a tennis game before, now I had none whatsoever. Laurence took it humorously. I suppose I did too. Every Saturday he reserved a court for the two of us. And every Saturday morning, after banging the ball back and forth for a couple of hours—little point left in trying to compete—we stopped by Bar None to see Francis. I hadn't been back for a full year. But that first Saturday morning, from the moment we walked in, it seemed clear that Laurence had. Often. He and Francis now seemed best of friends. Even made me feel like the outsider, the newcomer among the three of us. As we sat there drinking our Red Stripes and smoking a couple of Francis's cigarettes, my first time back in Bar None after a year, and I listened to the two of them, I learned something else: that Laurence was presently directing an off-Broadway production of his CLR James–inspired play of the Haitian revolt, and he'd cast Francis in the lead. Toussaint L'Ouverture. They were already rehearsing together three afternoons a week.

Of course I went to opening night. Laurence offered to comp me as many seats as I needed, but I went alone. What I was most curious to find out, what I couldn't stop pondering my entire subway ride uptown, was who he'd cast in the role of L'Ouverture's muse. Because it would not have been unlike my friend to fly his ex-wife over to play the part, the Senegalese actress I'd never met. But for some reason I could not identify, I suspected he'd cast Ashling in the role. Though whether Ashling ever acted a day in her life I had no idea. Tell you the truth I would not have been surprised to find Ksegna up there hanging in the chandelier.

L'Ouverture's muse was played by none of those women. And by the time we got to the critical scene I'd forgotten to check and see who the actress playing the part might be. Because now my attention was captured by Francis.

For his role he'd chopped off all his braids, and he'd chopped off his Jamaican accent too. Now he was French aristocracy. Or pseudo-French aristocracy, because now he was Haitian. Or, more accurately, now he belonged to Saint-Domingue, what the French called the former Spanish island of Hispaniola; Haiti, the play reminded me, was the island's original Arawak name, later reclaimed by the former Africans. When there were no longer any Arawak Indians remaining to remember it.

Suffice to say that L'Ouverture's problem, his confusion, no different from any of us, was that he could not make up his mind which of the tribes he'd come from. And there were so many he'd lost count.

I came away from the play pleasantly surprised by Francis's talent as an actor. Something else as well. Because although I'd read it in manuscript a few years back, I'd never seen the play staged. And I walked out of that theater once more impressed by my friend Laurence.

———————

Soon it was fall semester and I went back to juggling my adjuncts. Too busy for Saturday tennis. Laurence, I suppose, went back to his own one-day-a-week jaunt out to Princeton—or maybe he didn't, maybe he was still on leave—but in any case it had been a long time since we'd run into each other in Grand Central. On the tennis courts or anyplace else. It had been several weeks since we'd even talked on the phone.

That evening I was so exhausted that I almost didn't bother checking my messages. I dumped my books on the kitchen counter and flopped into bed. Then I got up again and hit the button. It was Laurence, sounding rushed: "Compère, having dinner tonight with my agent—young whippersnapper I told you about. I'm thinking surely she can place your novel on this side. Worth a try? In any case she's someone you want to meet. Say I bring her by for a drink, Bar None, half-nine?" He hung up.

I checked my alarm clock—almost nine already. Flopped back into bed and shut my eyes. Then I jumped up again and got into the shower. Opened the hot water full. Which came out ice-cold, turned lukewarm for a minute, then went cold again. But it left me half-awake.

Only after I walked through the door did it occur to me I'd never been in Bar None at night. Never been here at any time other than ten on Saturday morning. In fact I couldn't remember ever seeing anybody else in the place, other than the three of us. Now it was packed. Loud, smoky, lit by its yellow-blinking jukebox jamming Jimmy Cliff—bass so loud it had the beer bottles bouncing on the zinc counter—and, of course, not one woman. No female literary agent. No Laurence either. I looked over several black-leather-jacketed shoulders for Francis behind the bar, but it was someone else. And I almost panicked. Then I made him out in the far corner. Took me two full minutes to get to him.

I reached across the counter and we knocked fists.

"Stripe?" he asked.

"Dewar's-and-soda," I shouted back.

Even sounds literary, I thought.

"And Camels," I said when he slid the drink over.

"You and Lor catching Rudder tonight?"

"Who?"

"You homeboy, Rudder, concert tonight at SOB's."

Took me a second to register who Rudder was. And for the moment I was too preoccupied with other matters even to worry about missing our most popular calypsonian, in town for a pre-carnival jump-up.

"No idea," I shouted back.

Suddenly I was feeling wide awake. And self-confident—despite my thriftstore suede jacket, my primped-up company. Each of them looking like a GQ model. I was beside myself with excitement at the thought of meeting Laurence's agent. Had hardly had time to contemplate a US publication. Which was what I did now, lighting a cigarette, leaning back against the black-painted brick wall.

After an hour the smoke and leather jackets started thinning out and I got hold of a stool at the bar. Still too loud to talk to Francis. Still no women. No sign of Laurence, and no literary agent. By now I'd had a couple more drinks. Francis slid them over before I had a chance to ask. I noticed he wasn't writing them down, either, hadn't even started me a tab. Which made the scotch taste better still.

He slid me over another.

The guy on the stool beside me wrote *hi?* in the trail of water. I pretended not to see.

Then somebody covered my eyes from behind.

"Laurence?" I said. Seemed an odd thing for him to do.

I spun around on my stool: there he was, beside him the woman I took to be his agent. Her arm strung territorially through his, tall and blond and clad in black leather like everybody else. Just as primped-up and just as attractive. But I was so shocked by the two people who arrived with them that I hardly noticed.

"Discovered her eating at the table next door," Laurence gestured over his shoulder, happy as I'd ever seen him. "Like it's an invasion of rich white West Indians. Another member of our founding family!"

My cousin Rachel—she was the one who'd covered my eyes.

Of all my multitude of cousins, all my relatives, Rachel was the one I was closest to. Second cousins, but we were only a year apart in age. And up until the time we both left the island for good, we'd been inseparable. We'd grown up together—our houses shared the same backyard—though I hadn't seen her in years. Since I'd made the trip to visit her in Nice: Rachel came from the French side of the family. The founding family—one of them, anyway—but Laurence's statement was loaded with irony. Because by now *he* was as closely related to those first white French colonizers as we were.

And his irony didn't stop there.

There she was, her mound of shocking red curls, enough for three heads at least. Shining pale green eyes, spray of freckles across her café-au-lait cheeks, smiling—her extravagant lips—that mouth so familiar I wanted to curl up on it right now and drop asleep.

The guy beside her had on some kind of military uniform.

I got down off my stool and reached to hug her, but before I could manage it Rachel grabbed hold of both my arms, started dragging me out into the street. Going through the glass door I caught a glimpse of Laurence's face, his back turned to his agent.

Rachel pulled me along the sidewalk for several yards, running, laughing out loud. Then she stopped and shoved me backwards against the glass pane of a storefront window. Pinned me there. Reaching with both hands to pull my face down against hers, hard—for a second I thought she'd cut my lower lip with her teeth, same vulnerable place another woman had once split it with her fist—drowning me in a sea of insatiable, flaming curls.

Our childhood game, to be sure. Imitating star-crossed lovers we saw on the Roxy's big screen. But the people we were really imitating, trying to outdo, were our own parents—Rachel's mother and my father, that is—and we knew it.

The loser was the one to break the kiss.

I decided to play along, pressing my mouth back against hers, our lips opening, loosening—occasionally stiffening into smiles at the same time—tongues wrestling each other for several minutes. Until we were out of breath.

I looked down at her—still shocked by her appearance here, of all places—her eyes shining, reflecting the storefront fluorescent buzzing above our heads. Her smile mischievous.

"So who's the victor?" I asked.

"Both of us, as always."

"Or both defeated."

"Chut!"

We stared at each other—I was smiling so hard I could feel it in my cheeks—happy as kids again. Our faces a couple of inches apart, the back of my head and my shoulders pressed against the glass. Our breath misty. Chests breathing hard against each other.

With her mound of hair like that it felt like we were huddled into a small cave. Or hiding under the sheets.

"Truth is," she said, "I thought you'd want to kiss the bride."

"No."

"Oh, yes!"

"I don't believe it."

"True."

"Again?"

"Again."

"But this one's wearing some kind of focking military outfit. What's he, a captain or something?"

"Hardly. Twenty-two. Spanish boy. Met him in the Pyrenees in a show."

By which she meant horses, dressage. One of Rachel's distractions—pastimes, passions. Another was marriage: at twenty-nine, a year older than Laurence and me, she'd done it four times. Her Spaniard made four.

Which gave her two over Laurence, I realized.

And I was barred from the competition.

"The show was on his ranch," she was saying. "There's even a twelfth-century castle!"

I was only half listening. .

She went on, "Doing his year in the army. Which the Spaniards still require. At least he *was* in the army—until he scaled the barbed-wire fence and escaped, line of guards pointing bayoneted rifles at his back—you should've seen him!"

I shook my head, still not listening. Feigning disbelief, my eyes closed.

"We went straight to the public office—I scarcely understood a word mind you, Catalan—then the airport. They're the only clothes he has."

Rachel was working my eyelids open slowly with her fingers. Then she pulled my face down towards hers again. But this time the kiss was gentle, only our lips touching.

We stared, not speaking, a long minute.

"Actually," she said, "we're on our honeymoon. I made the mistake of telling him I'd never been to New York."

Rachel pronounced the been as if it were spelled bean. Some affectation the English left us with, we all had it. Like pronouncing either, I-ther. Like a-tall. Though there was more French in Rachel's accent now than I remembered.

She was wearing a button-up sweater that felt like cashmere, same green color as her eyes. Or the other way around. I could feel she didn't have anything on under the sweater either. Tweed skirt revealing the lengths of her brown, almost too-muscular legs, thin black ballet slippers on her feet. No stockings. No coat—with the temperature she should have been freezing—but it was as if she hadn't noticed.

I couldn't help thinking that Rachel looked more like her mother than ever, the way she had looked at Rachel's age. Exactly the same age Rachel's mother had been when she disappeared with my father, for several months, down the islands. Rachel's mother sailing her family yacht, because I don't think my father had been in a boat in his life. Other than the ship that had once delivered him, following five days of vomiting over the rail, to Oxford. But the scandal was less that my father had run away with his younger niece, than the fact that he'd seduced his own sister-in-law. For us, I suppose, God's conjugations outweighed those of His petty creatures. What we were: Rachel and I were eight and seven at the time. But old enough to know perfectly well what was going on. Old enough to console each other, and only each other.

And in perfect West Indian fashion, after five and a half months, our parents were back in their respective houses which backed each other and shared the same backyard. As though nothing had happened. Nobody mentioned it again. Except, occasionally, the two of us.

"He phoned me from his barracks in the middle of the night," she said.

I still wasn't listening properly.

"Absolutely distraught—I was back home in Nice, hadn't seen him in over a month. He was practically weeping. I told him to behave, make believe he was elsewhere. Make believe *we* were elsewhere. Turned into a challenge of course—the New York I mean."

She paused, "That's how this story begins."

Then her smile turned mischievous again.

"I assure you, I'm perfectly innocent!"

I looked at her for a moment. Just enjoying the sight of her, feel of her in my arms. Her warmth beneath the soft sweater.

"Can't you tell me something new?" I asked.

"I will. Now you must call me duquesa. Duquesa Raquel Maria Rubió. The Maria came to me as I was signing the certificate."

"Hideous."

"Think?"

"Specially Maria."

"Don't I know."

After a few seconds I asked her, "So why didn't you call?"

"I did. Your mother. Called her soon as we got to our hotel. She didn't have your number or your address. Told me both had changed. It's ungenerous of you, William. Poor woman!"

And my number was unlisted since the Philip/Ksegna incident. If Rachel would have thought to check the phonebook.

"You could've called home and asked Shay-lee," I said. "Or Oony. Even Minshall for that matter."

Or she could have simply called Laurence, though I didn't say that. She didn't really know him anyway.

"Never occurred," she said. "And in any case I wasn't worried. Not in the least. I knew I'd find you. Somehow. Even in this city. I simply knew I couldn't be here, in the same place, and not find you."

"And now," I said, "you have."

"My own true love!"

"Rachel—" I was shaking my head again, looking away, feeling suddenly like I wanted to weep myself.

"You just married this guy."

"Everybody gets married." She turned my face back to hers, held it that way between her palms. Looking into my eyes. "Everybody.

They'll never have what we have. None of them. Simply never know."

I pulled my face away again. Roughly.

"Lucky beggars," I said to the buildings behind her back.

"Chut!"

"Minus one Old Year's Eve morning," I told the buildings. "Minus three wajanks."

"A-tall! I won't have it you understand? I won't!"

She was angry, in a flash. She had every right. I don't know what came over me, how I'd let it happen. But suddenly all those familiar, contradictory emotions were welling up in me. As when you wake abruptly from a recurring dream. Panting. I couldn't hold them back.

"Kiss me," she said, "and shut up."

I did.

"Better," she said. "Far better."

Her smile again. And in the reflection of her eyes, I made out my own smile too.

Rachel had the lapels of my jacket balled up in her fists. She let them loose. Smoothened out the thin suede. Carefully. Until her fingers stopped trembling. Then she slipped her hands under the lapels and pressed her palms flat against my chest. Warm. Even through my flannel shirt. Pushing me slightly away, pressing me harder against the glass.

I held her tighter.

She looked up.

"Now," she said, "give me more. I always want more."

"You always want what you can't have."

"We all do. Yourself included."

It was the truest thing I'd ever heard her say.

"So shut up and do as told!"

I kissed her as though we were back to playing our childhood game. Several minutes. Until we were out of breath.

We stood there like that, staring at each other. How long? Somebody should have taken the picture for a postcard. I can see it as clearly as if I held it in my hand: black-and-white, glossy, slippery streamers of cars' headlights reflecting in the glass storefront. *Amore in NYC* the caption would read.

Suddenly I felt a shiver run through her. And I watched her eyes change from pale green to yellow-brown. In an instant. And in that same instant I watched their shiny green, plate-glass surface soften, then dissolve completely. Melt away into nothing. Drop into fathomless depths.

"Oh, William," she said, "do the horrors ever end?"

6

The rest of that night remains a blur. So don't hold me responsible for the accuracy with which I recount it. Because when we got back to the bar those three or four free scotches I'd downed on a stomach empty since my breakfast cereal seemed to descend—or ascend—all at once, and the champagne which followed didn't help matters. When we got back to the bar we found the three of them—Laurence, his agent, and Javier, Rachel's new husband—standing around my stool as if it were a table. Bottle of Dom Perignon in a bucket of ice sitting on top it. Laurence got a couple more glasses from Francis for Rachel and me. Those flat, impossible-to-drink-out-of champagne glasses. He filled them up, and we all made a show of touching them together and toasting the newlyweds. Francis raised his own glass behind the bar; Laurence made sure to keep him topped up too. Everybody in great spirits, Rachel fully recovered from her bout of despair, everybody perfectly happy. Except, apparently, Laurence's agent.

It was obvious, even to a drunk. Furthermore I was convinced I knew the look on her face. A look I considered myself something of an expert in. The one thing I knew better about women than anything else: that look of frustrated expectation. Flouted expectation. She'd had another sort of evening in mind. Other designs for her handsome, sophisticated star author (an English-accented-and-polished black man is something of a rarity in New York). As we stood there waiting for Laurence to dry off the bottle and refill our glasses, I found myself imagining the scene. Their dinner earlier in the fashionable downtown restaurant, which would have cost her the equivalent of one of my semester paychecks. All of it foreplay really. All of it understood before they sat down. Only the particulars of whose bed and how soon to be decided. Then, out of nowhere, she seemed to have lost him—to some frowsy, loud-mouthed, irritatingly vivacious West Indian sitting at the table beside them, some woman on her honeymoon, no less—and they hadn't even tasted their crème brûlée.

As I watched Laurence carefully refill Rachel's glass, carefully survey every inch of her at the same time, I was convinced I recognized the look on his face too: it was the very expression of entitlement with which his kneeling, redfaced compatriot had contemplated his muse.

What the agent didn't realize was that before that night Laurence hardly knew Rachel. Despite that both of them, in their own way, were quite popular. And both of them came from the same very small very insular place. In all probability, before that night, Laurence and Rachel had never exchanged a word with each other. In fact—and this revelation dawned on me with such impact that in my Dewar's–and–Dom Perignon floodlit frame of mind, it felt luminous enough to be called an epiphany—before that night *I* was really the only thing Laurence and Rachel had in common. But there was more to it than that. Because now I realized that for the first time since we were nine years old—since the Saturday morning he appeared on the precious clay court back behind the British Club wearing his homemade 12¢ cotton shirt, cheap drugstore racket in his hand—I actually had something over Laurence. And for a second I wondered if I didn't like it better than a US publication.

You've got to understand that while we were growing up all the boys were infatuated with Rachel. An unhealthy number of older, married men as well. Including, you'll not be surprised to hear, my own father—if you count one drunken Old Year's Eve in the British Club when Rachel had had no choice but to slap him. But maybe I should slow down here; maybe here I'm exaggerating somewhat. What I can tell you is that there was at least a moment—the moment Rachel hit sixteen or seventeen, say—when all the boys on the island, if they hadn't done so already, suddenly sat up and noticed her. And it's no overstatement to tell you that a good number of those boys quickly succumbed to conditions known to us by a few words which, even visually, seem far more suggestive than their synonyms in the *OED*. All of those boys went tootoolbay, assassataps, tarranjee-banjee over Rachel. Even the ones—and Laurence would have fit into this category, despite his early promise—even those boys for whom there were a couple of insurmountable barriers which separated them, absolutely, unconditionally, from a wealthy convent-educated French-Creole girl such as Rachel. Especially those boys. And a French-Creole girl such as Rachel was possibly farther out-of-bounds than her purely white English half-sisters. Before that night in Bar None, I was sure the three of us had never stood in the same room together.

What I can say is that there was a moment in our history when Rachel could have had just about any boy on the island she wanted. But she chose me. From the time we were kids, long before either of us had consciously made the choice, she was always with me. To the extent that everybody except us always assumed we'd grow up and get married. Soon as we had the chance. Despite the handful who'd always written me off as a buller. Despite the mild scandal of our equivalent surnames—even the Pope sanctioned the marriages of second cousins—and it certainly wouldn't have been anything new at home. As I've already told you the precedent was set for us by our own parents. But by the time they figured out we weren't going to get married after all, that we were going our separate ways, to separate corners of the globe—that Rachel was no longer "spoken for," that she was readily "available"—she'd gone off to live with her mother and sisters someplace in France.

So it's easy to understand how Laurence, having not seen or heard of Rachel for twelve years or longer, suddenly looking over to find her sitting there at the table beside him, could have had his attentions diverted so easily. But whatever it was that had been so upsetting his agent, she quickly left us. Complaining of a rotten headache she reached between two leather jackets and plunked her unfinished glass down on the zinc counter. Hurried out the door.

So not only did I miss my golden opportunity to have her "place my novel on this side," as Laurence had put it—making it sound as if it were as simple and straightforward a gesture as setting down her glass—I never managed to shake her hand. Never spoke a word to her. Never even found out her name. Goatmouth I put on myself and thoroughly deserved.

Javier and Laurence were smoking fat Cuban cigars. And now I lit one up for myself. The bridegroom had half a dozen of them stuffed into the breast pocket of his captain's jacket, a shocking white with an excessive number of shiny brass buttons, white captain's hat with its black patent-leather brim, and actual gold-braided epaulets. He looked more like he belonged to the navy than the army. And with his tan, against the crisp white uniform, he looked insultingly healthy. Rachel too, though the sun only enhanced her true coloring—both of them handsome, striking, even in this crowd.

The cigars, Javi explained to us in broken English he was endearingly shy about, were Rachel's idea. To counteract the smell of the drycleaner's chemical on his uniform. He seldom smoked them.

"Only Marlboros," he said, pronouncing it Mal-burros.

"Cigars like these," Javi went on, taking his cigar out of his mouth and holding it sideways as if to examine it for the first time, "are for pimps, and priests, and socialista-poets."

"And matadors," Laurence said, laughing with him. "According to the tourist pamphlet I once read."

Supposedly all the newlyweds had done since they'd arrived at the Plaza Hotel three nights ago was to eat and sleep. Two more of Rachel's favorite pastimes, and the two things Javi'd been most deprived of in the army. Every day after they'd awoken and bathed and eaten an elaborate room service breakfast, at three or four in the afternoon, they lay in bed making detailed plans to get them both new outfits. Rachel'd only brought a few things herself. But every afternoon, by the time they made it down to the street, all the stores were closed. So when they got back to their room later that night the captain's outfit was sent to the drycleaner. Three nights in a row. And truth is it reeked of the chemical. Even in Bar None. Still I couldn't help my suspicion that Rachel enjoyed Javi dressed up in his fancy outfit, her hero. I'm sure the Plaza had their own stores, probably with their own tailors, probably open 24-hours.

He was an outlaw, Javi explained, a fugitive. The moment he set foot back in Spain, they'd send him back to the army. Either that or throw him in jail. He'd already delayed his mandatory service five years. Already lost a pile of money trying to buy his way out. For the time being, he said, he planned to live with Rachel in Nice.

Of course he wouldn't allow Laurence to buy another bottle of champagne. Impeccably well-mannered. But instead of one bottle, he wanted to buy four, at the same time, one for each of us—or one for each of Rachel's husbands, I decided.

At first we thought that he was joking, or we'd misunderstood. But then Javi left to tell Francis as much behind the bar.

"Don't let's be ostentatious," Rachel said. "Call him off. Two of us've been drinking champagne since breakfast!"

But she gave me her glass and went behind Javi herself. We saw them arguing for a minute beside the bar, then I looked over again and they were kissing. Javi with his hands behind her back, one holding his cigar, the other beneath her sweater. Eventually they seemed to settle it with Francis. Javi handed over his creditcard and we saw Francis make his call, presumably to the fancy tandoori place across the street. A few seconds later a little East Indian boy who looked fifteen came running in the door, squeezing through the crowd, hugging three big bottles against his chest. He handed them to Javi. Strange thing was, the boy had on almost the identical outfit.

I thought I'd mention it to Laurence, but the image of the two of them standing there exchanging bottles, dressed in the same outfit, seemed so bizarre, I decided the alcohol had me seeing things.

Javi brought the bottles back. Gave one to Laurence and another to me. He took his cigar out of his mouth.

"Did you catch my younger brother?" he nodded at the boy hurrying out the door. "I have another who's the bellhop in our hotel. All of us in the same uniform."

He went on, "Raquel says she's had enough. She says she's drunk. I tell her she's beautiful when she's drunk. I tell her she's the most beautiful drunk I ever been on a honeymoon with. I tell her she's the most beautiful drunk in the whole New York. But she says she's had enough."

"Has she?" Laurence asked.

"Indeed. And very soon she'll embarrass herself—never been surrounded by so many flawless men in my life!"

"Pity they're of another persuasion," Laurence said.

"You can never be so sure," Rachel smiled at him.

"In any case," she said, "I'm well provided for, am I not?"

She wanted Laurence to know he was included, her three men.

Three of us busy untwisting the wires from our bottles, over-grown cigars in our mouths, still standing around my stool with the other overturned bottle in its aluminum bucket. We popped our corks, almost simultaneously, foam spilling, a lot of cheering around the room.

Javi took his cigar out of his mouth, raised his bottle and toasted "Goat-ham City," then he took a swig from it. Laurence and I clinked the foil-wrapped stems of our own bottles together and followed suit.

We toasted the newlyweds again. Room service at the Plaza. We toasted their drycleaners. We toasted all the tourist places Javi and Rachel hadn't been to. Don't ask me but that night it was very funny. Three of us clinking our bottles together.

Then Laurence refilled Francis's glass behind the bar, and we toasted him. We toasted Bar None. Laurence refilled Francis's glass again and he toasted us.

"To all-we wayward West Indians!" he said.

At some point a group of college frat-boys stumbled in. Loud, drunk, all wearing identical red baseball caps, white Greek letters stamped across their backwards-turned bills. Out-of-towners I de-cided. At first I thought they'd come into the bar by mistake. We heard them demanding Buds. Then two of them picked their way through the crowd towards us, squeezing into our circle.

"Mind if I pay your lady a compliment?" one asked Laurence.

He seemed pleased by the guy's mistake—anyway he didn't correct him.

"Not in the slightest," Laurence said, "fire away."

The guy turned to Rachel.

"I seen you from outside," he was speaking slowly, trying to re-member his lines. "And something just hit me. Like that perfume

—Impulse. You know, that commercial where the guy jumps off the bus and buys the lady he don't know from Adam a bunch a roses? Like that. I had to come in here and tell you something."

Rachel tipped her glass to him, offered a smile of encouragement.

The guy wobbled slightly on his feet. Forehead sweaty beneath the perforated, red plastic band of his baseball cap.

"You are," he said, "without a doubt, the finest lady I seen in a long time."

He took a breath, summoned his self-confidence.

"Correction," he said. "You are the finest lady I ever seen— anyplace, in my whole freaking life! And if I could get my hands on some freaking roses right now I'd buy em for you!"

He took a swig of his beer, pleased to have gotten it all out. And now he threw caution to the wind. Now he threw the floodgates wide open.

"Very fine lady," he went on. "And class. You got it, that's all. You got it written all over you."

He took another swig.

"Lady, you got more class in your earlobes than most white chicks got in their whole freaking cadavers. I mean, I ain't prejudiced or nothing, gimme a classy negress over a washed-out white chick any day a the week."

His friend nudged me. "It's true. JJ only scams black ladies."

"You don't say?"

"J-boy scammed a real live Miss Black Universe once. Met her in a disco down in Honduras. Wearing her title. Since then he's been obsessed."

"She wasn't nothing," JJ told Rachel. "Not next to you she wasn't. I mean it. You are the finest, classiest negress I ever seen. And believe me, I seen my share. I seen a handful. I seen a lot."

Now JJ turned to Laurence again, gave him a wink of complicity. "Know what they say, go black and never go back!"

I thought Laurence would hit him. But he was smiling—he seemed to think these guys were funny. And Rachel didn't seem bothered in the least, probably she'd been through it before.

Javi wasn't upset either. He was simply looking back and forth between the two of them like they'd landed from Mars.

I was the one who was angry—after getting past my initial shock that is, my momentary confusion. I actually felt like swinging at this guy, this JJ, or his friend, any of them. Just to shatter that privileged college-boy simplicity for a second. They'd almost brought me to blows a couple of times in my own classroom, kids like these. I was trying to calm myself down.

"Won't you write it in a letter to Mummy?" Rachel was telling JJ. "Just as you've said? Write it all down, then we'll send it in a letter to Mummy. She's sure to be pleased—I'm sure Mummy'd be thrilled to hear!"

"We'll tell her about Miss Honduras!"

"Absolutely," Rachel tipped her glass to him.

"Gimme a pen and paper and I'll do it right now," now JJ was shouting. "Gimme a freaking pen! What's your mom's name? I don't joke people, you hear? Not me. Joke people and you get your ass in trouble, that's my philosophy."

"Where you guys from?" the one beside me asked. "UK?"

I must have looked at him like I didn't understand his question.

"You guys Brits?" he repeated.

"We used to be," I said. "Now we're from the West Indies."

"Next stop on my itinerary!" JJ declared, the world traveler.

By now the rest of his group had made their way over. Four or five additional backwards-turned red baseball caps. Four or five additional sweaty foreheads. But they seemed to be headed out the door.

"This bar's fulla funnyboys," a mammoth one, face wide as a football, announced to everybody in the place.

He grabbed the back of JJ's jacket in his fist, started dragging him along backwards.

"No freaking way!" JJ said.

The frat-boys were gone. Off in search of a more appropriate bar. And we all felt relieved—I did, anyway.

How much longer we remained in Bar None ourselves I couldn't tell you. I remember somebody asked Rachel if she wanted to smoke, and a couple of joints appeared out of nowhere. Then I remember Francis bought us each a couple of shots, and we made him drink a couple of shots himself, all of us standing around my stool with four overturned bottles balanced in the dripping aluminum bucket, before we said good night.

We were the only ones left in the place at that point.

Then we were out on the street, the four of us, walking down Seventh Ave going who knows where, and Laurence stopped beside one of those sidewalk peddlers with his junk spread out on an old blanket.

He bent down to examine the stuff. Then Laurence picked something up, laughing out loud.

"Look here, William," he called. "This instrument belongs to you!"

We went over. He was holding up a dilapidated tennis racket.

"You're tight," I said.

"Think so? Watch."

He made a fist and punched it through the strings.

"Hand it over," I said.

Laurence pulled his hand out of the webbing and passed it to me.

Sure enough, branded into the wood along the handle—above the familiar, perforated, pea-colored plastic tape—not Wilson but Walgreens.

Our city of coincidences; her adopted citizens so giddy in love with her they believed without batting an eye.

The peddler had scraps of paper pinned under each of his items—the portable radio spilling half its guts, battered toy firetruck, ragged porn video, etc—his price tags.

The one that sat in the spot the tennis racket occupied read $50.

I was sure I hadn't paid twenty for it originally.

"Give you sixty," Laurence said.

The peddler's expression didn't change. Like he hadn't heard. Like he was deaf and dumb—or demented, I thought. Sitting there on the sidewalk with his legs stretched out before him, leaning his head back against the bare cinderblock wall. His black face filthy with a crust of gray-colored mud, or soot.

I let out a laugh.

"Eighty," Laurence said, laughing now too. "But that's it!"

The peddler remained silent.

Laurence removed his wallet, took out four bills, held them out.

I was still holding the racket.

The guy didn't budge.

Laurence waved the bills back and forth under his nose.

Suddenly the peddler grabbed them, threw them bunched up onto the sidewalk.

"Fuck-off back to wherever you come from," he shouted. "Bunch a you!"

The breeze started taking away the bills.

Rachel crouched quickly to retrieve them, pressing the back of her skirt against her with her other hand, and she tucked the bills into the peddler's shirt pocket. Folded his fatigue jacket back over them. She wrapped her arm through Laurence's and pulled him along.

———————

I can't remember splitting up, or how I got back to my apartment. Probably I took a cab. I think I remember climbing the stairs, I had to sit down twice, my racket heavy as a suitcase. All I know is that when I stumbled through my door, I was still holding it.

I managed to get my boots off but nothing else. Curled up under the blankets. And I'm sure I was out in a second.

Of course I had my dream. I hadn't had it in a long time. Months. But seeing Rachel that night brought it all back, made it certain. It wasn't a nightmare—far from it. Since I always woke up at exactly the point where the nightmare began. Always. At just the moment my dream turned into a nightmare, as inevitable as the "turn to violence" in Act III of a Shakespearean tragedy. My unconscious wouldn't allow me back into that territory: *it* was always careful to wake me up.

And the wonderful thing about dreams, the extraordinary thing about dreams, is that they're more real than real life.

It was Old Year's Eve. Rachel was sixteen and I was fifteen, and our families went together to the British Club to celebrate. As we did every Old Year's Eve. But this year was slightly different. This year, instead of one of the adults having to do it—they actually threw dice to decide the duty—Rachel would drive us home when the time came, at one or two in the morning. Because this year Rachel had just gotten her learner's permit. So when the time came we'd all pile into her mother's station wagon with the red L taped to the back window, and she'd drive us home, and Rachel and I would put the kids to bed. In addition to my own brother and Rachel's sisters, we always managed to pick up a few others.

Rachel also drove us to the club that night, following behind our parents in my father's Bentley, all of us screaming with excitement. Radio blasting that year's new calypsos for the start of carnival season, many being aired for the first time—Kitch, Rudder, Black Stalin. It was always something of a spectacle, walking up the long drive from wherever we found a place to park. Walking in the half-dark, the men in tuxedos and the women in hats and gloves and glittering gowns. With the blacks and East Indians gathered along both sides of the drive—they weren't allowed past the policemen posted at the club's wrought-iron gates—standing there for hours, gallerying the whites as we walked past. Some of them even took advantage of the occasion and set up tables or small stalls to sell their fried channa and cold drinks—doubles, shark-and-bake, salt-prunes, and tamarind balls—and most of the stalls had flambeaux posted beside them. Smoking and smelling of rank pitch-oil, casting long jerking shadows as we walked past, which added to the drama.

Of course part of the fun was hearing the spectators' comments:

"That is Hollywood, Papa!"

"Look Betty and Clark-self passing now!"

Or the ruder comments:

"That bamsee must be jelly because jam don't shake so!"

We weren't the only kids. But there weren't many other parents willing to make the sacrifice of bringing their kids with them; and, as I said, we always went home by one or two in the morning.

What I remember is walking up the drive with both our families. Rachel and I purposely let the others walk on ahead, her arm through mine. I was wearing my father's old tuxedo. Rachel her mother's backless gown, her hair loose, reaching down as far as her hips. But still with a slice of brown back visible where the dress clung. Her heels crunching on the gravel. So stunning that night she left the men watching from the roadside speechless. You could feel it.

Then I remember there was a sudden gap in the line of spectators, a couple of minutes of silence, pitch-dark, and at that point we passed an enormous poinciana tree, set a little back from the drive. With a group of five or six rastas sitting up in the tree looking out from the branches. You could hardly see them in the dark. And their heads were surrounded by thick clouds of gray smoke from their joints or whatever they were smoking, which hid them further. What I remember distinctly is that two of them looked the same, like identical twins. Sitting next to each other on the branch, and the uncanny part was they had their heads shaved clean. I can't tell you if it was because of their shaved heads—actually a familiar sight at home, nothing to do with fashion, but because the police made a regular habit of grabbing rastas at the slightest pretext and shaving off all their locks—I couldn't tell you if it was due to their shaved heads, or the fact that these two guys looked so exactly the same, or what it was about them that impressed me so. Maybe just the way they stared back at us, or at Rachel—the expression mirrored so exactly in both of their faces—but I just couldn't get them out of my mind. Long after we'd gone past.

For a long time Rachel and I had looked forward to this Old Year's Eve. For a long time we'd planned it out. Still, I can't remember dancing with her at all that night; there was hardly ever any dancing in my dream. Though Sam'd brought Byron Lee and his Dragonaires band from Jamaica for the occasion, as he did every year, and I'm sure Rachel and I must have danced practically every song together. At least every calypso. But I can't even remember kissing her at midnight. I suppose because I'd done all that half a dozen times before. Because that year my mind was focused, I was anticipating what was to come later on. We weren't drinking, either, Rachel and I. Because that night we were playing our parts as designated, serious, responsible adults.

The only thing I remember from the club is a moment when I was dancing next to Rachel. With one of my other cousins. Sometime after midnight. My father was dancing with Rachel—he'd been pestering her for a dance all night—and next thing I knew Rachel slapped him, hard, and I saw her picking her way through the other couples dancing, hurrying back to our table. With my father standing there by himself looking lost. And I remember, at that moment, feeling the distinct need to go over and help him.

At two o'clock we left the club and started with the kids down the drive towards the car—all the spectators and vendors gone home by now—and when we passed the poinciana tree the rastas were no longer sitting in it, either, and I felt relieved. We bundled all the kids into Rachel's mother's wagon, and Rachel drove us home. To her house, and when we got there I jumped out and unlocked the wrought-iron gates and swung them open, let the car in, and locked them back again. We got the kids into their pajamas and their teeth brushed and into bed, five or six of them on three mattresses fitted together on the floor of her sisters' room, and downstairs Rachel and I had a couple of shots of rum and we smoked half a joint in her kitchen, waiting for the kids to fall asleep. Rachel went back upstairs to make sure. Then we locked them in, walked around her house and across both our backyards—barefoot now, but me still with my tuxedo jacket on, Rachel a shawl over her shoulders—walking barefoot and leaving a trail across the damp grass over to my house, where we carefully locked the front door behind us again.

Our parents wouldn't be home until noon the next day. We had all the time in the world. We were in no hurry. We'd planned all this, and thought it all out, we knew the significance of what we were about to do, what it would mean to us for the rest of our lives. We'd chosen it for ourselves, and had waited for it, and now we wanted it to be unhurried, and memorable, and perfect.

It goes without saying we were also in love. It is highly possible that we'd been desperately in love with each other since we were eight and seven years of age.

Then, before we knew it, before we tasted our shots of my father's special twenty-year-old rum downstairs in the parlor, we were pulling off each other's clothes and sucking each other's bodies in places we'd never imagined, places lovers on the Roxy's screen were never seen to suck. As though we were inventing it now for ourselves. We were down on the rug in the parlor suddenly in a mad rush but not knowing exactly what to do or how to proceed, either of us, and we never made it out of that parlor until noon the next morning when our parents arrived. Though we'd planned for this part to happen upstairs in my bedroom.

What I remember is two contradictory things: how strange and impossible it felt when, after a few fruitless stabs—probably at Rachel's abdomen—she reached down between our hips and held me firmly and fitted me into some place which, much to my own surprise, much as I'd anticipated it, was hot and wet and startlingly soft; and then, a second later, how absolutely precise and accurate it felt when the two of us were fitted together. Like the most intricate key slid into the most intricate lock. Like they'd been made for each other waiting for this since the beginning of the world.

We lay there like that for a second—a few seconds, a minute, how long?—not moving a muscle. Astonished, I think, at just how perfect it felt. No amount of preparing could have readied us for this moment. No amount of planning.

I really do not believe we managed to move a muscle beyond that.

Suddenly a noise as when a jet breaks the sound barrier: they yanked the enormous wrought-iron burglar-proofing right out of the concrete wall. With their bare hands. Dropped it clattering to the concrete patio floor climbing over it with their bare feet and one of them punched his fist though the sliding glass door. Like punching though a spider web. Glass raining down around them like water on hot oil.

They were bareback, all three of them, all sweating like I'd never seen anybody sweat before in my life, every inch of their smooth dark skin, their exploding muscles, all covered by a second ragged iguana-skin of thick round drops of perspiration.

All three of them carried cutlasses.

We'd die before we let them pry us apart.

7

You won't believe me, but I got to NYU an hour early for my class the following morning. When I awoke, panting, and looked over at my alarm clock, it said five-thirty. I was still drunk, the room still spinning. But I knew I wouldn't be able to fall back asleep. I stood in the cold shower for as long as I could stand it, dressed, and went to the All-American Diner in Chinatown that was open 24-hours. Had their special $5.95 All-American breakfast: fried eggs and hashed-browns and bacon and sausage-links and toast and pancakes and half a gallon of All-American coffee. When I got to my classroom I had enough time to prepare all my classes for the day, and the only noticeable trace of last night was the tingling at the tips of my fingers due to lack of sleep. A couple of hour-long naps on my to-fro Bronx shuttles later on cured that, too.

The plan, I remembered as much, was to meet not at SOB's, but at the bar down the street so that we could have a drink before the concert. David Rudder had canceled from last night, or he was playing more than one pre-carnival jump-up, but Francis or Laurence or somebody—maybe JJ—had known positively that he was playing a concert at SOB's tonight. Rachel and Javi were leaving for Paris on their way to Nice early tomorrow morning. So they'd made us promise to get them back to their hotel at a decent hour. Whatever that meant—concerts at SOB's regularly ran till 3 AM.

The place down the street was already loud and smoky and filled with shouting West Indians. But after a minute I found my friends sitting at the bar, eating an hors d'oeuvre of jerked chicken-wings and drinking rum-cocktails, the latter which Laurence had instructed the bartender how to make properly. The three of them had been together since four that afternoon. When they'd break-fasted not at the Plaza, but in some uptown bistro Laurence took them to that was famous for their oeufs-à-la-something-or-other. There, Laurence told me, he'd taken the precaution of instruct-ing the bartender how to make a proper Bloody Mary.

That's how our evening began, in many ways a repetition of the previous one, except instead of champagne we took swigs from the bottle of Royal Oak Javi snuck into SOB's someplace beneath his captain's outfit. We figured they wouldn't frisk a serviceman. At least not one who spoke Javi's brand of Castilian Spanish. The four of us wining together with the bottle of rum sitting on the concrete floor in the middle of our circle, together with our piled up jackets. SOB's is a pitch-black bombed-out warehouse with a stage at the back, and that night, as with any night Rudder came to town to perform, it was packed with raucous, bawling, thoroughly happy West Indians. And we were among them. We jumped-up through Charlie's Roots' warmup; through Tambu's soca set, the three road-marches he had to his credit; then we jumped-up through at least a couple of hours of Rudder—"Hammer" and "Bahia Girl" and all his early calypsos—and three encores. Sweating in November, sweating profusely—so that after a while Rachel unbuttoned her sweater and knotted it be-tween her breasts, her navel and brown abdomen exposed above the tweed skirt, hair tied in a knot on top her head—and Javi stripped down to the marino he was wearing beneath his fancy jacket. After a while Javi was wining with as much abandon as any of us.

———

Bar None had just about emptied out by the time we got there, it was that late, and much to our disappointment Francis wasn't work-ing. But nothing could dampen our spirits that night. I got a round of ice-cold Red Stripes from the bartender, some guy we'd never met before, and Laurence used the payphone to call Delancy's for a car to take Rachel and Javi to the airport in an hour. Then they realized they hadn't checked out of their hotel. So Rachel called the Plaza and asked the concierge to charge everything to Javi's creditcard— reading the numbers off three different times, confounding him each time she repeated the number naught—then she asked the concierge to mail the things she'd left in her room on to her in Nice.

Then Javi realized they'd have to stop by the hotel anyway, to get their passports and tickets out of the safety deposit box.

Then they couldn't remember where they'd put the little key, and Javi took up his jacket where he'd tossed it onto the bar, started going through the pockets.

"Right," Rachel said when it was all settled. "The plan is to meet at home in three months' time."

Laurence was getting her a fresh beer. Mal-burros, in Javi's honor, for her three men.

After a second Rachel added as an afterthought, "I've put William in charge of all specifics!"

We'd agreed to it at some point during the concert—in the midst of our shouting, jumping-up, sweating—in the midst of our nostalgic revelry. Rachel saying she hadn't been at home for carnival since she was practically a child. Laurence said the same thing, which surprized me.

Probably half the crowd in SOB's also planned to return home for the festival. We heard them talking about it—"You playing mas with Minshall or Barbarossa this year?"—those few days when our local population is practically doubled by returning expats.

At some point during the concert we ran into an old friend, Alicia. She'd been in Rachel's class in the convent, just taken an apartment in the East Village. And during the course of our jumping-up together—five of us dancing in a circle to "Bahia

Girl," our arms hugging each other's waists—Alicia vowed to meet us at home for carnival too.

But the truth is that almost as soon as we'd agreed to the plan, I'd also dismissed it; I really did not believe that either Rachel or Laurence was serious. And even if they were serious at the moment, they'd never make it down—Laurence was simply too busy, Rachel too disorganized.

They both knew that I went just about every year. Every year I could get away, that is, and I usually managed. In large part because my friend Shay-lee always arranged to get me a cheap ticket. It was the only time I did return home. Not because I loved carnival more than anything, which I did, but because it was the only time of year I could return home. Only time I knew I wouldn't have to see my parents. My mother and father regularly "escaped the rabble" by flying off to Barbados for the week, together with their group of proper English friends: there were those of us who couldn't live without the festival, those who considered it vulgar and barbaric and wanted nothing whatsoever to do with it. An event, at best, to be tolerated for the "blacks."

My policy had always been to go alone. At least I'd never brought along any of my American friends, though each year a handful tried hard to convince me. I didn't want to feel responsible for anybody. Make sure they were having a good time, then to have to bail them out of trouble when they got into it, which seemed inevitable.

In addition I had my own friends at home, and I never believed in mixing. I liked the idea of keeping my two lives separate. And it was those few days of carnival each year that enabled me to keep my other life, my past, where it belonged: in place behind me.

Yet here I was, standing here in Bar None, a thousand miles away, actually accepting the proposition of bringing not only my friends, but my past back with me: Rachel and Laurence, to be sure. And in an odd way also Javier, since he represented the small army of men Rachel would seduce in an average woman's life, part of my past too. Then there was the bottle of Royal Oak we'd drunk at the concert, the Red Stripes.

Laurence raised his up in the air.

"Car-nee-val!" he said it the way we did at home, drawing out the last syllable.

We touched our bottles to his.

"OK," I blew a lungful of smoke over my shoulder, still far from convinced my friends would show up. "All you guys have to do is get there. I'll arrange the rest."

Those "specifics" Rachel had already put me in charge of.

Then, I suggested, when the festival was all over—after our day of rest and recuperation on Ash Wednesday—we could drive out to the village of Matelot. Leisurely hike into the rainforested mountains of the north coast, and we'd camp on the beach beside the Madamas River for a few days.

"It's paradise," I told them. "Perfect place to detox and clear our heads."

"We'll see a leatherback come up to lay?" Rachel asked.

She'd heard me talk about them.

"Maybe," I said. "If the wind drops. And we have a full moon."

It was the start of the laying season, I explained, and we'd have two or three nights. However long we decided to stay. Oony'd lend us her Suzuki, and I'd arrange to borrow backpacks and sleepingbags, canteens and whatever else we'd need.

It was my ritual every year after carnival. Except usually I camped out alone.

Rachel wanted to know about the Earth People, a family of rastas who lived up in the valley above the Madamas Beach, which they called Hell Valley.

I'd told her about them too.

"They'll come down from the valley to see us," I said. "Even take us up to meet Mother Earth, if we're interested. If she's in a receptive mood, that is, which you can never count on."

"They're not dangerous?" Rachel asked.

"They're the gentlest people you'll ever meet." My enthusiasm was bubbling through, much as I tried to hold it back.

"And it's true," she said, "the way they live?"

"They'll put on something when they come down to see us," I smiled at her. "Always do when they leave the valley."

It was what she meant, what everybody focused on.

"Pity," Rachel smiled back.

"They'll dress up for us in their cocoasack-skirts."

"Chut!" she said.

They'd made the news at home in a big way a few years back, especially after villagers in nearby Pinnacle discovered the Earth People's practice of living naked. The villagers were scandalized, rumors of orgies and incest. Of the satanic, self-proclaimed Mother Earth and all her "sons" which she kept as slaves, sexual and otherwise. Stories of the endless ganja they grew and smoked, which was the only true part.

But after the first headlines and outrageous full-page pictures, black circles pasted over their breasts and genitals—the photogaphers catching them in poses which made them look like wild African bushpeople, spliffs loose between their lips, hugely dreadlocked heads clouded in smoke—after all that, when the initial shock wore off, the Earth People were mainly ignored.

A common characteristic among West Indians is our short attention span. Or maybe it's our memory that's atrophied.

"Apparently she's been ill for some time, this Mother Earth," Laurence put in.

"She was very sick when I saw her a couple of years back," I said. "Too weak to stand on her feet for long without holding on to somebody. Or, when she's delivering one of her diatribes, leaning up against a post in the old cocoahouse."

I paused, "She suffers from a thyroid condition—goiter, hypertension, radical mood swings."

"So I've been told."

"And she only believes in bush-medicine, which is the main difficulty. Her husband—they call him Breadfruit—has taken over for the most part. Problem is, he doesn't have her vision."

Suddenly I was feeling awkward, the authority—or, oddly enough, as though I needed to establish some kind of authority. And suddenly we were all serious. But it only lasted a minute.

Javi wanted to know who were these naked people who smoked ganja, he pronounced it gang-ha. He'd put his captain's jacket back on, but hadn't buttoned it up, his marino still showing.

For some reason I chose that particular moment to try out my Spanish—managing to mix up the words secta and sexo—only adding to poor Javi's confusion. But I was happy to be laughing again. Suddenly excited by the possibility of all of us, including our new friend, meeting up again in a few months' time.

That is, if Rachel was still with him in a few months' time.

One thing for sure, I decided: if Javi and Rachel did make it down together, on time, it wouldn't be for a second honeymoon.

"Car-nee-val!" Javi was saying, and with his Spanish pronunciation he sounded like Laurence a few minutes ago.

Javi had his bottle raised in the air.

We clicked them together, the four of us, and seemingly on cue a dark blue Delancy's car pulled up outside the door.

II

8

That winter I kept myself busy. It had long since turned too cold for tennis, and much as I missed getting together with Laurence on Saturday mornings, our sojourns afterwards to visit Francis in Bar None, the truth is that I rather enjoyed not having to play. Somehow the spirit had gone out of it since the summer. That winter I added a couple of extra classes to my teaching load, stayed in and marked papers or read during the evenings, avoided the bars, enjoyed not having to play tennis on Saturday mornings, and I tried to put aside as much money as I could for our trip. Though I was still far from convinced my friends would show up. Or that it was such a good idea—my bringing them along, playing tour guide for Laurence, Rachel, and her husband. I wasn't sure how well they'd get along with my other friends at home, either, particularly Shay-lee and Oony. Of course, Rachel had gone to convent with both of them—and they'd been friends before that, since childhood—but Rachel hadn't been back to the island in years. Shay-lee and Oony knew Laurence too, though not intimately, and other than a few brief visits, he hadn't been back home himself. For that matter, Laurence and Rachel didn't really know each other. And you could never tell what might happen when you threw people together like that. Especially during carnival.

Despite my misgivings a month ahead of time I called my great-auntie, Miss Fletcher, at the Queens Park to make our reservations. She'd run the hotel since the day it opened its doors. In those days it was a posh place—Queen Elizabeth had come herself for the inauguration—a gem of a deco building. Now it was falling down, a boardinghouse for old people more than anything else, several of them quite mad, including a handful of distant relatives. Miss Fletcher always saved me my room, whether I called ahead of carnival or not. This time I asked for three rooms, and my auntie promised me three with balconies overlooking the Queens Park Savannah, as it's officially called. If Laurence and Rachel didn't show up, I told myself, I could easily palm their rooms off on a few tourists. And depending on how sentimental I happened to feel about my old auntie when the time came, I could even pocket a handful of local dollars in the process.

The hotel's location for carnival is perfect. Right across the street from the stands and the Savannah mainstage, focal point of it all. There's a modern Hilton high on the hill on the other side of the park—which I'm sure would have better suited Laurence, Rachel also—but that night in Bar None I'd told them straight away that if I was making the reservations, we were staying in the Queens Park. I wouldn't think of staying anyplace else.

I hadn't heard a word from Rachel since she left New York. Not that I expected to hear from her. Or, frankly, that I wanted to—either that she was keeping to our plans and coming home for carnival or not—because I truly did not know which would be better for all concerned. But during those last few months I'd been thinking about her a lot, certainly more than I had in previous years, and part of me was excited about the possibility of seeing her again. At home, on familiar ground. Fate would decide, and I had learned long ago not to try to manipulate fate. Leave her alone to her machinations.

I did hear from Laurence. Only a couple of weeks before it was time to leave. This time though, instead of leaving a message on my answering machine, he sent me a note through the mail. Written on the fancy stationery of the Majestic Hotel in Tangier. (He'd been sent there by the BBC to speak with Paul Bowles, in what would turn out to be one of that famous writer's last interviews.) Though I wouldn't have been surprised to hear from him in Tangier, Tokyo, or Timbuktu. Laurence got around.

His note read like telegrams did when people still used them, but the script was beautiful. I could almost see his elegant fingers shaping out the letters:

> *Not too late I hope to wish you*
> *a Happy Christmas, my bro.*
> *Arriving home for carnival eve*
> *of Sat 9 Feb. Will catch up*
> *with the gang at Queens Park.*
> *—L*

Which made me suspect he had spoken with Rachel. And I found out later that I was right. He'd sent her a couple of similar notes, from various corners of the globe, and when he got no response, he called her—three times before he could get her on the phone—calling, as a matter of fact, from the Majestic Hotel in Tangier. Rachel assured him she was coming.

————

The airport at home, a few days before the festival, is chaos. Inundated by expats returning to the island from "foreign." All of them dressed head to toe in new KC jeans outfits, squeaky new Nikes, each lugging a new boombox—each booming a different new calypso—and half a dozen oversized, taped-up and excessively-labeled boxes of presents from the mall. Customs has to go through every box. So in no time the place looks like the fleamarket on 25th St, everybody in the middle of packing up or unpacking. And, of course, they can never get it all back into their boxes.

Add to that the miniature steelband playing in the corner for a handful of tourists, all the locals meeting their friends and families who have managed somehow to get into the "quarantine" area from outside, taxi drivers hustling rides, food and drink vendors, people looking to buy US dollars, sell their carved coconuts and jumbie-beads and straw hats, the preacher on his soapbox already condemning the immoral nastiness of this car-nee-val you seem to be risking your life for and are presently clawing your way past people to get to . . . well, you get the idea.

In addition I happened to choose the wrong immigration officer. I knew him, recognized him as soon as I got near the top of the line. When it was already too late to change gracefully. We hadn't seen each other in twelve years or longer: Ganish Ramsumair, a dougla from quaint Temple Village, his father the pundit there. He'd been with Laurence and me in Father O'Connor's sixth-form special English. Ganish, like Laurence and me, had boasted he wanted to enter the literary profession; he, too, had wanted to become a "writer." To the extent that he'd forsaken his small village, where his straightforward and fairly prosperous future was already laid out for him, and he'd come to live in town, to attend the Catholic college. Though I remembered Ganish as not only a country-bookie, but something of the class fool.

He also recognized me, even before he looked at the name in my passport.

"Eh-eh, boy!" he said. "But you reach back from America. Come to pay we a visit in baboo-nation!"

Baboo being a derogatory synonym for dougla.

I managed a smile.

"You know," he leaned forward over his desk, resting his chin on his knuckles pensively. "I hear a good good story bout you! While back. Good few years ago it is already."

He paused, springs of his chair creaking, "I hear this story bout how you did pose as a negro-man. To get some kinda scholarship they was giving-way in one them fancy writing schools in New York. Columbia University, or someplace so. Any trut in that?"

I stared at him blankfaced.

"Boy, the story going round here was how you did paint youself black! With shoepolish. And people say how you put on a heavy West Indian accent for them yankees, and the blasted fools fall for it. Only a island boy could tink up a scheme good as that, eh? Only a scoundrel like we!"

Ganish steupsed, "But I hear it give you a helloffa time, when the polish couldn't scrub out. Not true? Boy, I did tell meself that if in America they does hand out money to people only for being black, then I could carry me rass in America too. And I ain't even bound to shoepolish meself!"

"It was a confusion with the application."

"Oh-ho."

"Wasn't any shoepolish!"

I could read the disappointment in his face, I'd lowered myself in Ganish's estimation.

"But you get trough, eh?" he said. "And I hear these days you writing plenty book in New York. Plenty big book! That the place, eh? Book like fire in you tail!"

"Not—"

"Come, nuh man. Speak the trut!"

I took a breath.

"I got my first novel coming out. In England."

"Yeah?"

Clearly this wasn't enough; Ganish wanted more, he wanted to hear about America. And suddenly I felt a distressing need to make up for the shoepolish story, despite its absurdity.

"My agent's trying to place it in New York."

"Oh-ho," he smiled. "Agent, eh? Sound like out the movies!"

"She tells me any day now."

"Man, you got to give me she name! That I could send she *my* manuscript when it finish. What she name is?"

"Well—"

"And what you book is about, eh? Plenty intrigue? Bubball? Plenty steamy sex?"

"Not—"

"You know," he cut me off again. " I got a good good one in me too. This book planning since we was wearing shorteepants in Padre O'Connor class. And boy, when I tell you this book a bestseller. This one a genuine Herness Hemingway. You want to hear? eh?"

He was holding on to my passport. Seemed reluctant to hand it back.

"Ever been by Penal Junction? Fyzabad? Them place is plenty action, oh G-o-w-d!"

Ganish opened his eyes wide, pursing his lips—and I could only think of our small, large-headed swamp-fish, the pag, popularly eaten in rural areas.

"Boy," he made a flourish in the air with my passport. "I going to tell you . . ."

There were, without exaggerating, fifty people waiting in line behind me. Fifty boomboxes. But instead of getting upset, half a dozen of them joined in. Elaborating Ganish's tale of Fyzabad.

————

Between Customs and Immigration, almost three hours. Night by the time I squeezed through the crowd pressed against the glass doors from outside. And all I had with me was my carry-on, and my duty-free plastic Bee-wee airlines bag, its two exempt bottles of scotch sloshing inside. One of which, with a little help from Ganish, was already a quarter empty.

Shay-lee and Oony were there waiting for me, drinking Caribs at the bar, sensibly located where Customs lets out. They jumped off their stools, three of us hugging at the same time. Shay-lee still in her Bee-wee outfit. Oony'd just come from mascamp, her jeans covered with paint and glue. She's a successful fashion designer— with her own line of clothes and her own factory to make them— which she shuts down during carnival season to oversee Minshall's costume production. For those few months Oony practically lives at mascamp, along with the other Minshallites.

She asked the bartender for a Carib for me.

"Surprise," Shay-lee pointed up at a portable radio, duct-taped to a post at the end of the bar. I heard the familiar sound of pan rasping from it.

"Semis," she said, "they just started."

"How's that?"

The semifinals of the Panorama steelband competition—they should have taken place on Sunday, five days ago.

"Mishap in northstand," Shay-lee smiled at me. "It nearly collapse."

"So what's new?"

"This time it almost happen in truth!"

She explained that on Sunday night, just as the first steelband was assembling on mainstage, people sitting in the upper right-hand corner of a jam-packed northstand began to feel the uncanny sensation of drifting even farther to the right. Most of them had already consumed their share of rum, and most of them ignored it. Not till a heavy-set woman got down on her hands and knees, her ample bamsee standing up tall in the air, and squeezed her head beneath her seat, did anybody realize the stands were collapsing. Several rows of seats were bending over backwards, and to the right—very, very slowly.

The woman let loose banshee-bawl and northstand was evacuated without mishap. Although, Shay-lee said, according to the *Guardian* the woman tried to sue the NCC, the National Carnival Committee, for a "sprained right cheek." When the magistrate performed the indignity of laughing at her she produced a certificate signed by the government doctor, verifying the injury in just those words. The magistrate ordered her free northstand tickets all carnival long in lieu of damages, and the semis for the northwestern region were postponed until Friday—tonight—while the faulty section of the stands was repaired.

"So we dragging you strait to the Savannah," Shay-lee said.

I couldn't be more pleased. This was an unexpected pleasure for me—two full nights of pan. Usually I arrived just in time for finals.

With traffic we had an hour's drive into town. But we were in no rush. Desperadoes, the Laventille band we all liked, was playing last. With eighteen bands before them, each with a hundred pannists, three-hundred-odd steeldrums on their wheeled aluminum carts. And each band had to be pushed up onto mainstage, they had to set up, play their tune, be applauded, then be wheeled down onto the track again.

Panorama made even the airport seem organized.

We drove past a sign posted next to the exit—famous, several of the calypsonians sang about it. This sign was sponsored by a group of notorious old ladies called the Marian Society—and Marian, of course, refers to the Virgin. The irony is that this group dedicated themselves to the prevention of unmarried mothers. In this case, "carnival babies."

CARNIVAL

WELCOME HOME
HAVE A HAPPY CARNIVAL
BUT DON'T LEAVE YOUR TROUBLES
WITH US: WEAR A CONDOM!

On the roadside not a mile from the airport an East Indian woman has a stall with some of the best doubles on the island. Shay-lee, who was driving Oony's car, stopped without my even asking. We collected our food and parked a little way down from the stall, facing the road, forest at our backs.

Our driver emerged from the car a couple of minutes behind Oony and me, changed from her airlines outfit into jeans, T-shirt, and flip-flops. Three of us sitting on the warm hood, the night air pleasantly cool, drinking Caribs, eating our doubles. A fried "bake" that's split and filled with curried channa—chickpeas. Mine and Shay-lee's with lil pepper, Oony's with plenty.

My mouth was on fire, traveling up my nostrils, bringing tears to my eyes. Which the beer only intensified instead of cooling.

We were talking about Minshall's latest infatuation.

"They call him Eddoes," Oony was saying. "Seventeen, but innocent as a twelve-year-old. Like he's never even been in the outside world."

"He's gorgeous," this was Shay-lee. "And don't talk about his body! He has Minshall bazodee, when I tell you. Following the boy round mascamp all day long like a lost puppy."

"He have any idea what Minshall's after?" I asked.

"Clueless," said Oony. "Which is why it's so funny. Eddoes trusts the world—loves the world—completely, unconditionally, like all of them. It's really very beautiful."

"So Minshall wants him to play King?"

"Practically redesigned the whole band around him."

"He'll play a great King too," Shay-lee said. "Once he gets over his shyness."

"Almost over it already. Specially with all the heckling they give him at mascamp."

"He's never played mas before?"

"Sure," said Oony. "Runs away every year and joins a band. Usually Fantasia, or Nevel Aming. But he's never played in a big band before. And he's definitely never played King."

"He just appeared one day at mascamp? Out of nowhere?"

"In his cocoasack-skirt, if you please," said Shay-lee.

"You're kidding."

"A-tall," said Oony. "He'd been traveling through the forest for three days. Hardly eaten anything."

She took a sip of her beer, put it down on the hood.

"Minshall was first to see him. Climbing out the bush behind mascamp early morning. Eddoes had just bathed in the river. Imagine: sun shining behind him, his long dreads and the skirt, skin wet, glistening, with *that* body—Minshall thought he was an apparition!"

"Come to save him," I said.

"The angel Gabriel," Shay-lee said, "come to announce the band to Minshall."

We were all laughing.

"Surprising he didn't call it Eddoes."

"Think you making joke?" Oony said. "He almost did!"

"So what's the band called anyway?" I asked.

"River," Shay-lee said. "Of course."

While we were talking a long-legged, ratty-feathered chicken appeared out of the bush to join us. Scratching at the dust around the tires at our feet. Type of chicken we call a clean-neck-fowl, I have no idea why—there's nothing clean about a clean-neck-fowl. We threw her little pieces of bake, which she tossed around in the air, then gobbled up. When we had nothing left to offer she made three low bows, one directed at each of us. Then disappeared. Her awkward, long-legged run back into the bush.

Well-mannered chicken, I thought.

A car pulled up to the stall. We heard the radio's blast of steel-drums as the driver lowered his window, ordered, then drove off again.

At our backs the cedars and bois-canot were enormous, running right up to the tops of the mountains. Canefields spread out in the low-lying, marshy fields in front. Stretching as far as the horizon. Where the green-gray land met the iridescent black bar of the sea. Canefields rippling to coincide with the headlights of cars passing in the distance—like the wakes of speedboats but inverted—fanning out in front. Which struck me as odd, I'd never seen it that way before. Like watching a film in reverse.

There was the faint smell of a far-off cook-fire. Or somebody burning cane trash.

We'd long finished our doubles. Shay-lee and I had drunk our beers, but Oony'd taken a few sips, let hers go flat on the hood of the car. That's the thing about Caribs—you have to drink them fast, and cold.

We sat there for a few minutes, not talking, just listening to the buzz of the night insects—almost deafening, when you listened for it—interrupted every so often by a momentary silence. Then the hollow wooden tok-tok of some kind of bird. Then the buzz again.

The car's hood was no longer warm. Oony shivered once, leaned forward and poured her beer out in a thin stream, splattering up in the dust.

"Let's go," she said. "Before we miss Despers too!"

I snapped as though I'd been asleep.

We jumped into the car, radio blasting Panorama again—Invaders had just started to play—headed for the madness of town.

Oony and Shay-lee dropped me off at the hotel's front gates. They went to park the car, I'd meet them in the northstand. When I got out I could hear one of the steelbands across the street playing onstage now, according to the radio it was Allstars. I stopped to listen for a second: the softly ringing pan, crowds in the stands shouting, their low roar growing as the band went into a run. I turned and hurried into the hotel. Looked around and took my key from the panel of hooks behind Miss Fletcher's desk. Climbed the stairs and let myself in.

I set my duffelbag on the bed and pulled out some fresh clothes. T-shirt and a pair of loose, baggy pants that reached to just above my ankles—only freshwater-yankees, and young-boys, wore "shortee-pants," as Ganish had called them. I'd bought these specially for the trip, at a bargain basement on 14th St called, appropriately enough, Kids' Town. But they'd only cost me a few dollars and they'd be comfortable in all the heat. In the bathroom I splashed some cool, rusty-smelling water on my smiling face—looking like a kid too, I decided, thoroughly happy. Pulled the front of my T-shirt up to dry off my face, no towel, then I grabbed the open bottle of scotch as a contribution when I joined the others, and I took off.

Only minor problem was that Miss Fletcher hadn't been around for me to change some money. I'd get some from Oony and Shay-lee when I saw them, but I needed a few local dollars to buy a ticket to get into northstand. Thing is you only need a ticket if you enter by the gate, which few people bother with. The police would never question a white boy like me anyway.

I crossed the street in front of our hotel, making a wide skirt through the knee-high grass and weeds around grandstand, heading for the drag. For the pan.

I stood with the tenors of Amoco Renegades, one of the big bands, feeling the power of the steeldrums all around me. Hundreds of tiny lights flickering in the distance around the Savannah's dark, wide-open expanse. In the mountains of the northern range, Cascade, St Ann's, Laventille to the east.

In the middle of the tune a guy standing beside me motioned for me to pour some of my scotch into his paper KFC cup. Which I did, sloshing a good amount onto the grass in the process, the pans lurching forwards. He tapped his friend on the shoulder, nodded in my direction, and his friend pulled a joint from behind his ear, lit it and passed it over—all at the same time we were pushing the pans. I smoked it for a couple of minutes, but when I turned to look for the guy I couldn't find him. Or his friend.

I didn't feel like smoking the joint by myself so I shared it with a pannist who was taking a break, sitting up on the crossbar of his cart, Renegades T-shirt draped temporarily across his shoulder. Then we each had a swallow of scotch. Which, jokingly, the pannist made a big deal about. Shouting above the music, holding the bottle high in the air—his thumb half-fitted over the opening, head thrown back—pouring the scotch out in a long, unbroken arch into his mouth. He didn't spill a drop either. Recapped the bottle and shut his eyes, shaking his head back and forth, beaded braids whipping against his neck.

Making as if he'd fall off his perch.

"Papa-yo!" he shouted.

Suddenly I didn't feel like carrying the bottle around anymore, and knew that if I kept it with me I'd continue drinking it. Things were under control, and I didn't want to lose control. Not yet, not on my first night.

I took a swallow and handed the bottle back to the pannist. Made a sign for him to keep it. He thought I was nuts, giving away half a bottle of scotch. And I probably wouldn't give it to a player of Despers, Invaders, or Skiffle Bunch. But I wasn't opposed to adding slightly to the demise of the Amoco Renegades. We knocked fists and I squeezed out between the carts, away from the band.

———————

Then I lost a couple of hours. Somewhere in the middle of the dusty Savannah. Somewhere on the drag between Renegades and Skiffle Bunch. They just flew away.

I found myself in the middle of Skiffle Bunch, a smaller band, pushing the pans, looking for a cousin of mine who was married to a guy who played first tenor for them. A black guy, also an accomplished jazz guitarist, another family scandal.

I talked to some players I recognized who told me they were both there, but I couldn't find either one. I found Melvin's cart, because I recognized the snapshot of their daughter—my niece Asha—that he had dangling on a string from a crossbar of the roof. But no Melvin. Or my cousin.

Then somebody covered my eyes from behind.

I might have guessed who it was if I thought about it for a second, since Celina, the cousin I was looking for—the cousin who'd moved back from Nice a few years ago—was her younger sister. And if Rachel was anyplace on the drag that night, she'd probably be with Skiffle Bunch.

I turned around, so pleased to see her that when we hugged I lifted her up off the grass for a second.

Then, without a word between us, we were kissing. Passion-
ately—and this time we were not playing our childhood Roxy
game.

We stood in the tall grass, in the shadows, Skiffle Bunch assembling noisily all around us, kissing each other. My mind going inevitably back to that last afternoon when Rachel returned from
convent—me sitting on her front step when her mother's wagon
pulled into the drive, still with its faded red L taped to the back
window—our last summer together on the island.

Rachel was eighteen and I would have just turned seventeen.
She got out of the car barefoot. Still in her convent uniform, the
pleated navy skirt and white long-sleeved shirt. Navy-and-red-
striped school tie loose around her collar. We hugged and she kissed
me on the cheek, well-behaved cousins before her mother. Rachel
handed me her suitcase and I followed her into the house, up the
stairs to her room. And in her bedroom she turned around and kissed
me properly.

At the top of the stairs, just as we were about to go back down,
Rachel told me she was dying to pee. She glanced over her shoulder and pulled me into the bathroom, locking the door behind
us. Rachel smiled up at me, shimmying out of her elasticized,
convent-issued bloomers. While she flipped up the back of her skirt
to sit on the seat. Stretching her long legs out towards me, kicking
her detested bloomers off the ends of her pointed toes. I watched.
Listened to her peeing. Smelled her urine spilling into the bowl.
Rachel looked mischievously at me unknotting her tie, pulling it
out from around her upturned collar, balling it up; she opened her
knees and stuffed it into the bowl beneath her. Smiling up at me
unbuttoning her shirt—*MSS* embroidered in navy cursive across
her left breast pocket—first unbuttoning the front, then the cuffs.
Her skin brown, rich, so wonderful against the shirt's whiteness.

Slipping it off and laying it temporarily across her lap. Now Rachel twisted her arms behind her back to unclasp her bra, bending forwards until it slipped off her shoulders, a small bundle of underclothes at her feet. I took a deep breath. Looking down at Rachel, her brown shoulders, breasts without the tan line, all of her the same smooth café-au-lait color. And over my shoulder I saw my own monkeyface smiling in the mirror too.

Rachel stood and slipped her shirt back on, buttoning up the front, cuffs flapping loosely around her wrists.

She grabbed her underwear and we hurried down the stairs. Jumping onto my bike, both of us. Me pulling on the battered straw hat, Rachel sitting across the handlebars, across my outstretched arms. Clutching my shoulders with one hand, her bra and bloomers in the other, headed for Huevos Beach. I was standing up on the pedals, pumping as hard as I could, two of us laughing like wicked kids. Like we'd just escaped the madhouse in St Ann's.

———————

Rachel had written me a long letter from school as the end of the year approached, describing in detail how it would happen. "A symbolic Extreme Unction," she wrote, "for both of us." According to Rachel this ritual would restore us. Instantly. Magically. Back to before. Both of us pure, unwrecked, practically—"technically," she wrote—virgins again. I was to choose something significant to bury for myself. And without thinking about it I'd stolen old Jim's straw hat, the yardman who'd worked for my father for donkey's ages—it had almost blown off a dozen times as I pedalled the bike. To me he'd always been the Jim of my own *Huckleberry Finn*. Rachel had her logic, I had mine.

At the beach we buried the stuff. Rachel's detested convent-issued bloomers, her wire-famed bra, old Jim's decrepit straw hat. All of it forever beneath the sand. Just as Rachel wrote we would.

But that's where her elaborate description broke off. The rest, I suppose, was left for me to interpret. Intuit. Yet to continue the "movie" in my imagination from that point had been so frightening that I couldn't bring my mind to comply. Much as I tried to force myself. That was the point at which fantasy—Rachel's words across the page—turned into a harsher past, a harsher reality. Stirring up all of those long-stifled memories. And I couldn't bring myself to face them.

Now, as soon as we'd filled in the hole and stomped down the loose sand, I was faced with that past again. That dreaded reality. As I watched Rachel turn towards me, slipping her shirt off her shoulders for the second time that afternoon—those brown, exquisite shoulders. Breasts. Slippery abdomen. As I watched her bend at her waist to unclip her skirt at the side of her hip. Watched it fall. And now I saw her turn and step out of the small navy circle.

I watched her walk, naked, beautiful, down towards the water.

Leaving me standing there still in my T-shirt and cutoffs—my bathingsuit, since I'd assumed, rightly enough, we'd be swimming at some point. Standing there with the sand still coating my arms up to my elbows, still hot and sweaty from our bicycle ride, the digging. My heart pounding. Desire, mixed with dread, pulsing through my veins. Standing there on the beach struggling to summon all of this aching desire into that numbed, washed-out, hollowed-out place in my middle: my absent center. Squeezing my eyes shut and trying to locate this place in my mind. Willing my fierce passion to flood this emptiness, this numbness. But feeling instead, as always, the same jittery panic. Same hopelessness. Rising up out of the same empty place, beginning to move up through my body in waves. My abdomen, stomach, chest—flooded, stifled, I could hardly breathe.

Then the images started flashing past—not a movie now—snapshots, slides. Flashing though my mind. Inevitably, unavoidably, jerkily: an image of fingers digging into a white concrete wall; a silent mouth gaping wide open, thread of spittle spilling over an extended lower lip; thick green-white chips of glass scattered among brown feet like chunks of hail; an enormous glinting blade, pressed against a tiny brown ear—an ear—and me thinking again the same absurd thought: *She'll lose it, he's going to chop her ear off by mistake!*

I opened my eyes, shutting off the slide show, staring down at the circle of footprints before me in the sand. But whose were they? Those footprints. Now I couldn't attach them to anyone. To any specific event, series of events. Then they began to make sense.

Slow, measured breaths.

I raised my head and watched Rachel wading slowly out into the water, waist-deep. She turned around to face me. Looking up at me over calm, shimmering water. Pale green eyes reflecting the same soft water, same green shimmering.

I pulled my T-shirt over my head. Unzipped my cutoffs and let them fall. Hurrying down the beach towards her—trying my best not to think, not to feel that small, lifeless weight shifting side to side between my legs—and then my calves, my thighs splashing, dragging for a few thankful seconds through the cool, green sea. My waist submerged beneath it. Hidden, gratefully, beneath the water. We held each other. My hurried momentum carrying us out a few more steps, chest-deep. Our arms wrapped around each other's shoulders. Hands exploring each other's bodies. Smooth slippery skin, mouths pressed together—sucking, loosening, opening.

Both of us anxious. Waiting. Both of us even praying for that so minor and basic of human/animal responses which—I knew, knew perfectly well—would never happen, could never happen.

Mind over body? Body over mind?

Human/animal over animal/human?

We found ourselves staring into each other's eyes. Our chests breathing hard against one another. I was holding Rachel up by her hips, her body half-buoyant in the chest-deep water. Her hands clutching my shoulders, legs wrapped tightly around my thighs. Squeezing. Trembling. Rachel's passion a physical thing in those trembling thighs. Our hips, abdomens pressed together, squeezed tightly against each other. Both of us perfectly, painfully aware of what was missing between them—between us. Missing. Always. That one small possibility that might have brought us together. Might have united us, finally, truly, forever, Rachel and me. Keeping us forever apart.

"I can't wait any longer."

Not even a whisper, her breath hot against my chin, against the side of my pulsing neck.

"I won't wait any longer, William!"

I couldn't find my voice. Not even my simple, wretched voice. Couldn't bring myself to answer.

"Feel me," she said. "I'm a mess. Positively trembling, all over. Just to touch you. Just to imagine what it would be like making love to you, William!"

She broke off. I was afraid that if I tried to say something I'd begin to weep. Again. And that would surely make matters worse. If things could get any worse than this.

But what Rachel said next turned my deep sorrow, my pain, into anger. Hot, biting anger. Anguish. Much as I'd prepared myself for years to hear just this.

"Or somebody . . . anybody . . . because it doesn't matter!"

She paused again, and then her words began spilling out.

"I just can't bear it any longer. It's the way I'm made. Don't you understand, William? It's what my body's telling me, demanding of me. I can't help myself, can't continue fighting it off any longer. Don't you understand? won't you?"

"No!" I shouted. "No! Why the fock should I?"

In the silence my words seemed to reverberate, echoing. Like I could reach out and retrieve them, hold them, pull them back. Out over the flat water.

"Because you love me," she said.

Now Rachel lowered her voice, calm and gentle for the first time since we'd entered the water.

"Because you love me, William. Because we love each other. Like no other two people ever. And you must believe me when I tell you nothing can change that. Nothing will, ever, you understand, change that. Get in the way of that."

Silence again. Fading echo over water. Soft slap of waves.

I could feel my tears welling up, in a few seconds they'd be streaming down my cheeks.

"What do you want me to do?" I asked, my voice faltering. "What would you have me do?"

Now my voice left me for good. I was sure. Now it had gone forever.

I was looking over her shoulder. Away at the sea. Out across the open, shimmering water. But it was as though I was looking into her eyes. Still. I couldn't escape them, not then and not now. Not since I was a boy seven years of age. Rachel had me trapped in those eyes.

"Forgive me," she said. "Forgive yourself, William. Please!"

She moved away. Shoved away. Past me. Wading into the beach.

I turned around to watch her go.

Then, just as suddenly, I found my voice. Out of nowhere. Called after her.

"At least you can wait until we leave. After the summer. When we're both," I swallowed, "off this rock. Out this focking place!"

She stopped. But she did not turn around. She did not look back at me, not even over her shoulder. Rachel did not answer me.

I knew she would though. Even before I'd said it I could be fairly certain that she would—wait, as I had asked her—asked of her. Another small consolation.

My life: a series of small consolations.

We had but a few wretched months of summer to make it through.

I watched her trudge out of the water, up onto the sand. Towards her clothes. Dripping, her hair dripping. Her shoulders, back. Rachel's exquisite black-woman's bamsee—because there was no doubt about its origin, because only that word could name it properly. Her almost too-muscular thighs, calves. Dripping, all of her. She seemed to be shedding the entire sea.

Trudging across the hole in the sand we'd just covered up.

How long? How many life times ago?

She grabbed her skirt and stepped into it, pulling it up around her, fastening the snap. Took up her shirt and shoved her arms roughly through the sleeves. Her head bent forwards buttoning it up. Trudging through the tall grass, the tall weeds.

I watched her go. Watched her disappear: the parallel pleats of her navy skirt shifting side to side with each step, white glow of her shirt against the dark grass, her wet orange hair draped across her shoulders like some small slaughtered animal.

She was gone. In my mind, in my seventeen-year-old heart, I believed she'd abandoned me forever. Standing there in the chest-deep water. Staring up at the empty, deserted beach. Only a gentle slap of waves. The water cold now, and I was the one trembling. Yet my passion—my useless, hopeless passion—had long subsided. Yet I did not want to get out. Ever. Never.

———————

One twin held Rachel from behind, her arm twisted painfully behind her back. With his other hand he pressed the blade of his cutlass awkwardly, absurdly against her ear. Rachel's neck kinked at a harsh angle. The second twin held me. Also from behind, pressing up against me from behind, his sweaty bare chest pressed into my back. But my hands were free, hanging down at my sides, useless. And with nothing else to do with them I cupped my genitals, clasped my own genitals—as though *that* could somehow protect us. Fend them off.

My captor held his cutlass flat, one end of the blade in each upturned, each clear-colored palm—its worn wooden handle floating in the air somewhere off to the side, seemingly far away—the sharp edge of the blade pulled backwards against my throat. Hard—it had cut the surface of my skin, maybe several times—I wasn't sure because I couldn't see. Not causing any serious wound, I could feel that much. Only a mild stinging sensation. Bubbling sensation at my throat as I breathed, as I called out to Rachel. Making a mess though. A mess—I could feel the blood thin and sticky and mixed with sweat running down my neck, over my chest. Beside my ears each upturned, each clear-colored palm clutching the blade as if wearing a thin surgeon's latex glove of glistening red.

Rachel had looked at me over her shoulder at one point, seen all the blood. She thought he'd slit my throat—I could tell by the look of horror on her face—and I was trying to shout to her that I was OK. Convince her that I was OK. My wound was only theatrical. It wasn't what it seemed.

The third guy was short, very black, flaming red eyes and mouth, enormous head of matted locks: he was the leader, ordering the twins what to do and when to do it. He wanted to fock Rachel first, he said, then they could have their turns, but first he wanted to smoke. A short glass straw pulled from his back pocket and lit with a Bic lighter, his cutlass tucked temporarily under his arm. Sucking at the glass straw—once, hard, and holding it in—for what seemed like a full minute. Until he exhaled an enormous lungful of thick, gray-white smoke. Smelling of ammonia, hospital disinfectant.

Now I witnessed for myself that scene from the cartoon *Hulk*. And it was no less horrific than when I'd seen it as a boy at the Roxy: his body, all of his muscles seemed to swell, instantly, to-gether, to explode within their own tightness—his skin turning blacker, eyes redder, mouth redder, wetter—and thick beads of sweat came squeezing out of every pore.

He was over behind Rachel, and the twin was beside her, still holding her arm but unbent now, his cutlass still pressed awkwardly against her ear. The small guy unzipped his cutoffs, but his legs were spread so wide behind Rachel they didn't fall to the floor. Hanging just below his hips, the two rounded top-halves of his sweat-beaded, deeply-black buttocks exposed. Burnt brown end of the glass straw sticking out of one of the pockets. He held his cutlass still tucked under his arm—now I was worried his cutlass would pierce Rachel's back unintentionally. But then he seemed to pause for a second, reach-ing out and putting his cutlass down on my father's desk. Carefully, gently, like he was afraid to scratch the surface. Now on the desk sat the cutlass and two shotglasses of rum, like an arrangement, floating, a still life mirrored in the shining surface of the desk like water.

He downed one shot. Wiped the back of his hand across his mouth. Downed the other. Then I watched him pause for an in-stant to examine his face in the polished wood.

He lowered his head and seemed to spit on his cock, seemed to work it up and down a few times fiercely with his hand, slap it a few times fiercely against Rachel's thigh—because his back was turned to me so I couldn't see. Only his wide, muscular shoulders, and Rachel's face, the side of her face. Her eyes squeezed shut, mouth gaping open, thread of spittle spilling over her extended lower lip. I saw her cringe, violently—saw the thread of spittle make a wide, slow-motion S through the air—and now it seemed as though Rachel heaved herself backwards onto him. Now I watched her body tighten for a second, turn to stone, then go complete loose. Limp. Her legs buckling beneath her. Only one arm remained tense, alive, stretched out before her, above her head, her palm pressed against the wall. Now it seemed as though Rachel held herself up by hanging onto the wall. And if it wasn't for those fingers, digging into the white concrete, I would have thought she'd passed out. The rasta behind her seemed to be holding her up too—or shoving her down—it looked like both at once. Rachel half a foot taller. And I couldn't tell you if he had his hands under the pits of her arms, or if he was holding her up from behind by her breasts.

I couldn't tell you if it went on for hours, or lasted a few minutes. It also seemed like both. Seemed to go on forever; and then, a few minutes later, it was over. Quiet. They were gone. Only a slight breeze rattling the leaves of the almond tree in the backyard, coming in through the hole in the wall where the sliding glass door had been. The burglar-proofing. Slight scent of hospital disinfectant still lingering in the air. Slight close human/animal scent. With Rachel and me left behind, discarded, lying there on the floor— we did not bother to dress ourselves, clean ourselves up—two of us pressed into a corner on the other side of my father's desk, rug bunched beneath us, our arms wrapped around each other.

And then, suddenly, light began seeping into the room. Spilling in, flooding the room like water. Gushing in through the hole in the wall where the glass door had been. That light seemed to roll over those chips of glass like pebbles on a beach. Seemed to make the same glass-tinkling noise. I could hear birds chirping in the almond tree. But they were chirping underwater. Then the sounds of our parents at the front door. Talking. Laughing. A key turning in a lock underwater.

9

We were with Skiffle Bunch on the far side of the Savannah. It would take us a good three-quarters of an hour to walk all the way around. Twenty minutes across the middle, which could be dangerous at that hour. I cannot tell you which way we went, how we got around. I remember Rachel saying that she was hungry, and suddenly I felt hungry also, and somewhere near northstand we drank a couple of cornsoups out of steaming styrotex cups. The woman carefully ladling in the chunks of chopped up corncob, thick bubbling splitpea soup, thick chewy dumplings. We drank our soup and we drank a couple of cold Caribs.

After the cornsoup an old rasta with a long gray beard invited us for a smoke. We were walking with our arms hugging each other's waist—we hardly let each other go the entire time we remained on the Savannah grounds—Rachel wearing a loose, white cotton dress with a faint blue-gray print of some kind of flowers, thin straps over her shoulders, her thin black ballet slippers. Her dress shortish, mid-thighs, which made her seem younger. And me with my baggy, ridiculous kung-fu pants. Making me feel jaunty and boyish too. Walking with our arms wrapped around each other. We must have looked very happy. We must have looked like young lovers. And in our own way I suppose we always were.

The old rasta with his long gray beard kept calling us his children. He had his dreads tucked up into a black woolen ski cap that swelled to the size of a second head. Bright yellow patch staring out of the center like a third eye: it said Caterpillar Tractor. The book of matches that he lit the joint with said Caterpillar also.

We went behind a couple of closed up foodstalls, somewhere at the side of northstand, and sat on the back stoop of one of them. Had a smoke with the old rasta who kept calling us his children.

Then we were walking around again, drinking a couple more Caribs to take the scratchy taste out of our throats, going who knows where, and Rachel told me she wanted to look for Despers. They would probably be somewhere on the other side of the Savannah. In the general area where, an hour before, we'd caught up with Skiffle Bunch. But we never found them. Never caught up with Despers. We never heard them play that night.

Rachel had no pockets. She was carrying her money around in a small change-purse with a snap, hanging by a thin chain around her neck. A bunch of money—wad of blue $20 bills as tightly-wrapped as her fist—the purse could hardly snap shut around them. It was a lot of money to be walking around the Savannah with at night. Yet I doubt that thought occurred to Rachel before I mentioned it. Now she wanted me to carry the money, dragging the purse out from under her hair, hanging it around my neck. Which I paid little attention to at first, then I must have decided it would be safer to spread the money out among my six pockets—my kung-fu pants had two extra pockets over the knees. I divided it up, carefully distributing the bills, three or four blues to a pocket. Thinking that if we got ripped off, at least we'd have a few pockets left.

But no sooner had I finished dividing up all the money, hanging Rachel's empty purse back around her neck, than we were walking between northstand and the line of foodstalls again. And for some reason we cut between two of the closed up stalls, plunging into pitch darkness. At that same moment we saw a thick crowd of people coming towards us. Out of nowhere. Sea of dark faces.

I can still see them coming. And I can still feel the smile on my face. As I let go of Rachel and raised my hands up high in the air —as if I were under arrest, as if to embrace them. I closed my eyes. Let the sea of people wash over me.

I did not feel a single limb brush past. Not a hand touched me. But when the crowd had gone, and I opened my eyes and dropped my hands to check, my six pockets were empty. My watch gone too.

Of course, Rachel still had her purse.

———————

We were back on the other side of the Savannah. There were no steelbands left on that side, and what we were doing over there I'm not sure—I suppose we were still looking for Despers?—but I remember Rachel saying that she was too tired to walk all the way around the Savannah again. We wandered out onto the road, got into a maxi-taxi full of people, all crowded in on top of each other. We had no money left so the driver must have let us on for free: it was carnival. We were young, white people. Could have been tourists, foreigners.

Rachel was sitting pressed against the sliding side door and I was squeezed in against an old black woman. Chewing her dentures, wearing bright red lipstick and a white straw hat and white plastic jewelry as if she were on her way to church—at three in the morning. Her jewelry kept clicking together with each pothole the maxi-taxi hit, her dentures making the same noise, clicking softly as she chewed. The woman reeked of the same Limacol toilet water my grandmother used to douse herself with.

Then Rachel was sitting on my lap, the maxi-taxi bumping along, and I was staring into her eyes. We were kissing again.

Then we were in my room in the Queens Park where for some odd reason it was "raining." Water dripping down through the ceiling, in three or four places around the bed, but missing it completely. Coming down harder through the ceiling in the bathroom. When we entered and saw it dripping down Rachel and I looked at each other and smiled, shrugged our shoulders. Too exhausted to contemplate it much—a pipe had broken someplace behind the walls? Anything was possible in the Queens Park. It seemed surreal but at the same time it did not feel strange or unexpected, and oddly cozy.

Rachel said she had to sleep. She was spent. She lifted her little purse up from around her neck, out from under her curls. Laid it down on the bedstand, a gesture that seemed to me like brushing her teeth before bed. I watched her curl up on top of the sheet in her white cotton dress with the faint blue-gray print of flowers. Her brown legs and the thin black ballet slippers, which she hadn't taken off. I thought to remove them myself, but the image of Rachel lying there with her face half-hidden beneath her mass of curls, spread out across the pillow and spilling over the far side of the bed, seemed to me so self-contained and so perfect, that I did not want to disturb her.

I was tired too but knew I wouldn't be able to sleep, and then I thought of the joint in my pocket and the book of matches the old rasta had given us. Which somehow they hadn't taken from my pockets with the money and my watch—unless that could have happened first? I sat up on my side of the bed, looking down at Rachel and enjoying the quiet, pleasant feeling the "rain" gave me, and I smoked half the joint and pressed it out against the side of the bedstand. Shoved it into the back of the little drawer with the Caterpillar matches, and I slept too.

———

We awoke holding each other. Still dressed except I'd taken off my T-shirt, Rachel still wearing her slippers. The "rain" still coming down around us, in five or six places around the bed, but missing us still. We could hear it dripping down harder inside the bathroom. Now we undressed each other, calmly, slowly, looking into each other's eyes and now kissing, now caressing each other's body.

"I love you to your bones," I said. "These clavicles." I ran my forefinger along one of them.

"Shuuu," she said softly. She did not want me to talk.

We were lying on our sides facing each other. Rachel reached and took hold of my shoulders and rolled me onto my back, and at the same time she shifted over on top of me. She kissed me and slid her mouth across my cheek behind my ear, then over my ear, kissing, breathing against it, sucking gently. Sliding her tongue down along the side of my neck. Now she pushed herself up onto her knees, straddling my hips, the softly gritty soles of her feet upturned and tucked under my thighs. She tossed her hair over to one side. Running her tongue down my chest, dragging her lips over a nipple, her hair brushing along my side, kissing my abdomen, sucking, gently, dragging her tongue along the faint line of hair stretching towards my navel.

Suddenly, firmly, I took hold of her shoulders. Stopped her. Cupped my hands under her armpits and pulled her up towards me. Rachel lying on my chest again but still with her knees bent beneath her, still straddling my hips, the soles of her feet pressing up against the backs of my thighs.

We lay like that for several seconds. Rachel raised her head off my chest and looked up at me. Out from under her heavy veil of hair.

"You must let me try. At least allow me to try."

She even laughed once. Rachel even managed to make light of my—of our—predicament. Our lifelong predicament.

"It's not as though I'm fresh out my convent uniform! There're things I could do for you now, things that I didn't know of then. Won't you let me at least try, William?"

I looked at her. Calmly—somehow I felt perfectly calm.

I could control the outcome of this. I could stop it, right now, as I just had.

Of course part of me wanted her to continue, wanted so much to let her go on—let her try, as she had put it—go on trying. For as long as she was able. Forever—what did we have to lose? What more was there left to lose between us?

Mind over body?

Wretched human over wretched animal?

We lay there for a minute. Only the water dripping down, birds beginning their chirping outside.

"There's something you don't know, Rachel. Something I've been wanting to say to you for a long time."

I paused, another minute, "Something I've been needing for years now to tell you."

We shifted onto our sides, facing each other. Rachel tossing her hair over the other side of the mattress.

"Tell me," she said.

I swallowed. Closed my eyes.

"What they did to you, they did to me, too."

Silence. Several seconds.

"I don't understand. What are you telling me?"

"They focked me, Rachel. All three of them," I swallowed again. "First the little guy, then the twins. One after the other. After they'd finished with you, they focked me."

I opened my eyes. Watched the color drain out of Rachel's face. She looked more frightened than shocked.

"But that's impossible, William."

"You saw the line of blood on my throat and looked away. You had your eyes shut. The whole time. Blanking it all."

I paused, "You had to blank it all, you had no choice."

She looked at me with her ashen face. A long time. Then, slowly, the tears began. Running down her cheeks and dripping onto the sheet. Like the water coming down from the ceiling around us.

"My love," she said. "My beautiful darling."

10

Her voice came to me out of a tunnel: I must have drifted off for a few minutes. Maybe she had too.

"I never even asked you when you got in," she repeated.

Rachel was looking out through the glass door. Past the open curtains, the balcony, her cheek still pressed against my chest.

I raised my head up off the mattress, propped it against the wall. Rachel had stretched out, pressing herself along the length of my side. We were half under the sheet, my arm circling around her back. Now I tilted my head to look out through the glass door with her.

Beyond the balcony, on the other side of the street, I saw the top of the samaan in front of grandstand. I could even make out a half-naked figure, asleep, high in a crook between two huge branches. His thin dark legs dangling down. Black sticks.

Suddenly I wanted to be him. Anybody but me.

"I got in yesterday afternoon," I said finally. "You?"

"Night before last."

After a breath she added, "Didn't you know? Auntie had the room waiting."

I thought for a second. "I made those reservations a month ago."

"She calls it the royal suite—something so. I think she's finally succumbed, poor woman, like the rest of them."

"She thinks you're Queen Elizabeth."

Rachel lifted her face off my chest and turned towards me—I could feel her eyes looking at me—but I continued staring out the window. Looking past her. I couldn't look into her eyes yet.

"Behave!" she said.

"I told her you're a Spanish duquesa. Only repeating what you told me."

She bit my shoulder, playfully, and we shifted so that we were facing each other again. Rachel throwing her hair off the other side of the bed.

We were smiling. Unbelievably, spectacularly, both of us were smiling.

"It is the royal suite you're staying in."

She laughed, "Then I pity the other guests."

Suddenly I felt a pang of guilt. "Where's Javi? You brought him, didn't you?"

She looked at me for a few seconds. Her expression serious again.

"I sent Javier back home. Just before I left to come down. He's back in the military, I suspect. But I don't know. He was very angry with me when he left."

"You can hardly blame him for that. Least you could have waited till after carnival."

"He was biding his time with me, William. Javier knew it as well as I did. He's back in his own country. Back where he belongs."

"You're sure?"

"Positive."

"I'm disappointed," I said. "I liked the guy a lot."

"So did I."

She paused, "He couldn't continue hanging on. And I couldn't allow him to. I've done him a favor, William. He'll realize one day, if he hasn't already."

We lay there.

"So what've you been doing since you arrived?" I asked.

"Sleeping, mostly. I'm upside down with the time change. Then there was the string of parties to see me off."

"Fiestaing the fiesta," I said, but the phrase felt wrong. Like repeating something I'd read in some book. Like all this had happened before.

"I spent yesterday afternoon at Daddy's," she said. "He has a house full of French guests, courtesy of Mummy, and I was helping him entertain them. Family gathering. Afterwards, Celly and Melvin took me to Apsara's for dinner. Seemed to go on for hours, one little tin plate after another. Then they dropped me back here, and I suppose they went directly over to the Savannah—Melvin, come to think of it, had his tenor drum on the back seat. They'd told me how semis had been postponed, but somehow it didn't register. I continued to think it all started tomorrow—today, that is."

"But you went over."

"Later on. When I got back to the room I decided to bathe, hadn't really cleaned up since I'd arrived. Felt filthy. I was just drawing my bath when I heard the pan across the street. Then I remembered."

"You mean you have a tub?"

"The royal suite you're forgetting. Anyway, I was just about to get in the tub when I heard one of the steelbands starting up, and I couldn't resist."

She paused, "And I knew I'd find you out there. Somewhere. Or you'd find me."

Her mischievous smile.

"I knew. I was waiting."

Finally a drip came down at the end of the bed, splashing Rachel's leg. Now she shifted closer and we held each other. Just listening to the water dripping down on the Cuban concrete tiles. Louder on the puddles that'd already formed.

Birds already making a racket outside.

"My God," Rachel said. She shoved out of my arms, sitting up. The sheet stuck to her back for a second. Then fell away.

"My God," she repeated.

"What?"

"I never closed the taps."

"How you mean?"

She turned and looked down at me. Biting her lower lip.

"I never shut off the bath water!"

Rachel jumped up and wrapped the sheet around her, grabbed her dress off the end of the bed and ran out. The door swinging to behind her. I heard her bare feet padding softly up the stairs. Heard her door open, close. Then I could even hear the faintly squeaky noise of her closing the taps in the room above. And after a few minutes the "rain" began to slacken. Slow to a gradual stop. After a few minutes I no longer had it with me. Only the birds kicking up their racket outside. Rachel's empty purse on the bedstand beside me.

———————

I slept. Till the phone woke me a few hours later. I was still half-asleep—groggy as I groped for the receiver, hanging on the wall above the bedstand—and for some odd reason I thought that it was Ganish, calling to find out the name of my agent.

It was Shay-lee, telling me that she was on her way to mascamp. Did I want to go? I could pick up our costumes.

"Besides," she said, "Minsh's been asking for you."

She paused, "By the way—we missed you last night! What happen? Miss Fletcher wouldn't let you out her clutches?"

"She wasn't even here," I said, then regretted it. "I spent the night on the drag. Ran into some friends," it wasn't a complete untruth. "I never made it to northstand."

"Smoke-up lil weed?"

"Little bit."

"We figured as much."

She let it drop. That was the thing about carnival—no questions—not too many, not among friends, even a number of married couples. Licensed excess Freud called it, the tribal cure. At least, that was the way it was meant to work.

Peter Minshall's mascamp is a former airplane hangar, part of the old American base, located on the gulf in Chagaramas. A few miles outside of town. The drive along the coast to get there—windows down, wind blowing in our faces—is startlingly beautiful. Looking out over the string of islands stretching off the point, across the Boca de Mono. Clear enough that morning for us to see the mountaintops of Venezuela looming in the distance.

Shay-lee stopped at a stall perched over the water for a shark-and-bake. The woman fried the shark up fresh before our eyes. Gave us our sandwiches wrapped in waxed paper, spotted with grease. Lovely—chewing up the gristle, sting of peppersauce, faint taste of shadow beni—chardon benit, an herb that grows along the roadsides like weed.

Cold Carib. Carnival breakfast.

We got to mascamp around noon. Where the workers, including Oony, had already been at it for several hours. A handful even working on costumes through the night. All for the love of mas.

They were all ready, Shay-lee told me, except for the Kings' and Queen's costumes—and these wouldn't be considered finished until the final moment, when they went on stage. Which meant Dimanche Gras on carnival Sunday, tomorrow night.

And this year, she explained, Minshall's once again unorthodox band would have two Kings: one "white," the other "black"; one "bad," the other "good." One of course played by the boy, Eddoes.

As usual there'd be lots of theater—Minshall's other trademark—endless drama.

Shay-lee and I went first of all to salute the master. There with a group of helpers working in a frenzy on Eddoes's costume. We hugged and Minshall made a little show for those standing nearby, laying on the accent as he liked to do—"Look the young writer reach quite from New York to play with we! Ya know, he go play mas in River!"—but he was distracted, elated and exhausted both. No rum on his breath though. That was a good sign. Minshall was in good form.

The costume was called Tic-tac-toe Down the River. The first part, tic-tac-toe, having a special meaning for us: it's what we call that boy's game of skipping a flat stone, in three hops, across the water. Eddoes's costume golden on a black background—to reflect the river at sunset, according to Minshall. It had 40-foot-tall wings sprouting from the backpack. And Minshall had decided only that morning that both wings would be covered entirely by gold and black "tiles." 4 x 4 inch mylar squares, which were being "ticker-taped"—the way price tags are attached to garments by white plastic ties—to the lamé material of the wings. The tiles would move with the costume. Throwing off light like sun off the river. Which meant hundreds of tiles, each of which had to be chopped out with a paper-cutter and attached individually.

Minshall has single-handedly revolutionized costume design. Not simply through his use of materials: aluminum and graphite rods, fiberglass, plastic, diaphanous fabrics—in addition to his tiles and method of attaching them. But more than any other innovation, by his use of a trailing wheel attached at a careful angle to the masplayer's backpack which—by using the actual weight of the costume as leverage—allows for their gigantic size. More important, Minshall's design allows his Kings to carry a costume

weighing a couple of hundred pounds in a way that seems effort-
less. Allows them to play their mas. Meaning that they can dance
their costume as if it is part of them. Not some enormous, obzockee
structure dragged behind, across mainstage.

And there was Eddoes, bareback, sitting quietly in the corner
on the concrete floor—he'd swapped his cocoasack-skirt for a pair
of cutoffs—little plastic gun in his hand. One of several workers
ticker-taping the gold and black mylar tiles to the wings of his costume. I could tell him right off, he was as good-looking as Oony
and Shay-lee had said. His impressive body, smooth muscles running across his back, down his long arms as he worked the gun.
Neat dreads and his smooth, boyish face. His gentleness, calmness,
qualities I associated with all the Earth People and felt immediately
in Eddoes's presence. It made him stand out from the other helpers
straight away.

Shay-lee took me around to say hello, and he looked at me and
smiled. Reached up and we knocked fists.

"All left!" he used the Earth People's inversion. Bent back to his
work again.

The other King's costume was called Samson-Mancrab. Played
by a guy I knew from secondary school, two or three classes behind mine. He'd gone on to study medicine in Canada. And because he always played mas with Minshall I met him every year in
the band. Unlike Eddoes though, Michael Defrates had played
Minshall's King several times, before he left for university. Michael
had played a great King too, taking first prize three years running,
unusual for a white boy. Of course Minshall was quick to bring
him out of retirement this year, since a white boy was exactly what
he needed.

Another nice coincidence was that Michael's father owned the
largest hardware store on the island. And because of that from a

child he was always fascinated with gadgets. Michael could collaborate with Minshall on Samson-Mancrab and indulge himself: the costume, Shay-lee told me, represented modern man. "Whose science and technology has cut him off from Mother Earth, bringing his slow destruction," she smiled, making quotation marks in the air—she was paraphrasing Mr Minshall.

Whereas Tic-tac-toe would be tall and shimmering and gorgeous and graceful, Mancrab would be bulky and ominous. A "techno-terror." And Michael had created a helmet that projected laser beams for eyes, a machine to billow forth chemical fog, flares to sizzle at the ends of mechanical claws, rockets to shoot skyward—even a TV which Mancrab would carry on his chest and on which he would actually watch himself, broadcast on the local channel, as he crossed mainstage. There were more theatrics he and Minshall hadn't even revealed yet.

Michael was there by himself at the opposite end of the hangar, beside his disassembled costume, drinking a Carib and making some final adjustments. He looked fairly relaxed, as though his costume was finished, ready to hit the stage. Shay-lee and I went over and he offered us beers out of his cooler. Shay-lee took one for Oony and we went to find her in the back room where the sewing was done; Oony was in charge of the Queen's costume.

There with her own team of workers and Aisha Brown, who'd played Minshall's Queen for years—first as kiddy-carnival Queen—taking more Dimanche Gras first prizes than she could remember. Three sewing machines buzzing away, and enough white silk and lace piled up around the room, it seemed to me, to dress the entire band. Aisha's costume was Mother Earth, but it would take the form of a popular West Indian folk character, washerwoman, always depicted in white. Endless petticoats and starched crinoline slips, her rustling sashay of a walk, with her white bundle of clothes balanced on her head, carrying them down to the river to wash.

The costume would also have two enormous wings, almost as big as Tic-tac-toe's, though there was no trailing wheel attached to Aisha's backpack to help her carry them.

"Minsh didn't want one," Oony told me, raising her eyebrows. "Said he wanted the costume to float across the stage, unfettered," Oony imitating Minshall, waving her arms like a seagull.

But the wings were a problem: nobody—not even Aisha—was sure she could carry so much weight. If any woman could do it though, she could. Aisha was six feet tall, a professional dancer— an athlete, all muscle. With a magnificent face that looked not only African, but as though she had Carib blood. Full of strength. Her posture—even out of costume as she sat behind the sewing machine—that of a dancer's, upright and confident. Aisha was as seasoned as any carnival Queen ever.

Oony put Shay-lee and me to work straight away. Cutting patterns which she'd already marked out in the white silk. And after an hour, after all the patterns were cut, she put Shay-lee, complaining, behind one of the sewing machines. Me to assist a woman, Aisha's daughter, who was bending wire to make the headdress.

But after a few minutes I snuck off. Went out behind mascamp where there was a huge willow tree perched beside the river, cool shady grass beneath it, and I passed out.

———

Shay-lee had the four boxes of our costumes piled on the backseat of the car. Each labeled with our names. When we got to town we went to the club to speak with Sam so he could give me our carnival passes. Every night during the festival the club was swamped— these passes were highly sought after. And they couldn't be bought;

Sam gave them out himself. But when we got into his office at the back, for some reason that surprised even me, I asked for five passes instead of four—Shay-lee and Oony had picked up theirs weeks ago. And when Sam went to write in the last name I told him Eddy Baptiste. I knew Baptiste was his mother's surname, the Eddy I pulled out of a hat.

Shay-lee and I thanked him, wished him a "santee maneetay"— sans humanité, our way of saying happy carnival, and we took off.

"You mad like toro!" Shay-lee whispered to me in the hallway. "They'd never let Eddoes in here, not those goons at the gate."

She paused, "He'd never want to come in here neither!"

"We'll see," I said. "Depends on the company he arrives in."

We drove to Sparrow's tent where we got tickets for the calypso show on Monday night, and a couple of extras just in case— we couldn't come to carnival without going to a tent.

Then Shay-lee stopped at a friend's house to pick up our jouvert costumes. Which amounted to nothing more than a pair of stubby horns glued onto a plastic hairband, and a bent wire tail attached to a velcro belt. The costume was just an excuse to play in a group, which you'd usually break away from after a couple of hours. In each of the brownpaper sacks was a slip that said *INCLUDES ALL THE MUD YOU CAN WEAR* and a flattened link-sausage of six Red Devil brand condoms.

At the box office at northstand I got tickets for Panorama finals tonight, and the Dimanche Gras show tomorrow. That is, I asked for the tickets and Shay-lee paid, since I still hadn't changed money. Which I promised to do, and pay Shay-lee back, soon as we got to the hotel.

I still hadn't seen my auntie. And suddenly I was looking forward to it. Hugging Miss Fletcher was also part of my carnival ritual.

But as soon as I pushed through the door my auntie started to cuss me. Bawling at the top of her lungs, from the other side of her desk—she almost jumped over her desk to get her hands on me.

"Listen here, boy!" she shouted. "I want you out from this hotel. You understand my French: get you little focking backside out from this hotel. Quick! All-you shitong yankees all the same. Get tight and smoke-up and don't know what the rass you doing. Embarrassment I tell you. If you mummy and daddy could only see! Flood-down the place. Open the focking taps and full the focking tub and don't close-off the water. Flood-down the whole focking place! Ever hear of anything so? eh? Ever hear of any damn foolishness like that? Jesus focking ages!"

Fortunately Shay-lee was there to fend her off me.

"Calm down, Miss Fletcher," she kept saying. "Calm youself down!"

But Shay-lee thought the situation was hilarious, fighting to hold in her laughter.

"Get out from this hotel! Damn shitong-yankees, don't know how the rass to behave civil!"

I escaped up the stairs, hiding behind the costume boxes and bags clutched in my arms.

Shay-lee walked in a couple of minutes later, still laughing.

"Boy, don't know what you did last night," she looked around at the puddles still on the floor, her eyebrows raised. "But like Miss Fletcher sit down on a coalpot!"

I'd already twisted open the remaining bottle of scotch. Taken a swig.

"Here," I offered.

"Not me," she smiled. "I'll wait for tonight. Besides, only focking yankees drink scotch!"

"God bless focking America!"

I toasted her.

"OK," Shay-lee said. "Listen up good: we meeting you here at eight o'clock sharp. Is that clear?"

She winked, "And don't forget you beautiful boyfriend!"

"Who's that?"

"Laurence, who else? Look, he left you a love note. Lucky I grabbed it out Miss Fletcher's hand—she wanted to burn it!"

Shay-lee handed me the folded piece of paper.

She shut the door behind her as I sat on the bed. Shaking the note open.

Laurence's careful, elegant script—who'd have thought the Queens Park had its own stationery?

> *Slight alteration of plans,*
> *my bro. Meet me at Hilton*
> *bar, upstairs, half 7. Some-*
> *one you want to meet.*
> *—L*

I stared at the note, oddly mysterious. But that was like him. I'd definitely be pissed off if he'd checked into the Hilton. Which was also like Laurence. And how would I explain that one to Miss Fletcher? Then I thought of something else: so long as Rachel was staying here, Laurence would be too.

I still held the bottle in my other hand. Took another swig and reread the note.

"Shit!" I said out loud, putting down the bottle and jumping up, rushing past the sliding door, out onto the balcony.

Shay-lee had just started the car, parked beside the front gate.

I whistled through my fingers.

She stepped on the brake, the car jerking forward and then back. Shay-lee rolled the window down and stuck her head out.

"Obviously you didn't read my love note," I shouted down. "Can you meet Rachel and take her over? I'll catch up with you guys later in the stands."

Then I winked down at her, "With my boyfriend!"

"Like last night," she said. "Better don't smoke-up nothing or you'll never find us—again!"

She pulled her head in and drove off. Her taillights crimson in the fading afternoon.

I stood there for a minute, leaning on the railing, looking out across the Savannah. First time since I'd arrived that I'd come out onto the balcony.

The squashed white circle of the horsetrack stretching out behind grandstand. Acres of tall yellow-green grass, breeze moving in parallel waves across it. Interrupted here and there by a cricket pitch, a giant samaan, perfectly symmetrical. From my balcony I could even make out the tiny, coral block-walled Fletcher Cemetery, near the center of the Savannah. That was the one piece of the Savannah grounds that remained private: only Fletchers and their direct descendants—those with documentation to prove it—could be buried there. We had our own key to get in; the cemetery was kept carefully locked up. Even though it was easy enough to jump the gate, and people did it all the time, in order to take care of necessities, especially during carnival. Once my mother discovered an entire family of douglas who'd set up house in William Sangor's—my namesake's—mausoleum. They'd been living there happily enough for weeks. And to prevent it from happening again, in a flap, my mother had the mausoleum razed.

Then I thought of something else, smiling to myself: one day people would jump the gate to piss and fock on top of my grave. Something to look forward to.

Almost at the same moment I had another thought—it was probably seven-thirty already.

I went back in, undressed, and got into the shower. Turning both rusted little wheels, squeaking, as many turns as they would go—but only a drip came out. Meaning one of three things: 1) the hotel was out of water, 2) my shower didn't work, 3) Miss Fletcher had purposely shut me off. And somehow I suspected the last. I stood there long enough to wet my face and dampen the top of my head. Got out and dried myself off with my T-shirt—still no towel. Trying hard, as I pressed the damp shirt against my face, not to contemplate the horrors of going through an entire carnival without a shower.

I went over to pull a pair of jeans out of my duffelbag, but decided on my kung fu pants. They'd be cooler. I pulled on a fresh T-shirt.

Somehow I had to change some money. I stuffed a US $20 bill into my pocket, along with two of the tickets for Panorama finals. The other ticket was Rachel's. On my way out I grabbed the bottle of scotch—my contribution, once again, when Laurence and I joined the others in northstand—tonight I was determined to get there.

I hurried up the stairs.

Rachel's door was locked, so I shoved her ticket under it.

———

It was already dark when I dodged past my auntie and out the door. The Hilton, as I've already said, is located on the other side of the Savannah. At the end of a long, steep, winding road, exhausting to climb. I could get there in a taxi in ten minutes though. First I needed some money. The foodstalls across the street hadn't opened up yet for Panorama. I started through the tall weeds, skirting grandstand, headed for the food- and drinkstalls set up along the drag. There'd be more activity over there, I decided, but I couldn't tell yet. From this direction I was looking at the backs of the stalls.

They were all open, each with their own sound system blasting the soca. As if competing to drown each other out. People wining in the dusty drag in front of the stalls. Girls in platform shoes and skin-tight jeans and chopped-off, frayed T-shirts. Most of the boys bareback, T-shirts draped over their shoulders. A couple wining up hard against each other, gyrating, going down to the ground. The girl holding her cup cool as ever behind the guy's neck.

I went over to a young rasta, sitting up on the counter of one of the drinkstalls, talking to the girl standing behind the counter.

"Smoke?" I said.

"Right on, brother," he shoved off onto the ground.

I followed him across the drag, behind the drinkstalls on the other side. Suddenly it was quiet, like we'd stepped into a different room. The rasta reached into the space under one of the stalls and pulled out a brown HiLo supermarket sack. We sat on a plank stretched between two rusted washtubs.

"This my office," he said.

He reached into the sack, pulled out a joint and lit it with a Bic lighter.

"Sample the product," he explained, pulling hard, handing it over.

Now I realized I'd pretty much have to smoke the joint with him. I leaned back against the plywood stall behind us, looking up at the lights blinking in the hills, took a drag, and handed it back. I had the bottle of scotch in my other hand, balanced on my thigh. Unscrewing the cap and taking a swig, I offered one to the rasta.

"Not me with the hard liquors," he said. "Them does bad-up you head. Me go take a Guinness in a space."

I took a drag and handed back the joint.

"Where you get them pants from, brother?" he pulled hard. "Wes' Mall?"

It was the American-style shopping center.

"No," I smiled. "New York. I live in NYC."

"Them pants the business, man! I see Lucky Chan wearing some pants just so in *Golden Dragon*. You catch it?"

I shook my head, exhaling.

"Good flick, and *Golden Dragon Strike Again*. Man, I got to get me some pants like that."

"They're cool," I said, then realized he'd take it the other way.

"They cool all right. One these days I go reach in foreign too."

"Good," I said, "because I got to give you US—didn't change money yet. Any problem?"

I was looking for the twenty, but had to check three pockets before I found it.

The rasta raised his eyebrows, adjusting his tam, studying the bill in my hand.

"How much of ganj you want, bro?"

"Few joints is all."

"Already wrapped? All them?"

"Give me what you got wrapped, rest in change. Truth is I need the change more than I need the joints."

He looked at me, puzzled. "I could give you the wrappers, man!"

"I prefer not to hassle—" I broke off.

"You the boss!"

He stepped on the end of the joint we were smoking, reached into the sack and pulled out a Skippy peanutbutter jar with about ten joints rattling inside. He unscrewed the lid, dumped the joints out and handed them over. Screwed the lid back on and stowed the empty jar away, then he took the bill from me.

I was already busy dividing up the joints between my pockets, why I'm not exactly sure.

"Leh me see if I could make some change for this breads now."

He took a stack of bills out of the leather purse he was wearing on his hip, almost all red dollar bills, few green fives, black tens. By the time he'd finished counting out my change there were only a handful of red bills left. Which he stacked together with the US twenty and slipped them into his purse. Snapping it shut.

I was busy dividing up the bills between my pockets, starting where I'd left off after the joints. Then I ran out of pockets and got confused.

The rasta was studying me with serious concern.

"Need to get you a purse like this, man."

"Yeah," I smiled, shoving the rest of the bills into my hip pocket.

"They got them in Wes' Mall."

Suddenly I felt as though we were starting our conversation over again. Like we'd just sat down.

The rasta looked at me, concerned again.

"Got any matches?" was the only thing I could think of to say. Besides, there was no point in having all the joints with no matches to smoke them.

He was leaning down, stowing his HiLo sack.

"Here," he stood, handing me his lighter. "Keep it, brother."

I followed him around to the other side of the stalls. Into the physical blast of soca. The other room. Already there was a crowd gathered on the drag—one of the steelbands just pushing into position at the end of the barber green.

"Thanks," I said, really thinking of the lighter, though my saying it a minute later didn't make much sense.

"Any time, bro."

I turned around and started off, then realized I was walking in the wrong direction. While I was sitting with the rasta I'd decided to walk across the Savannah to get to the Hilton. From here it'd be just as quick as walking back to the road to catch a cab. The Hilton, I recalled, had recently cut a series of steps into the hillside—a long, jagged, steep staircase—zigzagging its way up the hill and coming out just below some enormous green water tanks. Which I decided must be part of the hotel's water purification plant. But maybe they were just storage tanks? Then I thought of something else: maybe they weren't water tanks I seemed to remember a-tall, maybe they were the green tennis courts? Maybe that's what Laurence was doing up there? Playing tennis with one of his fancy friends? Because surely those courts were lit so the tourists could play at night.

But who the fock would be playing tennis during carnival?

The steelbands, camped out in various corners of the Savannah, were coming to life. The ones that made it past the semis last night left their carts and all but the tenor pans here. Pushed together into tight groups, instead of toting them on a flatbed all the way to their panyards, then back to the Savannah again for finals tonight. The tuners taking advantage of the time to double-check the pans.

I took a few swallows of scotch walking across, and with each swallow I felt a little more angry with Laurence. I didn't want to be going to the Hilton. A-tall. Not tonight. Not during finals. By the time I reached the bottom of the steps my face felt hot. Red with anger too, I supposed. I decided it would be a good idea to take a few drags to calm myself down. Of course I'd smoked almost the entire joint by the time I reached the top of the steps, exhausted, leaning onto the railing to catch my breath, where I discovered neither water tanks nor tennis courts. It was the putting green.

The bar at the top of the Hilton—faced in bamboo, with a false thatched roof above it—is part of a Polynesian restaurant called the Tiki Hut. For tourists there's a menu of Polynesian drinks, little stick umbrellas speared through chunks of fruit. But locals buy a bottle of whatever they're drinking like anyplace else. At the other end of the bar is a wall of pane-glass windows, like an airport tower, looking out over the Savannah, what had once been the old Spanish town, the port behind it. And up against the windows are a few small tables.

I found Laurence sitting at one of these.

There are two world-famous writers from the British West Indies. Neither lives here now, but they both come back for a visit occasionally. One of them is of African origins, the other East Indian. One a poet and playwright, the other a novelist and travel writer. It's the latter who has the added distinction of having been knighted by the Queen of England.

And it's this knighted novelist who was sitting with Laurence at the small table, discussing a collaborative project, the adaptation of one of his short stories to the stage, when I stumbled out of the elevator. Into the Tiki Hut at the top of the Hilton Hotel. Redfaced, blinking, more than a little dazed—wiping sweat from my forehead with one hand, half-full bottle of White Label sloshing audibly in the other—joints stuffed in every pocket of my baggy, kung fu, Lucky Chan trousers.

The famous writer was wearing tweed. Laurence an ash-gray blazer.

Suddenly I felt cold sober.

There were already two bottles in the middle of the round table, which made it easy for me to deposit mine among them. Laurence got up and we hugged, then I turned to the famous writer. His handshake surprisingly cordial, and he looked up and smiled at me the same strained, painful half-smile I'd memorized from his photographs. He was even smaller in stature than I'd expected. I had to fight back the urge to reach over the table and give him a bearhug, as I had Laurence.

I sat in the vacant chair that was waiting for me, facing the window.

As soon as Laurence said my name I could see the famous writer's mind ticking, working out my family tree. I had the feeling that after a few seconds he knew more about me than I knew myself.

"Your father's the lawyer," he said. "Island schol, 1948?"

I nodded.

I also knew that he'd gone to the government school, during the same years that my father had attended the Catholic one; in addition, he'd been the island schol two years behind my father.

"He's a Fletcher, is he?"

"Yes."

"You have a tough road ahead of you."

"Yes," I said again, though weakly, because I had no idea what he was talking about. He realized too.

"Laurence had your publisher send me a copy of your manuscript," he explained, "and I've just connected it with your surname."

Now he leaned towards me over the small table. Resting his chin on his knuckles pensively in the same way, I realized, that Ganish had done yesterday in the airport.

"Something there," he said.

Then he paused, and for a few seconds the only thing I was aware of was the low boom of the bar's air-conditioner.

"Problem is," he said, "nobody's going to pay much attention to a West Indian writer, who happens to be a wealthy white boy."

I could have answered yes or no to this and either, I realized, would have been appropriate. I said nothing.

"Let me give you a little piece of advice." He leaned back in his chair, smiling his painful half-smile. "Don't let them put your picture on the jacket."

Then, after a second, "Or get them to put on a picture of Laurence!"

"Give me permission to put on one of yours," I said, surprising myself that it came out so easily.

"If I had my druthers," he laughed, "this pag-face wouldn't appear on my books either."

I was happy not to have to say anything else. He turned to Laurence and they took up their discussion where they'd left it off. I was hearing them, making an effort to look from face to face, but I wasn't listening. Felt a little like an eavesdropper. I glanced up for a few seconds, past my own reflected image, out through the pane-window in front of me. In the distance I could see the flickering lights of town, ships in the harbor, and beyond the lights the flat, ink-black sea. I couldn't find grandstand or northstand from where I was sitting, but in the dark expanse of the Savannah I could pick out two or three pockets of movement, flashes of torchlights, which I knew were the steelbands getting ready. Coming to life. If I listened hard—above the boomboxes on the drag, the potcakes in the hills all around us barking in an unbroken conversation of their own—I could hear the gentle pinging of the pans. Different corners of the Savannah.

I pretended to follow the discussion some more.

The Hilton's air-conditioning was working overtime, must have been 55° F.

While he was talking Laurence used the tongs to put three rock-hard, crystal-clear icecubes from a beaded aluminum bucket into a crystal tumbler, all on the table before us, which he slid over in front of me. I found it astonishing how easily he handled himself. And I couldn't help thinking—as I watched his faintly pink nails go redder when he squeezed the little tongs, three times—how beautiful and elegant were his hands.

I was grateful to have something to do with my own hands, as I reached forward to uncap my bottle and poured myself a drink. Grateful for the ice.

Only after I'd put the bottle down again with the two others that were already there, did I realize what they were. For a few seconds I tried to imagine the scenario which would explain how those bottles got there, but I couldn't. I came up blank. First I'd assumed that one of the bottles was rum, the other scotch, that would make sense. Both were scotch. Both half-empty, square-shaped, both Johnny Walker. Except one bottle was Red and the other Black.

I was sure I was the only one to notice. But a few seconds later—again, without interrupting his conversation—Laurence leaned forward and slightly adjusted the three bottles with their backs pressed together, their labels facing outwards, one directed at each of us.

The scene was too ironic to touch. Too good even for literature, which is why it'll only end up in my novel: three West Indian writers, one red, one black, one white. Drinking their appropriate labels of imported scotch. Sitting together in the Tiki Hut at the top of the

Hilton Hotel, high above the dusty, hot Savannah. Where down below the people were coming together for their Panorama finals.

Down there, I told myself quickly, defensively, was where I wanted to be. Down there was where I belonged. Even if it meant not shaking hands with our famous novelist. Down there was where my heart was.

But even as I had this thought I knew it wasn't true either. Not altogether so. Nothing was true. There were no simple truths to be had, not for the three of us. And even the few seemingly straight-forward facts were suspect. What, quite possibly, the great writer had attempted to point out to me when I'd first sat down.

I turned my head and pretended to listen some more. Before I knew it the great writer was taking his leave of Laurence and me. He had a plane to catch—who would have thought? But it was the best time of the year to be flying to England, he told us. Not only did they put on special direct flights, his plane would be going back to the Motherland empty. He'd have it all to himself.

What I didn't realize is that I would still be sitting in the same chair, at the moment he passed above, high in the clouds, all by himself in his Bee-wee jet.

He took up the manuscript that was sitting on the table. Wiping a mirrored button of water away from the corner of its shiny black cover—Laurence's script, I supposed. Maybe his own.

He shook hands with both of us, and then he was gone.

Laurence and I did not say a word for five whole minutes. Laurence smiling—and I'm sure I was sitting there with nothing less than a monkey-grin on my own face. Stretching one monkey-ear to the next. I was still awe struck. Still stunned.

"You're a motherfocker!" I said finally.

"Cheers," Laurence raised his glass. "Welcome home!"

I felt as if I'd run a marathon. As if I'd just finished a carnival, not waiting for one to happen. Suddenly there was nothing I wanted to do more than to sit calmly with my friend in the Hilton's excessive air-conditioning, in the quiet of the Tiki Hut, and slowly drink a boatload of scotch. Exactly what we had on the table before us. Laurence had that ability, soon as we got together, to put me perfectly at ease. That comfortable, agreeable manner about him. And I knew that for months now I'd been looking forward to spending this carnival with him, as much as Rachel or anybody else.

She did not come up in our conversation that night. Not once. Probably we were both avoiding her on purpose. I couldn't say, at least I can't speak for Laurence. I do remember thinking that he'd probably checked with Miss Fletcher, when he stopped by the hotel to drop off his suitcase, leave me the note. He knew she'd arrived. And Laurence hadn't checked into the Hilton after all. He was staying with us, down below, our delightfully dilapidated Queens Park. No tennis courts, putting green, and definitely no water tanks.

My auntie, he said, had given him a perfectly tolerable room. According to Miss Fletcher, it was the room directly below mine.

What we talked about, surprisingly—the thing I've come away from those hours of drunken conversation remembering—was our fathers. Laurence knew that I'd broken off with mine, informally— though by now I suppose it was pretty much official—several years back. Since I'd left the island to study in the States. I tried to explain why, to myself and to Laurence. Botching it badly. Coming to the conclusion, once again, that it was just something I could not articulate.

Laurence was an only child. His father had abandoned him and his "mum" when Laurence was seven. This I knew already. Like most intelligent, black, middle-class West Indian men of enterprise in those days, he'd gone to foreign. To London (New York, Miami, and Toronto came later). Like most of them he had been successful. At least more successful than if he'd remained in the West Indies. And like many of those black middle-class men of enterprise who "made it" in foreign, Laurence's father never got around to "sending home" for his wife and child.

All of this I knew. What I did not know, and what took me completely by surprise, was that Laurence had always kept up good relations with his father. From the day his father left. A relationship both father and son prided themselves on. And when Laurence went to Oxford he'd made a point of going to see his father as soon as he arrived. It was, Laurence said—which surprised me too—one of the reasons he went to Oxford in the first place.

Over the years his father had drifted south from London and settled in Kent. Where he'd never remarried. Where he eventually became the owner of his own little two-story brick house—too big for a man living alone really—with its own little backyard and an enormous chenet tree, overshadowing both the yard and the house. Which, despite the miserable climate, actually bore its sour/sweet fruit every summer, and which his father had planted from seed. He lived just adjacent to the boys' orphanage where he'd started off doing carpentry work and general maintenance, and worked himself up to the position of head counselor to the boys.

Then, Laurence told me, for some mysterious reason—some reason Laurence did not understand at the time—he was sacked. This was a couple of months ago. But he'd gone on living in the little brick house with the chenet tree—it was actually contained by the orphanage's compound—as though nothing had happened. Except the orphanage no longer employed him.

All of this Laurence confided to me in his direct, easy-going manner. We'd already been sitting there a long time. How much of the scotch we'd drunk at this point I couldn't tell you. But by the time we stumbled out, several hours later, all three of those half-full bottles were empty.

At this point in his story, which had slowly got me sitting on the edge of my seat, for the first time since I'd known him, Laurence's voice began to falter. He was having emotional difficulty with this part. What he managed to get out was that he'd only just returned from England, from Kent. Not a week ago. His father, in distress, had actually contacted Laurence's mother—incredibly, his father kept up good relations all these years with her also—it was his mother who'd contacted Laurence. His mother who'd called him in New York and begged him to go to England immediately, to Kent, a place she had only ever heard about herself—she said it like it meant going round the corner for a bottle of milk, Laurence told me—and post his father's bail.

As much as I wanted to hear more I wanted Laurence to stop his story. It was coming too quickly. I'd heard enough for the moment. I needed to take a breath—though he was the one talking. Though all I had managed during all of this was to nod my head encouragingly. Laurence stopped. He broke off his story. But then he did something else I'd never known him to do before, and which he has never done again since. He made a request. Begged a favor of me. That sometime during the next few days I take the time out to go with him to visit her.

As I've already said, all three of those half-full bottles of scotch were empty when Laurence and I stumbled out of the Tiki Hut. And I don't know how many joints we smoked walking down the steep stairs that led from the putting green to the dusty grass of the Savannah. Then across. Let's say two, three. It's entirely possible that on top of the scotch we smoked three joints between us. All I remember is that crossing the Savannah we ran into a couple of pannists, walking with their tenor drums tucked under their arms. They looked happy, exhausted. Strange thing was, I knew one of them, I was sure, though I had no idea from where. He recognized me too.

Both pannists wore their hair neatly braided and beaded, slapping gently against the sides of their necks as they walked, and both had their T-shirts draped over their shoulders.

"Who won?" I asked.

"How you mean?" the pannist I knew answered. "We mash them up!"

"But who *we* is?" I asked, because without their T-shirts on I didn't have a clue.

"How you mean, Mr White Label?"

He steupsed, "Renegades, man. Re-ne-gades!"

11

I awoke the next morning staring up into Rachel's face. All rested and beautiful. Beaming. She'd let herself in. And now she kissed me softly. Smiled down at me.

It took me several seconds to figure out where I was, piece things together.

"Hello my love," she whispered.

"This heaven or hell?" I found that I could talk if I didn't move. "Or still the Queens Park?"

"Queens Park, I'm afraid."

"Then you don't really love me."

"You know I do," her eyes were shining. "Always. Forever."

"More than the others?"

"Not more, differently."

"But I don't want different, I want more. Quantity—not quality."

"More then. If you come to lunch with me. I'll give you whatever you want."

She kissed me again. "I'd give it to you anyway. Already have."

"I want to get married. Like we said as kids. Can't we, secretly? We don't have to tell anyone. Hardly think the Pope's keeping tabs."

"I don't think we could get married."

"We could live together then. If you're worried about offending the Church."

"I would if you wanted," she said, "live together."

"Would you?"

"Darling, after what you told me yesterday morning, I'd do anything you asked. I'm still in a state of shock, really. Can't put it out of my mind."

We were quiet for a second.

"Don't try to change the subject."

"I assure you," she said, "I am not."

"We were discussing living together. I was about to suggest Mexico. Where it's dreadful, where they kill you for crossing the street. Surely they'd allow us to cohabit in Mexico City."

She smiled, "Fell in love with a boy in Mexico. We couldn't go there."

"Helsinki then. Where it's cold and miserable. Where they promote free love, all the parks, front of everybody, minute the sun comes out."

"Fell madly for a boy in Finland. Fell in love with boys everywhere, sorry to say."

"Must be someplace."

"Doubt it. But I'll think over lunch. Promise."

"I'm sure you will."

"Come," she said, "the others are waiting for us. At Veni."

"Others? What others?"

"I sent Laurence on ahead with Shay-lee. Convinced them I'd be able to get you out of bed, into a taxi."

"Wonderful!"

I rolled over, facing the other direction. My head pounding.

"Don't be obstinate, dear."

"By the way," I said to the wall, "he's still alive?"

"Laurence? Indeed. Very much alive."

"I was afraid of that. The man has a constitution."

"Not like some others," she teased.

"Listen, he's tracking you, you know?"

"Course I know. He made that clear in New York. And don't think I'm not appreciative!"

"Fock," I said it to the wall, under my breath. Knew it was coming, but I felt the pang of jealousy just the same.

I turned around to face her again.

"You've got some competition," there was even an edge of aggressiveness in my voice.

"Have I?"

"Shay-lee. Told me so herself. Apparently she goes both ways."

"Does she?"

"She has hots for Laurence too. All the girls."

"Well then the rooster will just have to choose among his chickens, won't he?"

"You're making me nauseous."

"Then we'd better get you out of bed and into the shower," she kissed me a last time. "Because now we're going to have a nice lunch together. All of us. One big happy family."

"Like focking hell!"

She rolled me out of bed anyway. Slowly.

I'd managed to get my clothes off last night, my T-shirt in a ball, soaking in a two-day-old puddle of water. We stepped around it. Rachel walking me slowly towards the bathroom, her arm around my waist—a journey. Journey and a half.

I leaned against the wall next to the shower. My shoulder pressed into the cold tiles. Took a deep breath. Shaking my head, painfully.

"It doesn't work," I wanted to cry. "Focking Miss Fletcher shut me off!"

"Don't be absurd."

She reached in and turned one of the little wheels and water came gushing. A deluge. Rusty-smelling and orange-colored but it was water. Delicious water. I'd drink it up with every pore. And it pleased me as much as if Rachel had named the place for us to run away to, alone, forever, unhappy ever after.

She helped me under it.

Located in an old colonial house on Lucknow St, in St James, Veni Mange is one of the best restaurants in the world. French-Creole cooking, it's run by two flamboyant sisters whose mixture, I suppose, is everything but French. Veni is all tin eaves and moss-dripping fretwork and leafy ferns. Raised on groundsills above the grass and wide open so the breeze blows right through, with a lattice-sided gallery running all the way around. Always loud, always frenetic, always welcoming. And in the mist of the soca, in the midst of the shouting, little yellow-breasted birds flitted in to pick breadcrumbs off your table.

Tonight marked the official start of carnival. After lunch the restaurant would close for a week solid.

Veni has its own cart which follows the band, loaded down with many bottles of alcohol. The barman pushes it all day on Monday and Tuesday, drinks dispensed by his wife, who works in the kitchen. And because I was good friends with Roses, the younger sister, they always let me in. This year my friends as well.

We found them at a table in the corner of the gallery. Laurence, surrounded by four pining women: Oony, Shay-lee, Roses, and Alicia. He looked very pleased—Alicia was sitting on his lap—I'd half expected Shay-lee.

A startling mixture of African and Syrian, Alicia had been Oony's top model before she left for Manhattan. Very dark-skinned with the saffron tinge and extraordinary straight black hair reaching past her waist. Alicia has her own spirited West Indian personality to match. She also happened to be Carib's "postergirl" for that year, just as it sounds: her near-naked image thumb-tacked to the back wall of every bar in the country. Like the one around the corner from where we were sitting—who would drink anything else gazing up at that body? Now I found out she'd run into Laurence yesterday in JFK. They'd sat together on the flight over.

Everybody was drinking guava rum-punches, and judging from the number of used glasses on the table, they'd had a couple each already.

But I had to drink a Carib first, I got up and went behind the bar to get it for myself, then I managed to get down a rum-punch. Began to feel half human. Oony came around to our side of the table, pushed in beside me. She'd been at mascamp till four in the morning, she said, but Mother Earth and Tic-tac-toe and Mancrab were practically finished. Little left to do now but pack them up and truck them over to the Savannah tonight.

Oony wanted me to help her with the Queen's costume at Dimanche Gras, which I agreed to do. Afterwards, she said, Shay-lee and I could meet the others in the stands.

The restaurant was packed, food slow in coming. But after an hour, when it started to arrive, the plates kept coming for two hours straight. Roses, who seemed to be sitting at every table in the restaurant simultaneously, kept sending them over. We'd gone through the tedious process of looking at the day's menu and deciding and ordering, but Roses sent over whatever she wanted. Whatever, I suspect, was left in the kitchen, and we shared it all around. We didn't hold up on the rum-punches either.

First there were hors d'oeuvres of stuffed crabbacks, allopies, chip-chip cocktails—a tiny oyster that's drunk by the dozen with lime and peppersauce. Bowls of steaming callaloo. Bull-jhol and zaboca, an old slave dish of salted cod with avocado-pear.

Then there were a series of main courses, which kept on coming and which we kept on sharing around. Curry goat and buss-up-shot—"busted-up-shirt," an East Indian bread. Barbadian-style flyingfish with coocoo—cornmeal and ochroes. Cascadoux, a thick-scaled river fish, delicately steamed with christophene. A Portuguese garlic-pork dish called cavinadash. Pepperpot, a Guyanese meat stew cooked with casaripe—in the days before refrigeration it served as a preservative. And whatever else I'm forgetting, all of which came accompanied with bowls of rice cooked with pigeonpeas. Bowls of steaming ground provisions: tanya, cassava, green fig, eddoes.

Bowls of soursop icecream for dessert.

By the time we'd finished our lunch most of the restaurant had cleared out. Only the bar still packed, still rambunctious. Mostly men, who weren't at all pleased that we'd monopolized the women—including Alicia, leaving them little more than her poster.

She and Shay-lee decided together that my hotel room would be the place of congregation tonight. The place where everybody would meet to dress, or undress, for jouvert. As I handed over my key, which they demanded, the image of Miss Fletcher flashed before my eyes—all four and a half feet of her, hands on her hips, cussing—but it wasn't as though Shay-lee and Alicia had given me any choice. Our jouvert costumes were all in my room anyway.

By the time our marathon meal was finished it was time for Oony and me to leave for mascamp. Start trucking the costumes over to the Savannah.

This time it was Shay-lee who promised to meet us later on the drag.

Oony and I got up from the table, a little reluctantly, just as the waitress arrived with another tray full of rum-punches.

Oony didn't want to drive. The old Suzuki, her other car, which her handyman used at the factory. Her good car she'd generously offered to Shay-lee so she could chauffeur us around. I didn't want to drive either, and not only because I was half-drunk. I didn't want to be driving on the left, in a right-hand-drive car, shifting with the wrong hand on top. I agreed, despite myself. Stalling, knocking over a garbage bin, before we managed to pull out onto the road.

We got to mascamp just as Minshall was putting the finishing touches on Eddoes's bodysuit, a small crowd gathered around to watch. His suit the shade of dark chocolate, to match his own coloring, made of skin-tight latex. But Minshall was using an airbrush with gold paint to highlight the features and musculature of his entire body. Down to the finest details, including his genitals. I was thinking—it's as though he's carving out his own inverted David in black marble. Little did I know, as I'd hear from Oony later, that Tic-tac-toe was meant to call up that biblical story. The result, by the time Minshall cleared the little pistol and put it down, silenced the compressor and stepped back to examine his labor, was to create an Eddoes who stood before us more naked, his body more extraordinary, than if he'd shed his clothes.

We gave Minshall a small round of applause, and he bowed while Oony hugged him around his waist, and Eddoes raised his left fist in the air, smiling too.

It was late, almost eight already, when Dimanche Gras was supposed to start. Eddoes and the others jumped up on the back of the flatbed on which the three costumes were loaded. I started climbing up also, then I overheard Oony telling Aisha and Minshall to ride with us. In the Suzuki. And I realized I still had her keys in my pocket. That now I'd be taking into my hands the lives of our Queen and band-leader to boot.

We were unloaded with the three costumes assembled and ready in our corner of the barber green within an hour. The costumes held up by wheeled aluminum stands welded to the height of the masplayers. That way, when the time came, we could slip into place in the lineup, rolling the costumes in lunges towards the stage, like the steeldrums in Panorama. When we reached the top of the barber green, at the bottom of the ramp, and it was our turn to cross over, two helpers would hold the costume up while a third helper pulled the wheeled stand away, and the masplayer stepped underneath. Then the costume could be buckled on.

But the judging of the Kings and Queens was the finale of Dimanche Gras, and before it came the whole plethora of calypso competitions. There were calypsonians we wanted to hear—Stalin, Cro Cro, Gypsy, Chalkdust, not to mention the two female sensations that year, Denyse Plummer and Drupatee Ramgoonai—but in order to catch them we'd have to sit through dozens of bellowers and groaners first. We'd hear most of the calypsonians we wanted to catch tomorrow night in the tent anyway.

For a while it was amusing sitting there with Minshall's group, listening to the comments of people strolling along the drag, checking out the costumes. Greatly amusing when they suddenly caught sight of Eddoes in his bodysuit:

"Oui papa-yo! But the man naked! Toe-tee and all ringing in the breeze!"

"Look a lovely bamsee for you, sweetness! Leh we see if the standpipe could show lil 'preciation and stand up too!"

Oony and I got a couple of Caribs, found a quiet place on the grass not far from where our group was parked, and we lay back to relax. Looking up at the stars and the lights in the hills around us— no point in expending too much energy before jouvert.

Oony was telling me the story of River. The tale told by the band. Mr Minshall's theatrical myth-making. He'd written it up a couple of weeks ago—in his own exuberant, flourishing hand—in an article printed in the *Guardian*. Greeted, of course, by the usual mixture of excitement and outrage.

What Oony didn't know—at least I don't think she realized herself how closely Minshall's story retold the cosmogony of the Earth People—was that I was already familiar with it. In fact I'd heard it retold with greater and greater embellishments over the years, as the story grew and invented itself—as it came to life in the Earth People, as they lived it—ever since my first visit to the valley. As Oony spoke, paraphrasing Minshall, there were even moments when I could have been listening to Mother Earth herself. Moments when Oony, unknowingly, slipped into Mother's own language.

River was her story. Passed on to the "prophet" Minshall, through her "weak" son, Eddoes. Though I'm sure I'm the first to put it so succinctly:

In the end of life there was only the Mother, earth. She was all darkness and slime, the forest, the dark waters—the devil, the serpent. Walking in the dark forests with a balisier for a staff. Mother took dirt from the earth and water from the river and placed it in her womb, and she put out flesh: two sons, twins, but opposite to each other in every way. She gave them their own planet to share, the sun, and they lived there for a long time until they began to feel lonely for their Mother. They returned to the earth and entered into her womb/moon, and Mother put out more flesh. Sons and daughters, the two races, black and white.

The white son was the stronger, he invented science, and he went with his race to live in Europe and America. The weak son had the black race, and he went to Africa and Asia.

The strong white son called himself God, the Father, and using his science he attempted to control the earth and her nature. He made a religion of material, of greed, and he tried to take the earth for himself. Soon the black race was also living under the religion of the strong white son. Their skins were black, but inside they were white, and they had forgotten the nature of their Mother. The world became one white race, and even though they were still black and white, you could no longer tell them apart. All of this the white son called good, he called it love. Because he had turned the world upside-down, he had perverted it, and he called his Mother and his weak black brother the devil/evil. He substituted the love of the Mother, her nature, for his religion of greed.

Wars were fought in his name of the Father and love. In the midst of plenty, which the white son had made through his chemicals, there was famine. The tomatoes which he had grown through his science, without earth, gave no nourishment, because through his chemicals he had taken out the nature from those tomatoes. They looked like tomatoes—even redder, oranges oranger—but they gave no nourishment, nor did any of the fruits and vegetables which he produced in such great quantities in his laboratories, and the world starved. His science polluted the sea, and even the fish that he grew in his laboratories began to poison him.

In a last attempt to take the earth for himself, the white twin used his science and his chemicals to wage racial war against his black brother. He believed that if he could destroy all of the black race, he could also destroy his brother, but those black people whom he killed were white like himself. In his fury he also killed white people, because you could no longer tell them apart. He nearly destroyed the whole world. But he could not kill his brother, who had fled to the protection of his Mother, living with her in the valley of death, beside the river of death, with only a handful of his true black descendents, who were People of the Earth.

The white son finally arrived at the hidden valley, Eden, and he came face to face with his black brother. He used all the strength of his science and his chemicals to try to kill him. But the white twin who stood as tall as a giant, as tall as King Kong, was now the weak one.

His black brother was standing in Eden on his side of the river, with his Mother beside him and the last true members of the black race. As foretold by the Book from the end of life, he reached and took up a small, smooth stone from the bank of the river, felled and killed the great giant, his brother.

It is the day of death, and the river runs red.

It is the first day of the People of the Earth.

It is the day of we beginning.

My job was to pull the wheeled aluminum stand away, while two big guys held up the enormous wings, and Aisha stepped in under her backpack so Oony could strap it on. Three large metal buckles. Aisha grimaced as the strongmen shifted the weight of the wings onto her back and shoulders, and for an instant we were afraid she'd crumble under them. A-tall. Her dancer's neck and head went up straighter, and we watched her take several deep breaths—blocking out the screaming Savannah crowds—entering her Mother Earth persona. Meanwhile Oony slipped the ruffled blouse over Aisha's shoulders, pressed the velcro snaps together in front, covering the canvas and the aluminum bars of her backpack, and Minshall draped the long lace veil over her arms. A second later one of the strongmen fitted on the headdress, the white sequin-glittering bundle of washer-woman's clothes.

It went like clockwork.

During all of this the soca was blasting. Now Aisha picked up the beat. And in what called to my mind the instant when an enormous leatherback turtle, after that tedious process of laying her eggs and dragging herself back down off the beach into the water again—

freed from the constraints of gravity, from her own tremendous bulk and weight, back again in her own element, in her world—takes off swimming, flying through the crystal water, power and grace and liquid light: Mother Earth moved out onto the stage.

The crowd went mad.

Aisha moved differently from the women who'd crossed the stage before her. Her sashay of a walk seductive but not vulgar. Nothing strained—despite the weight she carried—nothing jarred or awkward. Aisha was herself on the stage in her exquisite costume, moving back and forth to the soca, extending and opening her lace-draped arms at each side of the stage to embrace the crowd—and the crowd responding each time with an explosion of noise. She was Queen of the Bands. Queen of Carnival. Nobody needed to hear the judges' decision.

Since Aisha had been last in the lineup, she was first to cross the stage coming back. The crowd went on screaming. By the time she got across for the second time she was dripping in sweat. We supported the weight of her wings and rushed her down the ramp. Helped her out of her headdress, then out from under her backpack, transferred to the wheeled stand again, which I pushed into position between the two big guys.

Exhausted, Aisha went down in the dust in her huge, lace-ruffled gown. Oony and Minshall reached to hug her, help her to her feet, and somebody handed her a bottle of water. We wheeled her costume along the barber green, back to the flatbed and loaded it up—all while the other Queens made their second crossing.

Everything had gone so smoothly that without anybody actually saying so, the decision was made to stick with the same team: the same two strongmen would hold up each of the Kings' costumes when the time came, and I'd pull the wheeled stands away for Michael, then Eddoes to step into their backpacks. Cross over the stage.

Michael's costume was just what it was meant to be: huge, bulky, ominous—the techno-terror. Lots of theatrics to win the crowd over. Send them into a series of explosions of noise. When he ignited his red laser-beam eyes. When his machine began to spill forth its chemical fog. When he reached down and ignited the television on his chest—and the crowd saw the image of Mancrab crossing the stage, as he crossed the stage—his prick the whiplike television antenna. All the while Michael danced in his costume moving to the soca like the carnival King he already was.

Since Eddoes was last in the lineup, he'd be first coming back, with a couple of minutes to rest between crossings. Our worry was that he had never done it. But in his scandalous bodysuit, when he stepped into his backpack and took the weight of his enormous, glittering wings—stretching up 40 feet above his head—he certainly looked the part.

Fortunately the process of getting him into his costume was simpler and quicker than for Mother Earth or Mancrab—no straps to buckle on or aluminum bars to cover up—the wings simply rested by their own weight on his shoulders. Because of the way the costume was designed, that trailing wheel attached at its angle to his backpack, it was far lighter to carry.

Where Minshall had disappeared to I have no idea. Until now he'd hardly left Eddoes's side. Suddenly he was gone. The other helpers too. It was only the two big guys, one at each of Eddoes's shoulders, helping him support the weight of his wings—with a crowd of spectators pressed all around us, pointing, shouting—and me, standing there still holding the aluminum stand. Because I had no room to wheel it out of the way. There was a long minute while we waited for the penultimate King to reach the other side of the stage. For the crowd around us to clear away so Eddoes could move up the ramp.

I noticed his right hand trembling. At his temple, under his dreads—gold-dusted and woven in gold thread—I could see him sweating. I let the stand go and pulled a joint and the Bic lighter from my pocket, lit it, and pressed it between Eddoes's lips. He pulled hard, exhaled, pulled hard again. And as he exhaled a third time and I took back the joint, he smiled a big wide-mouthed smile and I could see his lips moving—"All left!"—but above the blasting soca and screaming crowds I couldn't hear him.

He moved out.

Eddoes danced his costume. Played his mas. Better than any of us could have hoped. When he reached center stage and turned to the crowds at either side, first grandstand and then north—his enormous, glittering wings—he even did a scandalous jook of his hips and groin as the soca reached to tempo, his left hand raised above his head, index finger pointing skyward, and the crowd let loose. His bodysuit so detailed, it looked as though his toe-tee and all were ringing in the breeze in truth. The crowd roared. On and on.

Then, suddenly, it was over—our hearts dropped like dead weight out of our chests. Eddoes was crossing back for the second time—doing his scandalous jook before a screaming northstand—when he turned and one of his bare feet seemed to catch on a floorboard, or he lost his footing on a piece of debris thrown to the stage, and he stumbled to one knee. A fallen angel: Eddoes went down beneath the weight of his wings.

Competition rules state that the Kings and Queens must cross the stage "unassisted." So how could Eddoes get back to his feet, alone, under the tremendous weight of his costume?

He did. As though it were a move calculated to take us all beyond the point of emotional excess. He flexed his bent right leg—we could see his muscles straining, shaking for an instant, a flash of concentration on his face—and slowly, surely, he raised his costume up. Unassisted. Danced his way off the stage.

———————

I was by myself, walking back to the hotel. Everything had gone Minshall's way that night. Mother Earth had taken Queen, Mancrab and Tic-tac-toe tied for King. Because no matter how obvious things looked there was no accounting for these judges' tastes: the prizes often went to the most obzockee, coskell costumes in the lineup. (There was also, it goes without saying, no small amount of prejudice directed at Mr Minshall, a white man, a shameless homosexual.) But it had all worked out, as well as any of us could hope, and I was happy to have played my part. Now I wanted to be alone for a while. Quiet. I felt sensually saturated, overloaded. I'd go back to my room and rest for a while. Take a shower. Catch an hour's sleep if I could manage it. Till the others showed up and it was time to get ready for jouvert.

My legs could hardly carry me up the stairs to my room—if I didn't get some rest I'd never make it. But when I reached into my pocket and felt around I found it empty. No need to bother checking the others. I'd given my key to Shay-lee and Alicia. Why? I couldn't remember exactly. Now I was locked out. What time was it? I looked at my wrist—no watch. Now I leaned my forehead against my locked door for a second, took a deep breath. OK, I told myself, you'll get something to eat—*potato roti, no pepper, cream soda*—then you'll come back to the hotel and wait for the others. Maybe chat-up Miss Fletcher, sweet-talk her little bit, get back on her good side. Maybe auntie'd let you lie down in *her* bed for an hour?

I started back down the stairs.

Things weren't half bad outside. Cool. Suddenly quiet, pleasant. I'd go for a walk.

Since morning the front windows of the hotel had been boarded up with hurricane shutters. The front glass doors covered over with sheets of plywood, screwed directly to the aluminum frames. All of the folding aluminum chairs where the old people sat in a long line on Sunday mornings after mass had been carried inside. Even the two curved concrete benches which usually sat on either side of the hotel's entrance had been stowed away. It would have taken four big men, straining, to even budge them.

As I looked down the row of buildings on this side of the road—a government ministry, Barclays Bank, couple of apartment buildings—I saw they'd all boarded up their lower windows with plywood or corrugated aluminum hurricane shutters. Tables, chairs, umbrellas and all loose objects carried inside. The buildings stripped down and boarded up, hatches bolted tight, like a great ship going to sea.

The odd thing is that our island's too far south from the warm waters of the Gulf Stream to be threatened by actual hurricanes. The storms never reach us. We're a safe harbor, located far enough down the backbone of islands. But on this West Indian island we board up once a year for a human hurricane.

In the cool air you could feel the lull before the storm. The sudden stillness. Yet in the apparent vacuum you felt an electric charge. Foreboding: some catastrophic, atmospheric event was about to take place. Even the birds were quiet. They knew. The potcakes up in the surrounding hills. An eerie silence.

I crossed the road and walked along the line of plywood food- and drinkstalls. They were all open for business, apparently, their plywood shutters raised, but the proprietors were nowhere to be found. The stalls abandoned, in the middle of things, the scene apocalyptic. As I walked along I began to make them out, asleep in chairs or makeshift cardboard-couches in hidden, dark corners. One woman stretched out on a blanket on the dirt directly behind her stall, her loose cheeks fluttering with each exhalation.

A small group stood before one of the foodstalls—tourists. Only people around who looked half alive. They wanted phoulorie balls. Their spokesman, a southern American, pronounced it pay-lore-high, in three distinct syllables, reading the word off the pamphlet held in his hand. "Fried balls of dough doused in curry sauce, spiced with pepper and green mango," he read. "An East Indian–Caribbean delight, together with doubles and roti." The others laughed. But the woman preparing them didn't appear amused. She looked drugged. Or like she was doing it in her sleep.

In a few hours, and for the next two days and nights, she'd be moving triple-speed. She'd have those phoulorie balls fried up and served on the sheet of waxed paper, yellow-flecked liquid dripping down, spoonful of peppersauce slapped across the top—whether the yankees wanted it or not—before the guy could read the word off his pamphlet.

After the line of foodstalls came the oyster carts, flambeaux lit with their long-tongued yellow flames licking the air, but the oystermen had vanished.

Then came the line of battered pickup trucks, bright red or green peeling paint, each of the beds piled high with a mountain of coconuts. The vendors—rail-thin douglas, barefoot, dressed in rags—stretched out across their piles of nuts. Snoring. Their cutlasses still for the moment, embedded in a nearby husk. Young, pale green, jelly-nuts, their water sweet: nothing could quench a thirst so well on a blistering carnival afternoon.

There were even a couple of highfaluting vendors with signs that boasted *COLD NUTS!!!* Beside these trucks huge fiberglass tanks filled with water, the surface covered with bobbing coconuts and blocks of ice. Gently, hollowly knocking together—it was the only sound you could hear.

The last of these cold nuts would go for ten CC dollars on Tuesday afternoon. The vendors remaining with their trucks until they ran out, their pockets inflated. Then they'd head back home to the south of the island—Naparima, Suparee, Mayaro—where there were vast fields of coconut palms. Where once there had been a thriving copra industry. As before that there'd been the vital cocoa commerce, before that the cane. Now the nuts were good only for their water, free to anyone willing to expend the effort of climbing the trees to pull them down. During most of the year they were hardly worth collecting. But this was carnival, when even coconut water went for a premium.

I wandered along the roadside, following it around the Savannah's periphery. Nobody out now. No car horns blowing. No one shouting, talking, humming a calypso. Not even a lone pan trilling softly in the hills. Even the soca temporarily silenced. Catching its breath, resting up too.

On the other side of the Savannah I walked past the small zoo of silenced animals, the cage of hunched-over, dumb macaws. To the botanical gardens, with the white, brightly-illuminated prime minister's residence perched on the hill above it. Beside the big house, I knew—hidden now by bush and darkness—was St Ann's, the crazyhouse. On our island the PM and the mad people are neighbors.

There's a story of how the police raided Hell Valley and dragged Mother Earth into St Ann's. And how Mother—much to the doctors' and nurses' dismay—convinced half the patients to shed their pink-striped gowns. "Mother Earth Hosts Orgy for St Ann's Crackpots," the *Guardian* reported. Then how the Earth People, wielding cutlasses and dressed in their cocoasack-skirts, had made their way along the string of mountains in the northern range, directly to the prime minister's house. Not to discuss the matter with him personally. The Earth People climbed over the stone wall around the prime minister's backyard, to avoid St Ann's security guards posted in front. They entered and exited by the same back door, rescuing their leader, and the guards never noticed.

An important moment for the Earth People's developing mythology. And it had been the prime minister himself, scared out of his black skin, who watched on a television monitor as the tribe of seemingly wild grass-skirted bushmen, and their naked leader, climbed back over his backyard wall. He warned his chief of police never again to bring Mother Earth to St Ann's. Leave her alone in Hell Valley where she belongs.

"Back Behind God's Back," the *Guardian* reported.

After walking for a couple of minutes through the botanical gardens, I found my favorite spot. I used to ride my bike here to study as a boy. We called it the oval. Like a cricket oval, though nobody ever played cricket here. It was too small for that. A wide, shallow, grass-lined crater that could have been left by a meteorite. With a circle of wooden benches around the lip. There was always a peculiar energy about this place, and it felt even stranger tonight. In this lull before the storm. Even the vagrants who make a permanent residence of the benches were gone. I was all alone. As I stretched out and shut my eyes.

———

My friends were all waiting for me in my room when I got back. Applauding as I stumbled in, still half-asleep. They'd picked up a couple of stragglers along the way, Alicia's younger sister and her boyfriend. My bed shoved sideways against the wall to make a couch.

Laurence sitting squeezed between Rachel and Roses, Alicia sprawled across all three of their laps. On the bedstand beside them four unopened bottles of rum: two of Vat (light), two of Fernandes (dark). They were passing around a fifth bottle, taking turns drinking thimble-sized shots out of the cap. Shay-lee tossed her capful over her shoulder, took a swig from the bottle and handed it to me—and I realized that Oony, her girlfriend, was the only member of our happy family not present.

Another half-dozen half-empty bottles of Carib clinging to every available perch around the room. Joint passing too. My family seemed so far ahead of me already, I wondered if I'd ever catch them up.

They'd pieced out the six jouvert costumes on hand among them. Alicia's sister and her boyfriend added two, but Shay-lee had left hers someplace. Some of them wearing the stubby red horns, others the velcro belts with the bent wire tails. The girls, with unfailing ingenuity, had made necklaces out of the sausages of Red Devil condoms for the boys.

Shay-lee and Alicia—I realized after a minute, in a bolt of panic—had raided my duffelbag in order to *undress* the entire group: there my bag sat in the middle of the floor, beside a puddle of muddy water, nearly empty. Alicia and her sister both had on my T-shirts, what had once been my Levi's longpants. Now they were cutoffs, short-shorts. The clothes they'd shed piled against the wall behind my bed to make a cushion. Roses wearing the dress shirt I'd arrived in two days ago, unbuttoned, front tail tied between her breasts—minus the sleeves and collar.

Through the open sliding glass door, tied to the railing of my balcony, I could see the string of their multicolored bras and panties. Knotted together and hanging down like the tail of a madbull kite. Like the ladder the princess made to escape her tower—for a second I considered the possibility.

Shay-lee announced, "Doesn't William look primpy-primpy?" and she turned me around and stood me before her, brandishing her little curved nail-scissors. Now—while I tipped the bottle back and took a serious drink of Vat—Shay-lee chopped up the clothes I was wearing. My beloved Lucky Chan trousers. History.

Shay-lee rubbed my face with a piece of coal. Alicia fitted on a plastic headband with the stumpy horns. And her sister—who I suddenly recognized in a flash of déjà vu, some vague carnival— hung a necklace of condoms around my neck.

———————

The night was alive with people, flashing in and out of the street-lights. Most, like us, dressed in rags—dirtymas, mudmas—their faces and bodies blackened. Or painted head to toe in devil-red. Bright baby-blue. Some wearing oldtime jouvert costumes: mokojumbies on tall stilts, caped Midnight Robbers, Dame Lorraines in frills and petticoats—flipped up to reveal stiff pink dildos. Fancy Sailors shaking canisters of talcum over our heads, busting gunpowder-packed bamboo-cannons against the sidewalk. Fire-and-smoke–breathing dragons. Bats. Imps. Pitchfork-stabbing jab-jabs. Or jab-jabs attached to their jabbless-cohorts—by thick, rusty chains. And jab-molassies, of both sexes, wearing only tattered underwear, horns and tail— already dripping in putrid-smelling used motor-oil and molasses.

Explosions of fireworks, car horns, whistles—and soca every-where, coming at us from all directions.

We were headed over to the Roxy, meeting point for our jouvert band. For years this wonderful old deco cinema remained aban-doned, falling down, left to rot. Now it was fully restored—an enormous, two-story KFC. Multiple awnings of the Colonel's smiling face on a background of red-and-white stripes, flapping over the windows. But we still referred to it affectionately as the Roxy.

While we walked an open bottle circulated, joint passing. Alicia and her sister had on their sunglasses, plastic squeeze-bottles hanging around their necks, rum-and-coke crackling with ice. For a while I found myself walking between them, two exquisite sisters, an arm around each of their waists. I'd caught up quickly, already running a nice head.

Then, not ten minutes after we'd left the hotel, we heard shouting. Wrong kind of noise. Incongruous. We stopped and turned around: Alicia's sister and her boyfriend, standing under a streetlight. We saw the crack of a slap across his face—freeze-frame for an instant—and he was gone. Dissolved into the night. Alicia's sister dissolved in tears, squeezed between Alicia and me.

"Fock him!"

We started off again.

That was all. One fleeting moment of anxiety, bad vibes—a moment of ugliness—and it was gone. Smoothed-over. Everybody pleasant again. Our big happy family.

It had officially started.

———

Chinese Laundry was already blasting soca when we arrived. Thick mob of revelers wining in the street around his big-truck, spilling over the grass-covered roundabout in front of the Roxy. Car horns blowing, squeezing through the crowd.

They swallowed us up. Like a hot seawave of energy—of soca, naked limbs, whistles, smoke, diesel fumes, sweat.

In addition to Laundry's eight-wheeler DJ big-truck, loaded top to bottom with giant speakers, we had our own metal band—our own "engine room"—a pickup loaded with percussionists beating cowbells with pieces of rebar, car brakes and hubs, pots-and-pans. Covers of aluminum garbage bins. Rubbing pieces of rebar against the washboards strapped to their chests. Another mob pressed against this pickup—beating the ever popular bottle-and-spoon—wining against each other down to the pavement.

Last came the small dumptruck hired by the band, carrying its load of ochre-colored mud. Sufficient in quantity, by the time the sun rose in a few hours, to coat the several hundred masplayers of our jouvert band. And the several hundred others who stumbled into our path. Four or five guys already clinging to the sides of the truck, bareback, wearing motorcycle goggles or swim masks, their buckets dripping. Already dripping themselves—if you went anywhere near them you knew what to expect. You took your life into your own hands.

Without warning we were on the road, Chinese Laundry leading the way, our mudtruck taking up the rear. Everybody chipping together—a way of dancing and walking at the same time, hardly picking up your feet. Skidding them across the asphalt. Staving up your energy, all of us chipping in time to the deafening soca. And under the hard-pulsing music—the heart-pulsing music—faintly, you could hear the thousands of feet. Chipping in rhythm together—*shu, shu, shu*. That sound would remain the soft unconscious underbelly of our music for the next two days and nights. If it wasn't for chipping, like treading water between sprints, even the strongest of us would dead-up long before dawn.

I'd left the hotel carrying a bottle—somebody'd walked off with it already. But Laurence had gotten a wine-skin from someplace, hanging around his neck. He'd filled it with white rum, and every couple of minutes one of us would take a turn shooting it into our mouths. Or into the wide-open mouth of anybody else who came around. Spraying as much rum over our faces as we managed to get into our mouths.

Rachel kept buying snowballs of crushed ice in pointed papercones, without the syrup or condensed milk, which we kept passing around.

Grabbing out handfuls of ice to rub across each other's foreheads, along each other's backs and necks.

We'd already lost Shay-lee and Alicia. Roses had been dragged off by a gang of grease-glistening musclemen, including the two who'd helped earlier with the costumes, wearing only stumpy horns and red thongs.

I was chipping between Laurence and Rachel. Somebody grabbed me around my waist, from behind, and Laurence and Rachel chipped on ahead, arms wrapped around each other's hips.

For a second, in the dark, I thought it was Oony, happy to see she'd come out after all. It turned out to be Alicia's sister, whose name I still blanked on. Only when a jabbless sitting up high on one of Laundry's mammoth vibrating speakers cupped her hands around her mouth and shouted down to us did I remember—Jennifer.

Two of us chipping arm in arm behind Laundry—the band headed downtown, along Abecromby St—when suddenly we got jammed up in an intersection with a steelband. Crossing from the other side.

Jennifer shouted and grabbed my hand, pulling me behind her. Towards one of the wide, wheeled carts with several pannists up there beating, jumping, their locks flying. They were beating out the chorus of this year's chutney hit, "Indian Soca." From Drupatee Ramgoonai, her sweetly militant cry to the nation for douglahood.

Screaming out the chorus—rhythm of Africa and India/blend together in a perfect mixture—Jennifer fixed my two hands onto the crossbar of the cart. At the same time she squeezed in front, locked between my arms. Both of us leaning onto the aluminum bar, pushing the cart as we walked. Chipping in time to the soca.

But more than anything else—more than anything I was aware of—Jennifer was back-backing her half-exposed bamsee against my crotch. She was squeezed into my own chopped up Levi's, little that remained of them. And because of the way she was built, her wider hips, she'd had to leave the top snap undone, zipper pulled halfway up. Wearing my own shredded Despers T-shirt—split down the front and knotted between her breasts—her dark-sienna abdomen exposed to the top of her half-open zipper. Gyrating and jostling and jooking-up—shoving backwards against me at the same time—my own hips shoved forward, riding Jennifer's bamsee from behind.

Like holding on to one of those machines that busts up the sidewalk.

How long it lasted I'm not sure. Maybe half an hour. All I can say is that I did not want it to stop.

Suddenly Jennifer looked back at me over her shoulder, through her dark sunglasses, flipping her long wet hair out of the way. She reached back and held my crotch. Smiling wickedly. Several long seconds. Turned her back to me again.

Instantly I became aware of my own profuse sweating. The heat. Noise. I felt suddenly lost, confused, dizzy—too quickly drunk, too quickly high.

I let go of the aluminum bar. Pulled my T-shirt up over my head. Wiped it across my face and flung it into the gutter.

Jennifer put my hands back on the bar. Roughly. Held them there. Her back-backing. Jamming up hard against my crotch. Then she looked at me over her shoulder again, reached back and shoved her hand into my pants.

I shut my eyes—and in a flash, in my mind—we'd switched places: Jennifer was the one standing behind, shoving her wet face into my back—I could feel the soft knob of her nose pressed between my shoulder blades. And I clutched my own genitals.

I opened my eyes: in her sunglasses, reflected twice, I saw the expression of horror on my face.

Jennifer pulled her hand back. Like she'd shoved it into a coalpot. At the same time she spun completely around to face me. Still caught between my arms—between my sweat-dripping chest and the cart's aluminum bar—walking backwards.

"What happen?" she shouted into my face. "You ain't like me? Can't handle the heat?"

She put her hands on my chest and shoved out from between my arms. Under. Away from the cart.

I half-turned behind her. Stumbling a few steps, one hand still holding the bar. Searching for her in the dark.

Then the bar of the cart behind caught me in the kidneys. Winding me. I went down on the asphalt. Rolling, by reflex, out of the way of the cart's wheels. I tried to stand, went down on one knee. Tried again. Went down again—and this time I went down so hard my nose hit the blacktop.

I crawled the remaining distance over to the curb, four or five yards, towards the concrete sidewalk. Pulled myself up onto it— like pulling out of the water into a rocking pirogue. I sat on the edge of the curb with my head down between my knees, eyes closed, panting, catching my breath.

My head spinning. I couldn't remember where I was. Lay back against the cold concrete, gritty against my bare shoulder blades, sneakered feet shuffling past.

———————

Somebody was pulling me by both hands onto my feet.

"Willy-boy!"

I opened my eyes: my friend Vincent. Smiling. Shoving an over-sized tan-colored pacifier back into his mouth. Short, brown-skinned, completely bald—huge bulging eyes, huge bulging beer-belly. A brilliant architect, I hadn't seen him in years. He was painted head to toe in bright blue, wearing only baby diapers, nippled baby bottle sloshing with rum hanging around his neck.

After he got me standing, after a wet bearhug around my waist, he reached to the sidewalk to retrieve his biscuit-tin, which he proceeded to beat with a wooden spatula. We stumbled, my arm draped across his shoulders, over to a battered pickup crowded with musicians playing instruments more or less the same, wearing more or less the same outfit—bright blue paint and baby diapers. Five or six others stumbling in the street behind the pickup.

One of the guys in the truck passed me down a half-empty bottle of white puncheon-rum, the hard stuff, and a soup-spoon. Which I proceeded to beat. And after a minute another oversized, bright blue diapered baby—instead of the pacifier he had a snorkel in his mouth, mask on his face—jumped off the truck with a can of paint and a huge wide brush. Painted me head to toe, bright blue like the rest.

———————

At some point, way downtown, end of Fredrick St, I found our jouvert band again. Roses and one of the musclemen who'd helped with the costumes—three of us stumbling together, arms slung over each other's shoulders. The rest of our group, they told me, had disappeared hours ago.

Then I found myself walking alone. Dragging my feet. My sloshy sneakers like two wet bricks. I felt I couldn't take another step. Only the soca shoving me forward. For a time I walked next to our slow-moving mud-truck, holding on to the side. Then, with an extreme effort, I climbed up and threw myself in. With five or six others —men, women, all the same now. Not that there was much mud remaining in our truck at this point. Enough for us to wallow in and squirm over each other, happy pigs in a trough.

Last thing I remember the sun was coming up. So bright it was painful. I was on my feet again. We were all the way back at the Savannah. Crossing mainstage. I was surrounded by a mob of revelers, tribe of people I didn't know. Never seen them before in my life. Jumping-up together, wining against each other to the unstoppable soca.

Chinese Laundry parked somewhere beside the stage.

A solid mass of humanity, indistinguishable, embracing each other. Covered, head to toe, in every imaginable nastiness: axle grease, baby oil, flour, Quaker Oats, tar, mustard, peanutbutter, Hershey's chocolate syrup. In addition to the paint, mud.

This—I told myself, I proclaimed it every year, every jouvert morning—this could save the world.

Standing in the middle of mainstage, my head thrown back, staring up at the blinding sun.

12

When I opened my eyes I found Shay-lee beside my bed. Wearing the band's black T-shirt and what looked to me like a cocoasack-skirt. She'd shaken me awake.

"Bubulups!" she said.

I stared. A long minute.

"What the fock?"

"How you mean?"

"Please explain," I swallowed, "the skirt."

Her brow furrowed, "Obviously you haven't checked out your costume."

I hadn't even looked in the box. Never did before carnival Monday morning—which, by now, I understood was today—content to wear whatever costume Shay-lee and Oony had picked out for me. The section we'd all be playing mas in together. Which, far as I was concerned, was all that mattered.

Shay-lee brought my box over and set it on the bed beside me, smiling, tossing the lid off onto the floor.

"Ta-dum," she sang.

I pulled myself up, painfully, sitting sideways on the bed with my back pressed against the wall. My bed still in the position my friends had shoved it into last night. Scattered on the mattress around me articles of clothing I didn't recognize. On the floor between my duffelbag and a puddle of muddy water, the tattered remains of my Lucky Chan trousers—which, nostalgically, I did recall. Beside them my sneakers, wet-looking but relatively clean.

My body—I examined it now, naked except for the sheet twisted around my waist—relatively clean too.

Miss Fletcher always left the bottle of Vim, scrubbrush, and a stack of towels next to the standpipe in the alley behind our hotel. Once again I'd found my way to them instinctively. Nothing else could explain my semi-pristine state.

Other than the two nasty-looking purple bruises across my knee-caps—monkey-knees—my body appeared to be in far better shape than my throbbing head.

I leaned over and examined the contents of my box: the band's folded black T-shirt, beneath it the folded square of sacking—which, I now presumed, was my own skirt.

"That," I said slowly, "is our costume?"

"That's right," singing it out.

"Minshall's lost his head. It's too much."

"Too little, you mean."

I looked at Shay-lee again. Standing there with her hands on her hips, smiling down at me.

"We always wear T-shirts on Monday, right?" she said.

Monday mas was low-key for all the bands. Everybody leaving the larger, unwieldy parts of their costumes at home—their head-dresses and standards. In Minshall's band we wore the bottom halves of our costumes, or shorts, and the band's T-shirt.

"So?" I asked.

"So here's your T-shirt." She pulled it out and tossed it at me, egging me on.

"So?"

"So for today, as usual, we wear our T-shirts. But Mr Minshall's instructions for Tuesday mas, at least in our section—and ours, let me tell you, is by far the largest, swamped the whole band . . ." She paused for drama here, enjoying herself. "Mr Minshall's instructions are to come Tuesday wearing only bag-skirts."

It took me a second to take this in.

"Bare-breasted?"

"That's right," singing again.

If our costumes were modeled on the Earth People it made sense. They wore their skirts whenever they left the valley, primarily when they made their annual pilgrimage into town to "put out the faith." But the female members went bare-breasted above their skirts. Usually sufficient excuse for the police to round up the entire group—lock them in jail for a few days—until they agreed to return home without a fuss.

"You'll be arrested," I said. "The women, maybe the whole band."

"Minsh's counting on that too."

"I'm sure he is."

"Anyway," she said, "for today we have on our T-shirts. Breasts covered."

Shay-lee squeezed her own breasts through her T-shirt, winking at me, "Perfectly decent jamettes!"

She pulled my skirt out of the box, tossing it into my face. Beneath it I saw the black Speedo.

"So young man," she said, "get your skirt on and get downstairs. Everybody's waiting. And best put some powder on that nose."

"What?"

"Looks like you fell on it."

At the doorway Shay-lee paused to look at me over her shoulder.

"Hurry-hurry-run-fuh-curry," she sang. "Band's meeting at ten sharp!"

———

I couldn't get over everybody's cheery spirits. Despite the lack of sleep. Hangovers. All of them dutifully dressed in their cocoasack-skirts and T-shirts. Stretched out comfortably on the old green sofa in the lobby.

Laurence, I saw, had on a white River T-shirt, while ours were black. And for a second I wondered how he'd engineered that one—he'd certainly be better off beneath the sun.

I was sure he'd ended up with Rachel last night. It made me instantly angry. I was trying to calm myself down.

They were already on their feet, eager to get going. And as I pushed through the hotel's plywood-covered door, stumbling behind, I attempted to focus on something else. Few steps across the street and I had it in my hand: an ice-cold Carib.

Since Minshall's mascamp is located outside of town, the band has a meeting point at the top of Aripita Ave, twenty minutes' walk from our hotel. Along the way we passed groups of masplayers from other bands, their colorful costumes trimmed in gold and silver tassels. Their cheeks and forearms glittered. Shining in the sun—prettymas.

With us in our cocoasack-skirts, eliciting comments as we went:

"Eh-eh, but the man wearing he mummy's old-dress!"

"Is a band of vagrants if you ask me!"

But by the time we got to French St everybody stumbling along with us had on the same T-shirt, same sack-skirt—comfort in numbers. That's the mechanism of mas.

We found Alicia and Roses waiting for us at the cart. Roses had her bartender mix a rum-and-coke for Shay-lee, gin-and-coconut water for Rachel, scotch-and-sodas for Laurence and me.

At the top of the street NecroNancy, our DJ, already had the soca pumping, a crowd jumping-up beside her truck. The tassa-rhythm-section already going at it, already sweating up a storm. Their pickup loaded with tilak-stamped, barebacked, dhoti-clad East Indians. Beating their tiny tassa drums—lightning quick—scraping graters, clapping tiny finger symbols above their heads. Charlie's Roots getting ready on another big-truck, David Rudder's backup band. They'd perform live for us on the road: Rudder was a staunch Minshallite himself, he even composed a special calypso each year for the band. He'd take turns on Roots' truck with Tambu—policeman-turned-soconian for the carnival season—who'd give us a dose of the louder, younger, speeded-up brand of calypso. The jump-and-wine variety.

Our three sources of music, all day long on Monday and Tuesday. We'd alternate beneath the three.

And before we finished our first drink we on the road. All two thousand of us, chipping together to the soca. The idea was to make a quick sprint to the Savannah and across mainstage before things got too jammed up. As we approached, peering down the gap between the two stands, I could even make out the sanitary people, still cleaning off the stage from last night. As soon as our banner-carriers reached the bottom of the ramp Rudder was singing "River is Mas." And just as the band started across the stage Minshall appeared, together with his gang of cohorts, including Oony and the stars—Aisha, Eddoes, Michael—everybody dressed in their cocoasack-skirts and T-shirts.

Before long we left the Savannah behind us, dust rising in our wake. An energized mob of masplayers pounding our way along St Vincent St, headed for downtown. Our group of friends were chipping together behind Roots' truck, Tambu singing "We Ain't Going Home," with Rachel arm in arm between Laurence and me, Alicia on his other side. Oony with us now, back with Shay-lee, two of them chipping together.

Rachel stood on her tiptoes for a second—leaning onto Laurence's shoulder and shouting something into his ear—and she pulled me off to the side of the road. Towards a back alley.

She informed me, smiling, that she needed to have a "serious" talk with her cuz.

We walked a few blocks away from the band, until it was quiet, sat down on the edge of the sidewalk. Rachel stopped a boy passing with a snowball cart, asked for one without the syrup. She was wearing her change purse around her neck again.

I stretched my legs out before me. Examining my monkey-knees. They'd been painful when we started out. Now, few scotch-and-sodas later, they only hurt when I thought about them.

I was in pretty good shape, except for one thing: I was still jealous of Laurence. Still angry.

I took out a joint and my Bic lighter—our sack-skirts fairly sophisticated, with velcro belts and a pouch sewn into one hip.

Rachel turned towards me.

"I've been worried about you," she said.

I blew a lungful of smoke over my shoulder.

"Really?"

"Yes, really."

Suddenly I didn't want to smoke anymore. Pressed the joint into the sidewalk and shoved the remains back in my pouch. As if on cue Rachel tossed her snowball into the gutter, its papercone standing up, pointing back at us, ice melting in a trail down the concrete ditch.

"I'm sure you were tormented the whole night," I said.

We sat there for a few seconds.

"And just what are you talking about, William?"

"Forget it!"

A minute of quiet. Only the faint noise of the band in the distance. Breeze blowing through the weeds growing out of cracks in the sidewalk.

"I didn't sleep with Laurence last night," she said. "If that's what has you so upset."

"What?"

"I went back to my room. Alone. As a matter of fact, it was long before sunrise. I have no idea what became of Laurence!"

I was relieved to hear it. Extremely so—it surprised me how much. I took a deep breath.

Rachel continued, "I can't stop thinking about what you told me the other morning. Can't put it out of my mind."

She paused, "I wanted to tell you yesterday, but I never found the right moment."

We were quiet for another minute.

"Put it out of your head," I told her.

"I can't."

"You have to. It'll spoil your carnival."

"I'll find something. Then I'll stop."

"It's what we do," I said. "You and I. We worry about each other."

"I had no idea, William. That they did those same horrible things to you." She put her arm around me. It felt cool through the T-shirt. "How could I *not* have known? I don't understand it. All this time I've been thinking only about myself. Selfishly feeling sorry for myself. How you've suffered, all these years."

"We've done it together. I should've told you long ago, it would've been easier. For both of us. Possibly."

"Darling," she said.

She looked at me for another minute, then took her arm from around my shoulders. Turned away. Now we both sat staring into the gutter, watching the trail of water from her snowcone, zigzagging its way down. You couldn't hear the band any longer. Only the breeze blowing through the weeds growing along the curb.

We sat there for a long time.

"Want to go?" I said finally.

"In a moment. It's nice sitting here. In the quiet."

I needed to get back to the band. Give myself over to the music again—the mindless, blind energy. Blank this conversation—it certainly wasn't what I wanted to be thinking about on carnival Monday morning.

"Oony has me helping with the Kings' and Queen's costumes tomorrow," I said. "When we cross the stage. I'm on orders to remain sober."

I paused, "I have to take full advantage of today."

"They're stunning," she said after a second, "those costumes. What's the boy's name?"

"Eddoes?"

"Never seen anything like it, really. Minshall's outdone himself this time."

"It's the combination: Eddoes is a natural."

"And he's so beautiful!"

"He's the best-looking boy I've ever seen."

"Where'd Minshall find him?"

"He found Minshall, as a matter of fact."

She turned towards me again.

"Seems a child. How old is he?"

"Only seventeen, according to Oony."

"He *is* beautiful," Rachel was smiling. "And the bodysuit—I'd love to see how he gets it on!"

"I'm sure you would."

"I'd like to meet him," she said. "You have me fascinated with these Earth People."

I looked at her.

"He's good friends with Oony and Shay-lee. They'll be happy to introduce you."

We sat for a few more seconds.

"Let's go," I said. "Before the band gets away."

———————

The first twin was taking his turn behind her. The short rasta had finished his, now he was holding Rachel by her arm for the other one, the first twin—both of their cutlasses set aside on my father's desk, Rachel far beyond the point of struggle—but I can't be sure of the exact sequence. It's all out of focus. All I know is that without my even noticing, the twin standing behind me, pressing his sweaty bare chest into my back, holding the blade of his cutlass between his hands and pulling it backwards against my throat—they'd switched places. Somehow. Without my being aware. The second twin and the little black rasta. Because suddenly those forearms attached to the clear-colored palms holding the cutlass were black, not chocolate-brown, and they were pulling the blade harder against my throat—or I was pushing my throat harder into the blade—because that's what my body wanted to do, tried to do instinctively to lessen the pain. To somehow bend forwards at my waist. But I could manage it only by arching my shoulders back, shoving them backwards, harder, into his sweat-dripping chest. Except with the little rasta it was his face pressed into the middle of my back—I can still feel the soft knob of his nose pressed between my shoulder blades—shoving my throat harder into the blade.

But I cannot really tell you about the pain. Because in truth I don't remember it. What I can say is that the most painful memory is not the little guy, with his head of wild dreads, the first one, the leader. Him I scarcely remember. Despite that he was the first. For both Rachel and for me. The most painful memory, the one that has remained with me, came later. Looking over at the second of the twins behind Rachel, while the first twin took his turn behind me. Because in that bizarre moment—in my memory it's only a moment, an image of pain—in that surreal moment of juxtaposition I became that boy. That twin with his shaven head over behind Rachel.

In my mind, in that moment, the twins merged, they became one, and I became them. That one over behind Rachel. Behind me.

Whatever it means, if it means anything at all, I do not know.

Our parents wouldn't let Rachel shower, or clean herself up, until after the doctor examined her. We must have tried to explain to them, in whichever way we could, what had happened. Maybe it was obvious, only by looking at us—at the shattered glass, the burglar-proofing flung to the patio floor outside, the wrecked state of the parlor, our own nakedness, the dried blood on my throat and chest and the backs of my legs—maybe, with all that, we didn't have to explain anything to them? What I remember is that neither of us made any attempt to hide our nakedness before our parents. Neither Rachel nor me. As though, after what we'd been through, any embarrassment was a trifle. When our parents entered the parlor we simply stood there, stunned, paralyzed, on our feet now but still hugging each other. Until Rachel's mother walked slowly over and Rachel let go of me and took hold of her. And after several minutes she told Rachel that she could not shower until after the doctor examined her. Then Mummy went over to Rachel's house to fetch her some fresh clothes, and she brought them back. The children, Mummy whispered, were still fast asleep. My father nodded to me and I understood and hurried upstairs and showered quickly and dressed, pulled on shorts and a T-shirt.

We all drove over to the doctor's house, all of us—Rachel's mother and father and my father driving his Bentley, all of them still dressed up from last night, and me—everybody except Mummy, because she went back over to Rachel's to wait for the children to wake up. But when we got there, early on that Old Year's morning, we were told that Dr Robert had just left on an emergency call to the hospital (he and his wife had sat with us at our table in the club last night)—his wife met us at the door, tying her nightrobe around her, and she told us about the call to the hospital. Then she took us through the house and the kitchen and out to the back porch, where we waited for a long time, in silence, maybe an hour, until the doctor got back. All of us sitting on the back porch beneath a poinciana tree that had bloomed early, covered in orange flowers, petals on the bare ground around the thick trunk. All of us sitting in aluminum patio chairs waiting in silence, staring into the pool that seemed hideously blue. Reflection of the flowers hideously orange. Artificial. Motionless. A photograph of a pool and a tree.

Then the doctor arrived. Rachel's father and my father stood and the doctor took them inside—we could see the three men through the kitchen window, talking—and then they came back out to the patio again. Dr Robert told us that he'd just admitted the wife of the new Barclays Bank president, an Englishwoman, to hospital. She was in bad shape, he said. Very very bad.

Then he explained—as though he already knew our entire story—that after the three badjohns left our house, they walked to the end of the street and pulled the burglar-proofing off the front window of the house recently rented by the new Barclays Bank president. But the doctor wanted us to know that that house was alarmed, directly to the station, and within minutes the police arrived—even on Old Year's morning—and they had the three boys behind bars. They were already locked up.

The doctor took Rachel and her mother inside the house. They went into the doctor's own bedroom—Rachel told me this years later—and he examined her.

Then we all went home.

13

By the time we'd caught up with the band again Shay-lee and Laurence had disappeared. They'd gone off together someplace, and Oony was in trouble—not only distraught, drunk. And Oony seldom drank more than a couple of Caribs. I let Rachel go and put my arm around her and we chipped along together. Oony handed me her rum-and-coke and after I tasted it, I had little doubt she'd had too much. Little doubt about how the rest of my Monday mas would be occupied. And it was only two or three o'clock—the band would be on the road till eight tonight.

I drank most of Oony's drink, then the two or three others after that. Trying to keep her under control I was getting drunk myself. But by this point Oony could hardly walk on her own. We were chipping behind Nancy's big-truck, crushed in with the mob, and I don't know where our other friends had gone. Then I looked over and some guy who wasn't a member of the band—brown-skinned, wearing a marino, purple anchors tattooed on his biceps—had his arm around Oony on the other side. I didn't know him, and I was fairly certain Oony didn't either.

I started to pull her off to the side of the road.

The guy wouldn't let her go—and suddenly it was as if I was trying to pull Oony away from him, like he'd been hassling her. He was drunk himself—and probably he'd been running his head for twelve hours straight.

I made a second attempt to veer Oony off towards the side of the road. This time the guy reached across her and put his hand on my chest, grabbing my T-shirt in his fist, shouting into my face.

"Wha happen?"

He shoved me backwards.

Eventually the song ended, the guy let Oony go and turned around for a second, and in the same instant I pulled her over to the side of the road. The guy spun around—we saw the vexed look on his face—but by then he'd been caught up by the crowd and carried away.

Oony and I hurried around the corner, then a few blocks until we were away from the band. Leaning against the wall of somebody's frontyard, catching our breath, and Oony used the bottom of her T-shirt to wipe her face.

"I know it's only for a few days," she said between sobs. "But I can't help myself!"

"Think about something else."

"I just can't."

"You have to. It'll spoil—" I cut myself off.

"She slept with Laurence last night!"

I paused, feeling despicably pleased. Despite myself.

"Try and forget it," I said.

We stopped a skinny girl lugging a plastic bucket sloshing with ice and drinks, waited while she fished out a lone club-soda which she assured us she had. Oony felt better after the soda, and we started off. But we were all the way up in Belmont, and Oony lives in St Clair—not only on the other side of town, other side of the Savannah. Eventually we flagged down a pickup loaded with children, crowded into the back of the trunk. Costumed as burrokeets, papier-mâché donkeys, worn so the kids appeared to be riding them. They'd come out as a section of one of the adult bands, and now they were headed home. We climbed up and rode the rest of the way with them on the bed of the truck, the kids cheering Oony up.

The driver dropped us off in front of her house, blowing his horn, the children shouting and waving good-bye. I walked Oony around the side, in the back screen door, and down the hall to the bathroom. Got down on my monkey-knees to untie her sneakers, helped her out of her costume and in under the shower. Then I dried her off and I walked her down the hall again to her bedroom.

Oony slid under the sheet, towel wrapped around her. Wet hair framing her brown face.

"Don't forget," she said, "you're helping me with Mother Earth tomorrow."

"Have I ever let you down?"

"Plenty times," she smiled. "Not today."

She pulled my face down to her and kissed me.

"And you won't tomorrow," she said. "Understand?"

She'd already shut her eyes.

———————

My intentions were to go back to the hotel. I'd checked Oony's clock on the way out, already past five. By the time I caught up with the band again there'd only be a couple of hours left. Better to go back and get some sleep. Till it was time for the tent.

But I'd walked only a few blocks before I ran into Poison, the band famous for all the wild young-girls. Their scandalous bikinimas. Coolie Caravan was the DJ on their big-truck—blasting Denyse Plummer's "Get on Bad"—and let me tell you the young-girls were doing just that.

I stood with the crowd gathered on the sidewalk—a gang of boys enjoying the spectacle—telling myself more than once to turn around and go back to the hotel the other way. Suddenly, in the midst of the white bikinis, I found two sack-skirted Minshallites. You couldn't miss them. And when they got closer I saw that they were Rachel and Laurence. They saw me too, and they came running.

Before I knew it they'd dragged me into the band, three of us chipping arm in arm together.

Over the music they explained they'd just come from depositing Shay-lee at Oony's house. They'd caught a cab into town. Shay-lee had gotten word of Oony's condition, and she was worried—she'd gone in to nurse her. Then Laurence and Rachel had run into Poison, just as I had.

Rachel knew several members of the band. And now she squeezed the sunburned shoulder of the guy in front of us, and I was introduced to "another French cousin." Soon I realized that the masplayers jumping-up around us—the four or five young-girls in their white bikini-costumes, and the two sunburned boys with them, including my cousin—were all speaking French. All Rachel's friends. All of them, I learned after another minute, staying at her father's house.

"Mummy," Rachel told me, "organized everything for them from Nice."

We stopped at a roadside stall for cold Caribs. Our happy family shouting a mixture of French and broken English. Everybody excited, redfaced, sweating.

As I handed out the beers I found myself admiring a tall, very tanned brunette wearing a very small white bikini—top so sweat-soaked you could see two brown areolae through it—silver tassels at her wrists and ankles to call it a costume. She slid her sunglasses down her nose, looked at me over the rims. Made it clear that she had noticed me too.

A second later we were chipping together behind Coolie's big-truck.

And half a dozen Caribs after that we were still holding on to each other.

Monique, from the French island of Martinique—but between her broken English and the blaring soca it took me a minute to get it straight—two of us laughing together. Monique let me know—despite that she presently resided in Paris, despite that this was her first carnival—she was a West Indian: she knew how to wine, to free-up sheself. With me feeling more than ever the freshwater-yankee, trying my best to keep up.

During a pause in the music to refuel the Coolie's generator she ran into a bar and came out with a big styrotex glass full of ice. Monique turned her back to me and lifted her hair off of her shoulders with both hands, calling out instructions as I rubbed a chunk of ice along the back of her neck, across her brown shoulders, along the ridges of her spine and under the curves of her bamsee, all the way down the backs of her legs. Until I found myself kneeling on the hot asphalt, on my monkey-knees, for the second time in an hour.

Monique pulled me to my feet, pulled my T-shirt up over my head and wiped it across my chest. Then we were both rubbing icecubes over each other.

We jumped-up with Poison and the "French posse," as Laurence dubbed them, until we reached their mascamp on Cipriani Blvd. Coolie, shouting instructions for tomorrow morning to his masplayers one final time, shut down the PA system. Our ears ringing.

Rachel's house, where Monique and the others were staying, was on Rust St. A short distance from Poison's mascamp but in the opposite direction of our hotel. We split up with the plan that everybody had exactly an hour to shower and change, we'd stop by Rachel's house on our way to the tent to pick them up. Just how we were accomplishing this I couldn't tell you—since Shay-lee was no longer with us to chauffeur us around in Oony's car—and carnival Monday night is the hardest night of the year to find a taxi. Which we couldn't all fit into anyway. But that was the plan.

———————

We stopped for a proper drink at one of the stands across the street from our hotel. We'd been drinking beers all afternoon. Rachel wanted to use the toilet, and Laurence needed to get some money, so they left me there for a moment to go up to their rooms. I warned Rachel not to lie down, not for a second, or she'd never make it. Instead she got into the tub, and when Laurence got back he said she was staying in. But she promised to meet us later at the club.

Now Laurence told me to turn around and take a look at our vehicle for the night. Parked in front of the hotel, like an apparition, I found an enormous white Cadillac. 60's model, convertible, all smooth curves and pointed fins and shining chrome. The driver wearing a matching white shirt-jack—impeccably starched and pressed, you could tell even from the other side of the street—leaning up against his car smoking a cigarette.

Mr Ferguson, Laurence explained, was the same taxi driver who'd brought Alicia and him in from the airport. Laurence had told him to come back and look for us, that we'd make use of his services again. In fact Laurence had just given Mr Ferguson three hundred US dollars, organized to have him drive us around for the rest of the night. Or morning. However long we managed to keep going.

Now Laurence gave the proprietress of the stand we were leaning against—another newfound friend, the phoulorie balls woman—another crisp US twenty dollar bill. Asked for phoulorie balls and a couple more scotch-and-sodas.

The two of us spilled into the back seat of Mr Ferguson's shining white Cadillac, still unshowered, still wearing our cocoasack-skirts, me still bareback. But hardly had we started out when I shouted for him to pull over. There was a girl standing in front of the Roxy handing out free T-shirts. And Laurence and I pulled them on. The Colonel, goateed and smiling, exclaiming *Finger-lickin' good!* into a cartoon cloud, plastered across our chests.

Rachel's father came to the door. Still wearing his white Speedo, silver tassels at his wrists and ankles—he'd played with Poison too.

My uncle explained that he'd just dropped his French houseguests at the club for dinner. Where Sam was putting on a special carnival Monday night barbecue—New York strip steaks and spareribs, flown in specially from Miami.

My uncle wouldn't let us leave until we had a drink.

Back in our car with Mr Ferguson Laurence and I decided there was no way we were eating spareribs and steaks and french-fries. We had him U-turn in the middle of Maraval Road, head out towards St James where, on the sidewalk across the street from Smokey-and-Bunty's, there's a woman who makes the best baigan rotis on the island—Hindi for eggplant, which the rest of us call melongen.

We ate our rotis sitting at a picnic table on the sidewalk in front of Smokey-and-Bunty's, a fairly crude local bar. The waiter known as Mums, a quite mad—and just as famous—transvestite, not a tooth left in her mouth, also wearing Poison's white bikini and silver tassels. Though clearly she'd assembled her costume herself. Mums brought us Caribs, sashaying splendidly. Our picnic table sandwiched between two mammoth, vibrating speakers, blasting the soca. With a group of drunks and vagrants—joined occasionally by Mums—wining together in the middle of the street. But things hadn't even warmed up yet. In a couple of hours the mob of revelers, most still in costume, would effectively cut off traffic along Western Main Road.

The club was still quiet, nobody even at the door to check out passes, which I'd left in the hotel anyway. We looked for the French posse. First out back on the grass around the pool where they were doing their barbecue. Sam saw us and got up from his plate of ribs, came over to say hello. He walked us, his arm around Laurence, over to one of the outdoor bars. Told his bartender to give us a round. Sam was sure that the French group was still there, but Laurence and I looked all over the grounds and couldn't find them. Then we checked inside the club, nobody even on the dancefloor yet. We decided they'd made their way to the tent on their own.

The show had already been going for a couple of hours by the time we walked in. I'd left those tickets in my room too, but this late in the performance we didn't need them. The tent jam-packed, mostly with middle-aged men in unbuttoned shirt-jacks, their marinos showing. Sitting up on the backs of their folding aluminum chairs, drink in one hand, program fanning away in the other. Giving fatigue to the calypsonians. A handful of beet-red tourists in Hawaiian shirts.

No French posse.

Crazy was the calypsonian shouting onstage, running around like a wild man, constantly whipping back his frazzled, waist-length bush of hair. Wearing nothing but a leopardskin-loincloth, beating his bare chest like Tarzan. The more the crowd taunted him, the wilder he got.

Laurence and I made our way to the bar at the back, where we found ourselves standing across from Eddoes. There with a rasta-farian friend, Brother Resistance, who'd performed earlier. The inventor of rapso—rap-infused-calypso—his lyrics frequently militant and biting. Yet Brother Resistance is one of the gentlest men you'll ever meet, a long-time sympathizer and advocate, I knew, of Eddoes's mother.

I left Laurence in the drink line and went over to say hello. Eddoes still in his sack-skirt and T-shirt, drinking a Guinness.

"The man with the spliff," he said.

"Just happened to find one in my pocket."

"Wha?" he laughed. "Save my life you know. Me did feeling plenty geegeeree to go across them stage!"

"That was only to give you the edge."

"Think so?" he steupsed. "Me ain't accustom to them kinda crowd, unnastand?"

"Well you better get accustomed," I said. "Minsh'll have you playing King every year, after last night. You watch."

"We go see bout that!"

I asked after Mother.

Eddoes studied my face for a second, took a sip of his Guinness, then he steupsed again.

"All this time I telling meself—but you know this white-man, nuh!" He paused, "You been in the valley before, not true?"

"Last time was a couple years back. I didn't make it to Madamas last year."

"I could remember."

"You were a little boy then," I said. "Now you reach King of the Bands!"

He looked away, "I coming up."

"So how's Mother?"

Eddoes shook his head, "She good good these days you know. Very good."

He was speaking with the Earth People's inversion.

"The sickness?" I asked.

"Plenty sufferation. Some days she don't even leave the house.

Not even to take she breakfast. Weak, I tell you. And get them spells—you know, the malkadee, faints—fall down on the ground all the time. You there talking with she easy like that and she fall down. Just so."

"And Breadfruit?" I tried to change the subject.

"He OK."

Eddoes took a sip of his Guinness, "You know, Mother wasn't so please bout me coming in Rome to play in the carnival neither."

Rome was town, civilization.

"How you mean?" I asked.

"She did vex! Cuss me two days straight, when I tell she I was thinking to come in and join the band."

Mother was dead set against the festival—the excessive drinking, sexual abandon. She held no restraints on the Earth People, even her own sons. They were free to come and go as they pleased. But playing mas in a carnival band was another story.

"Think she knows you played King?" I said. "And bust the trophy?"

He laughed. "Don't know yet, but she go find out! Mother go cuss plenty when she hear bout that, I could tell you."

"A-tall," I said. "She'll be proud."

"You tink?"

"How you mean? She'll be angry to start with, but she'll get over it."

"I feel so."

"After a while Mother'll see it for what it is."

He nodded.

"She'll come round," I said. "You watch. Next thing you know she'll be praising Minshall!"

Then I remembered she was dead set against homosexuals—another of Rome's perversions.

"All left!" Eddoes was smiling again.

Laurence brought me over a Carib. I introduced everybody.

The calypso show was winding down, several of the seats vacant already. Brother Resistance was about to leave for another engagement.

"Let's get back to the club," Laurence said. "Before the stampede."

What the hell, I thought, turning to Eddoes again.

"You know," I said, "I got a cousin wants to meet you."

———————

Now there were three of us, like pageant queens in our sack-skirts, sitting up on the back seat of Mr Ferguson's shining white convertible. Joint passing between us. Every few minutes someone on the roadside whistling, shouting out—"Look Charlie angels!"

Sitting up on the back seat like that we wound up taking a tour of the whole town. Because every few blocks we ran into another big-truck, pounding out the soca, surrounded by revelers. Or a steelband—Monday night pan-around-the-neck. Or we ran into police barriers, stretching across the road. Mr Ferguson calmly making another eight-point, squealing U-turn. We had him stop at a couple bars along the way. Laurence insisted we pass by the Roxy again, pick up a T-shirt for Eddoes.

Earlier it had taken ten minutes to drive all the way in from St James to the club, two minutes between the club and the tent. Now to drive between the tent and the club again, it took two hours. Though we could have probably walked it in twenty minutes. Almost as long as we did walk, in the end, since Mr Ferguson couldn't get within half a mile of the club. Cars parked all the way along both sides of the winding drive, another line of cars stuck between, horns blowing, radios blaring.

The line to get in the front door seemed just as long. Fortunately there were a handful of kids lugging buckets sloshing with ice and drinks, circulating among the crowd—mostly freshwater-yankees, passports and passes ready in their hands.

Finally, when we got near the top of the line, the two black guys standing in front of us got into an argument with the two black thugs posted at the door. Shouting for ten minutes. Cussing. Threats.

Eventually the bouncers shoved them aside, roughly, and three of us made an attempt to storm the door.

"No dread-heads coming in here!" the one blocking our way said to Eddoes.

"I got some passes tucked in this skirt someplace," I said, feigning as if checking my pouch.

"We were all just here," Laurence told one of the doormen. "Sam paid us the courtesy of buying us a drink. Go ask you boss-man!"

"No dreads inside here," the guy shouted into Laurence's face. "And no upstart niggers, neither!"

"Listen," I shoved my way around Laurence. "My skin's white, OK? Just let me go look for our friends—we don't want to be in this focking place anyway!"

I was already walking. Shoving my way between the two thugs.

Then I was sitting on the ground, still between the two doormen. Only now they were floating above me—two wide, black, balloon-faces. Bright strobe flashing behind them.

I felt like somebody'd hit me over the head with a shovel.

Suddenly, in the air above me, fists were flying—the two young guys in line in front of us, slugging out at the two bouncers. Then I realized I was being pulled to my feet. I had an arm slung over Laurence's shoulder, the other over Eddoes's, and they were dragging me down a dark corridor, crowded with people—horrified expressions on their faces as we went past.

They dragged me across the crowded dancefloor, Byron Lee and his band playing onstage, out through the door at the other side of the room. Carrying me all the way out back onto the grass, where they put me on a lounge chair beside the pool. But there were so many people in the pool, most still in costume, you couldn't see the water.

Laurence pressed a paper napkin to my eye, held it there for a minute. Then he got an ice-cold Carib which he wrapped in the now red napkin, pressing it against the side of my face.

That was the first time I felt the pain—I shoved the bottle away.

Laurence laid me back on the lounge chair, pressed the napkin-wrapped bottle gently against my eye.

There were people crowded all around us, shouting, dancing, music pumping from inside the club—I could feel it vibrating along the arms of my chair.

Eventually Laurence left Eddoes there to nurse me, and he went back inside to see if he could find Rachel and the French posse. He came back alone in ten minutes.

Suddenly I looked up and over the heads of people in the pool, on the other side, I saw four uniformed policeman. I nodded and Laurence and Eddoes looked over.

The policemen were searching the crowd. With them one of the thugs from the door. *He* held a blood-red napkin to the side of his face—or so I thought—but when they got closer I saw that it was a dripping NY strip steak.

Laurence and Eddoes already had me on my feet. Dragging me across the tennis courts, out the back gate.

———————

We had Mr Ferguson drop Eddoes off at Minshall's house. Shouts of "All left!" Knocking our fists together. Then he drove us to

Smokey-and-Bunty's, but the closest he could get was three blocks away. Mums shrieked when she saw me—my eye, I could hardly see out of it now—an arm slung over Laurence's shoulder.

"Ayeee!" she bawled. "Look me doux-doux! How them could mash-up he pretty face so?"

Mums dropped her empty tin tray to the sidewalk with a clatter. She ordered the people sitting along one side of the picnic table out of the way, shoving them off the seat, so I could have a place.

Mums laid me back on the bench. She stood above me, frazzled, adjusting her bikini top.

"Oh me lossie lossie! Oh me lossie lossie lossie!"

Everybody laughing—especially Laurence.

She turned around and shoved her way through the people crowding the door. A minute later she appeared again carrying a piece of roasted rachette—the flat, mitten-shaped cactus that grows along the seaside—applied, in the old days at least, to cuts and bruises. Bush-medicine. An ancient Amerindian remedy.

She laid my head on her lap. Pressing her roasted rachette gingerly against my eye. Explaining to Laurence—could I invent this?—how she'd been using it earlier to soothe her "jouvert monkey-knees."

Mums swooned over me. Fussing. Adjusting her dirty bikini top. A handful of beet-red tourists came over to watch—like she was performing some exotic tropical ritual. Meanwhile the speakers on either side of us continued pounding the soca. Revelers went on wining in the street.

———————

When we got back to Mr Ferguson he was snoring away in his marino. Stretched out on the front seat of his car, his shirt-jack laid neatly across the dashboard beside him. He jumped up and started buttoning it on, still beautifully pressed. Laurence and me spilling into the back seat of his car, blinking, sun stinging our eyes.

He dropped us off in the alley behind our hotel, the front street already closed off. We tipped him every crumpled bill we could pull out of our pouches. Then Laurence and I stood, an arm over each other's shoulder, watching Mr Ferguson make one last squealing eight-point U-turn. He waved to us over his shoulder.

"Enjoy the car-nee-val!" he sang. Like it was just about to begin.

Laurence and I dragged ourselves around to the front of the hotel. Where we found Rachel, Shay-lee, and Alicia sitting on the step, waiting for us.

They'd bathed, eaten, slept twelve hours—with one minor interruption for Rachel—then they'd awoken and bathed again. Eaten again. Sitting there on the front step looking perfectly rested, young, lovely.

They'd already heard the story of our little mishap at the club. According to Rachel, the four uniformed policemen had come by the hotel only a couple of hours ago, still looking for us. Making a row. Waking up Miss Fletcher and everybody else.

Our efficient Miss Fletcher called Sam on his cell phone. He assured her there'd been no trouble.

"I can vouch for those boys," he apparently told her. "Especially Laurence—just saw them swimming in the pool."

———

The only way for the two of us to keep going was to keep going. We already had our costumes on anyway. And we left immediately, headed for Aripita Ave.

"We already late!" Shay-lee said.

She was right. Already headed downtown. When we got to Aripita Ave the band had left. It wasn't even eight o'clock.

After hurrying for half an hour we caught up, making our way slowly towards our cart, past the other sections. All the masplayers in full costume now—wearing elaborate headdresses, toting tall driftwood-standards. On Monday the band organizers attempted to keep us in our sections as much as possible.

Sections of Fisherpeople, Chip-Chip Gatherers, Planters for the Nation. A gorgeous section of older obeahwomen, Bush Tea. Another of younger Washerwomen, cohorts to Mother Earth. Even an infamous section of Ganja Growers, trailed by their cloud of smoke.

When we got to the cart—to our Putting out the Faith section—we were the only six masplayers still wearing T-shirts. Laurence's and mine depicting a smiling Kentucky sticking out even more. We pulled them up over our heads, the girls somewhat reluctantly. Stuffed them into a space at the front of the cart.

Laurence wasn't prepared for this, and you should have seen the look on his face. And even though I knew what to expect, it was still another half-hour before I could restrain myself from staring boldfaced at all of those breasts—slippery and shining and lovely looking beneath the sun—bouncing all around us. But before long those breasts began to seem natural, rather than sexual, as Mother Earth would have said. Mechanism of mas once again.

There was only one stressful moment the entire morning. And it occurred after the band had already been on the road for a couple of hours. Just as we reached the intersection of Woodford St and Tragarete Rd—just as I had predicted to Shay-lee yesterday. But by the time we saw the flashing lights I'd already grown so accustomed to our natural state of undress, that it didn't cross my mind. Not until I saw the group of eight or ten uniformed policemen, bootoos raised in their fists, posted before two camouflage-painted vans, parked front bumper to front bumper across Tragarete Rd. Red lights spinning on top.

They cut us off. The band coming to an immediate halt.

Meanwhile a tiny chief of police, standing at the top of a short stepladder, shouted into a megaphone the size of a small Christmas tree.

He ordered the music shut down: Roots, Nancy, and the rhythm boys.

Now he directed "all you womens carrying you bosoms outside" to file into the waiting vans.

Chaos erupted. Women screaming, looking for some piece of cloth to cover themselves, or pulling their sack-skirts up into their armpits. Running in the opposite direction down Tragarete Rd.

It only lasted a moment. Because at that same moment the minister of culture and education—also a popular TV and radio personality—happened to walk by. Dressed in his space alien costume from Wayne Barkley's band, headed towards their mascamp on Woodford St.

The minister told the policeman to behave himself.

"These ain't colonial times," he said. "You can't lock-up people again for enjoying theyselves!"

Then the minister, a large man wearing a green, antenna-bouncing costume—he looked more like a galactic bug—picked up the little policeman by the stepladder he was standing on. Walking off with him and his Christmas tree–sized megaphone, around the corner and down Woodford St. Gang of bare-breasted Minshallites cheering behind.

A minute later the soca was cranking again. The two vans, still with their red lights flashing, pulled out of the way to let us pass.

We jumped-up with the band until we reached Mahatma Gandhi Square, a small park in the shape of a triangle, where the band stopped for lunch, the music quieted. Roses had a huge pot of still warm pelau on the cart, and now she piled up heaping paperplates for our group, eaten with plastic spoons sitting on the grass.

Afterwards, lying on my back, staring up through the dusty leaves of an almond tree, I noticed a couple of gray clouds. Moving in from behind the mountains. We might have a shower later on to cool us down, and by then we'd be needing it.

We'd been lounging on the grass nearly an hour when a pickup pulled into the square, loaded with Minshall and his theater group, the dancers. Now Mr Minshall spoke into his own megaphone, calling all of his Putting out the Faith masplayers over to the truck. Our section. He had a special plan for us, in addition to having us bare our breasts. Now he ordered us all to remove our sack-skirts too. Of course we were wearing our Speedos under them—black or white, depending.

In a carefully orchestrated, elaborate ritual which seemed a sober extension of jouvert's mudmas two nights ago, Minshall painted each of our skins the opposite color. Each member of his Putting out the Faith section. In addition to his theater group. Head to toe.

Minshall baptized each of us as our other. As the opposite race.

Loaded onto the back of the pickup were two enormous vats of paint. Two wide paint brushes. And following Minshall's instructions two lines of masplayers formed behind the truck. As he coated each of us with paint that smelled of freshly kneaded dough before it goes into the oven, Minshall, in his deep theatrical voice, pronounced:

"The river shall wash you clean!"

He painted another masplayer:

"The river shall wash you clean!"

It was water-based paint that dried in a few minutes beneath the sun. Now my black Speedo matched the rest of me. Laurence's white Speedo matched the rest of him. We put on our sack-skirts again, pressed our velcro belts together around our waists.

As Minshall finished his baptism ritual one of the band organizers, shouting into the PA system on Roots' truck, called us into sections. At the same time, mysteriously, bolts of red silk were unloaded from the pickup Minshall and the dancers had arrived on. No one knew what they were for, not even Shay-lee. She said that Minshall had not even told Oony what the bolts of silk were about, though she'd gone with him to the airport to pick them up, shipped from China.

As the various sections grouped together the music cranked up. And as the band started off again the bolts of red silk were simultaneously unfurled. Several bolts per section, each bolt a hundred yards long. Unfurled, stretched out, these long strips of silk were carried overhead by our shouting, wining, chipping masplayers.

We danced the long strips of red silk. We became the river, and the river flowed red with blood.

Minshall's standard strategy, for carnival Tuesday, is to cross main-stage at sunset. The costumes always look more spectacular in that light. And sunset, according to that morning's *Guardian*—Tuesday, February 19, the Day of Death—was to occur at 5:47 PM. At that moment, or as close as possible as we could get to it, the Battle of the Sons would take place.

Just before we went on stage the flatbed loaded with the Kings' and Queen's costumes would pull into the Savannah. And I'd help Oony get Aisha into her costume as Mother Earth, then Michael and Eddoes. Or the other way around, since the Battle would be the opening theatrical event, and Mother Earth would be the very last masplayer to cross the stage, preceded by her group of cohorts.

But in order to get to mainstage by sunset we'd have to start over now, at only a little past three o'clock. Reports reached us that the Savannah was already chaos. As it always is on carnival Tuesday afternoon. Dozens of bands already jammed up.

Even before we got to the end of Charlotte St, before our sneakers could step on Savannah grass, we came to an abrupt halt. Soca shut down. Strips of red silk carefully folded into squares or rolled up. Slowly, in what seemed a solemn, vengeful silence, we filed into the Savannah. Masplayers looking for some soft, cool spot to sit. We'd be there for a while: we had the entire circumference of the Savannah to pass around before we got to mainstage.

After sitting for a few minutes Shay-lee, Rachel, and Alicia decided they were going back to the hotel to use the toilet, relax. Laurence said he'd go with them. The Queen Elizabeth Suite had a rotating electric fan on one of the bedstands, and they planned to sit in front of it. On the cool, Cuban-tiled floor—under our layer of paint we felt even hotter. They'd meet me back here. *I* didn't feel like going back to the hotel. A-tall. I was feeling restless. Anxious. Especially after our burst of excitement jumping-up beneath the strips of silk. I wanted to keep going, needed to keep going, and this waiting around in the Savannah—as it did every carnival Tuesday afternoon—bothered me tremendously. Frustrated me. Even angered me.

In truth I didn't know what I wanted to do with myself. Not until the rest of my group had wandered off, and I'd been sitting there by myself on the grass for another half-hour. Not until I heard a gang of six or seven sack-skirted, chalk-white guys shouting out, running past. Headed for the pit at the side of mainstage: Poison was crossing.

They were already well past the stage by the time I caught up with Monique and the rest of the French posse. Wild again, same as yesterday afternoon. Redfaced, shouting, dripping in sweat. Same as all the other Poison masplayers. They'd just crossed the stage, after several hours' wait. And if I haven't said it already those few frenzied minutes of crossing mainstage on Tuesday afternoon are the highlight of our two days and nights of carnival.

That was the level of everybody's spirit. The level of the speeded-up soca pounding out of Coolie's big-truck. That was the vibe when I finally caught up with Monique—after, I now realized, having searched for her for nearly 24 hours.

They all had a good laugh when they saw me. Monique shouting out something in French, grabbing my blackened shoulders and planting a passionate kiss on my blackened mouth, shoving her tongue inside.

I couldn't remember if we'd kissed yesterday afternoon.

They were drunk and happy like everybody else, the French posse. But there was something different going on with Monique and her friends. Different from the other masplayers. Different from yesterday: a glazed, flattened look in their eyes. Slowness in the way they were moving, half-second behind the beat.

Whatever it was I can tell you that when I finally caught up with Monique that afternoon, when she grabbed my shoulders and kissed me, I wanted to be with her—wherever she happened to be at the moment. And when she shouted into the ear of one of her friends, my French cousin, and he unzipped his belted pouch and produced a large white horse-pill that looked to me like a Tums, and Monique shoved it into my mouth and kissed me again—leaving me little choice but to swallow it—I did. Happily.

If it was hex-ta-sis—as Monique pronounced it a few seconds after the fact—that was fine. Wouldn't be the first time I'd swallowed it.

Twenty minutes and a couple Caribs later I was in good shape—or bad, very bad—depending on how you look at it. Depending on whether you live in Rome or Hell Valley. Twenty minutes later I'd forgotten Oony, River, my friends—everything and everybody in the world besides Monique.

We were chipping, or stumbling, arm in arm behind Coolie Caravan, along the main road on the other side of the Savannah. Hilton shining in the sun high above. Monique pulled me off the road onto the grass, saying she had to pee. Then I suppose we were wandering around looking for someplace semiprivate, a tree or a parked car to duck behind. And although we seemed to trudge through the tall grass for little more than a couple of minutes next thing I knew we were standing before the tall, coral-block wall of tiny Fletcher Cemetery. Which for some reason struck me as humorous. Laughing out loud, kissing Monique at the same time, pressing her back against the coral-block wall.

I told her that all my relatives were buried in there. All the way back to the first of my forefathers. My namesake. First Fletcher to set foot on the island.

"We must pay a visit," she said. "We must wake him up!"

I took her hand and led her around the wall to the front, where we found the wrought-iron gate already shoved in, one of the hinges pulled clean out of the wall. Monique ducked down and pulled me through the gap at the side of the gate. Now it was her turn to shove my blackened shoulders against the inside wall, thrusting her tongue in my mouth.

Hardly had we stumbled a few steps before I found the bronze plaque.

Monique yanked down her white bikini-bottom, stretched between her knees, taking hold of both my hands and leaning backwards over it. Yellow urine catching the sun and bouncing up off the shining plaque like golden beads. Monique staring into my eyes, smiling at me maliciously, deliciously, waking up a long dead William Sangor Fletcher.

———————

Two of us were stumbling arm in arm along the line of food- and drinkstalls in front of our hotel. Our phoulorie balls woman. Despite my state of mind I knew exactly where we were headed. Which direction I was steering Monique.

We stopped to look over at a group of people on the other side of the street. They seemed to be calling to us, waving, shouting. Now they were rushing across the street towards us—two white boys and three white girls. I recognized them, but not exactly. Suddenly the girls were pulling Monique out of my arms. Roughly. And I was pulling her back.

They were her friends, the French posse. Shouting to her. Monique shaking her head.

But no matter what they were telling her I wasn't about to let Monique go.

Suddenly many more people were pressed all around us, everybody screaming, hurrying in the direction of grandstand.

I heard a shout, "Run, nuh! Minshall ready to cross!"

The French posse turned their backs to us, running with the others in the direction of the stands. Leaving Monique and me standing there, arms wrapped around each other, struggling to keep our balance. Battered by shoulders rushing past.

We were rolling around in my bed, still shoved against the wall. Lying on the bare mattress, the sheet tangled around our legs—everything streaked with black paint rubbing off my body. Through the open sliding glass door, beyond the inward billowing curtains, I heard three distinct explosions—three pops—a roar from the crowds following each one. And somewhere in the recesses of my fuddled mind I understood that they were the rockets of Mancrab's arsenal. Battle of the Sons—it had begun. The crowds shouting. Rudder singing "River Is Mas."

I lay on my back with my legs spread wide across the bed—one bare foot planted on the cold Cuban tiles in an attempt to keep the room from spinning—and Monique was kneeling over me. Her head between my spread thighs, dark hair fallen forward so I couldn't see her face. Only her brown shoulders, moving up and down, her bobbing head. A buoy, several yards away, and I was swimming towards it. But the longer I swam, the harder I stretched to reach for that buoy, the more it receded from my grasp.

I closed my eyes. Fighting to find a focus.

Then I heard Monique shout something in French—exasperated, angry—and when I opened my eyes again she was curled up at the other end of the bed. Beside my blackened leg. She lay there in a fetal position, her face still hidden from me by her hair, hands cupped between her thighs.

I pressed the side of my face into the wall, streaked with black too, looking across at Monique—her beautiful, trembling body—weeping, or so I thought. And now I wanted desperately to reach down and take her into my arms. To comfort her. We could hold each other and feel comforted. Both of us. Until the hurt passed.

Then she seemed not to be weeping. And as the trembling of her shoulders increased, as her hands moved faster between her thighs, and her entire body tightened around her cupped palms—rigid, straining, her shoulders covered with a film of sweat—I knew Monique wasn't crying at all.

I should have looked away but I did not. I watched. I forced myself. Made myself endure every second. Until she reached the peak of her excitement, and she held it for several tense seconds, and then her shoulders stopped shaking. Her body slowly growing limp. Giving out.

Then I knew that she was asleep.

I rolled out of bed. My Speedo caught around one ankle—I kicked it off. Stumbling out onto the balcony.

As soon as I stepped past the sliding glass door the roar of the crowds seemed to treble in volume. Rudder beneath the clamor "River Is Mas."

I stood there, leaning on the railing. My mind reeling.

Then, with a jolt, the sound of a fistful of gravel thrown onto a galvanized roof. The clatter came again. I raised my head. Felt the first hard ping of a piece of gravel against my forehead. Another at the side of my neck. And when I raised my hand before my eyes and examined my upturned wrist, I saw the pale pocks left behind each piece of gravel as it struck my blackened skin and seemed to stick, seemed to melt.

People in the street in front of the hotel were shouting, running for cover. Jumping into parked cars and slamming the doors. It was coming down, in sheets, hard—coughing up the dust at the roadside and beating it back down.

Only Minshall could have planned it, only he had those connections. The rain, a tropical storm, would not last. The sun had disappeared for the day, but the sky surrounding the gray cloud overhead was still crystal blue. Still bright. The air hot. Humid. Steam rising from the still hot asphalt of the street against the pelting rain. A temporary nuisance for some, welcomed cooling for others. Sufficient in duration only to wash a few painted, inverted masplayers clean. To give them back to themselves, more thoroughly and poignantly back to themselves. As they emerged on the other side of the stage, other side of the river.

I wasn't among them. But despite it all, or in spite of it all, I did not feel that I was far away either. The same rain pelting them was pelting me on the top of my head, my back and neck and chest and shoulders. Same pool of dark-ribboned water collecting at my feet.

After a few minutes it began to slacken. But I waited for it to stop completely. There was no longer the roar of the crowds, or soca, or any sound other than the splash of water spilling off the hotel's roof, landing in the puddles below. I watched the hot ground and the asphalt of the road steam up some more. And when I turned around and stumbled past the sliding door, fully restored to myself too—yet in no way that I could imagine—my bed was empty.

14

Sun streaming past the open curtains. Churchbells. Birds chirping. As I rolled over I could still hear the soca pounding in my head, vibrating at the tips of my fingers. I got out of bed and pulled on my remaining pair of pants, the khakis I'd arrived in. Stepped out onto the balcony. Shielding my eyes from the bright sun.

The garbage had already been picked up. Overnight. All the bottles and aluminum cans, discarded bits of costumes, headdresses and standards thrown into the gutters. All magically cleared away. Fresh dew on the Savannah grass. Cut through the middle by a girl meandering across, barefoot, her oversized dress loose around her sinewy frame, yellow bundle balanced on her head. Across the street a man was using a crowbar to disassemble one of the plywood stalls. But he was doing it carefully, almost delicately, as if attempting not to make too much noise. Taking his time.

I watched for a few minutes, went back in and got into the shower. Standing beneath the lukewarm water long enough, I hoped, to put the soca to rest. But when I got out I was still hearing it. Still pulsing in my fingertips as I pressed a T-shirt to my dripping face. I shaved. Then I put the razor down to examine my eye. The slightly submerged spot of dried black blood pressed against the cornea. Like a fat, misshaped period. Full stop—that was appropriate. No swelling at the side of my face though. Wonders of Mums's roasted rachette. A yellow-brown, semitransparent scab over the bridge of my nose. My face tanned, with a sprinkle of new juvenile freckles across my cheeks. Rosy after two days of the sun. I looked healthy, in better shape than when I arrived.

I pulled on my remaining clean shirt, light blue with long sleeves and a button-down collar. Rolled the sleeves up to my elbows, left the tail hanging out of my khakis. Downstairs in the cafeteria a couple of boarders were still eating breakfast, old men in bedroom slippers, one wearing pajamas. Back in the kitchen I recognized a cook who piled me up a plate of congealed scrambled eggs, corned beef hash sweating orange grease beneath a red lamp. Dry toast. Instant coffee laden with condensed milk. A feast.

When I got outside three men were taking the plywood shutters off the windows. A line of old people sitting in the folding aluminum chairs, observing them over their shoulders. All their foreheads marked with gray splotches. I recognized a couple of them, including an aged Dr Robert, but my hello went unacknowledged.

At the end of the walkway the two curved benches were back in place, Rachel sitting on one of them. I slid in beside her.

She jumped slightly, turned to me and smiled.

She was wearing a hat, the old-fashioned kind of white straw, kerchief for a tie, knotted into a floppy bow beneath her chin. Her mound of curls spilling out from underneath.

"I notice you're wearing a hat," I said.

She laughed. "Isn't it dreadful? Belongs to Miss Fletcher. We're going to mass together."

"Really?"

"Why not?"

"Yes," I said, "why not."

And after a second, "Can't believe you woke up for church though."

"Couldn't sleep. Leftover excitement I suppose."

She paused, "And now you're up you can come with us."

"Like focking hell!"

"No need for blasphemy, dear."

"It's just that I haven't been to church in years."

"And you think I have? But you know, the ashes were always one of the rituals I liked, morbid as it sounds."

Truth is that as a boy, as the acolyte pressed to Father O'Connor's side holding the little crucible, Father making his tiny cross on the recipients' foreheads—dust-you-came-unto-dust-you-shall-return—I'd also been fascinated by the ritual. Though I didn't tell Rachel that.

"I've had a row with our Miss Fletcher," I said. "Don't think she'll be going with me to mass or anyplace else."

"Don't be foolish. I'm going in to find out what's keeping her."

I sat there watching the man across the street, still taking apart his plywood stall. He was up on top of it now, bouncing slightly, waving his crowbar in the air like a conductor's baton. Suddenly the stand collapsed and he ended up sitting on a pile of plywood, cloud of dust rising around him. Startled look on his face.

Some of the old people clapped.

Dr Robert called over, "Mind you don't sprain your bamsee!"

"Or get in splinters," the old man beside him laughed. "You'll have to operate."

"Indeed," the doctor said.

After a minute Rachel returned, pulling me off the bench, onto my feet. She fixed my hand in the crook of her arm like we were going courting. Rachel in her church hat.

"You're taking me to mass," she announced. "Miss Fletcher has an emergency. Woman slipped in the shower. She's complaining of a sprained right cheek."

"It's going around," I said.

We walked for a few minutes.

"Listen," I told her. "I'll take you over, but I'm not going in."

"Fine. Maybe I won't be able to either. We'll see."

A group of schoolchildren hurried past, wearing their uniforms, emerald skirts or shortpants, starched white shirts. They'd just come from church, all their foreheads marked with splotches. Two of the boys were trailing behind, laughing. I watched them spit into their palms then grind them into their foreheads, removing the ashes. The nun with them—dressed head to toe in white like a washerwoman, her veils blowing in the breeze—saw also. She gave each of them a proper zobell, hard flick behind the ear.

Now the boys were rubbing their ears, complaining, the nun hurrying them along.

When we got to the cathedral on Richmond St, I let go of Rachel's arm. Tucked in my shirttail. And we continued walking, straight into the church. Still arm in arm.

It was packed, third high mass for the morning just beginning. The priest, a young black man I didn't recognize, circled the altar with one of his acolytes, blessing it with incense. Slinging out puffs of smoke with each step. You could smell it all the way at the back of the church.

A family squeezed tighter together, the mother taking one of her children onto her lap, so Rachel and I could slide in at the end of the pew.

We had a wait. The ashes wouldn't be dispensed until after mass.

I started wondering about it, our receiving the ashes. What effect they'd have on our souls that is. I knew it was an unthinkable offense to receive holy communion in a state of mortal sin, which was surely the case for Rachel and me, hundred times over. For starters, every time we missed Sunday mass. I sat there making calculations, visualizing the figures written on a chalkboard:

$$
\begin{array}{r}
12 \text{ years} \\
\times\ 52 \text{ weeks} \\
\hline
624 \text{ mortal sins}
\end{array}
$$

But maybe they weren't cumulative? those mortal sins? Anyway, they could be wiped away with a single confession. Couple minutes of mumbling. Clean slate. All those heaped-up, exponential sins.

If you could bring yourself to go to confession, that is, and I certainly couldn't. Doubted seriously Rachel could either.

But maybe it didn't make a difference, for the ashes?

As it turned out it didn't, through no fault of the ashes or the marked-up slates of our souls. Because after a few minutes Rachel reached and took hold of my hand, her palm suddenly cold, clammy. She leaned over, brim of her hat cutting me across the temple.

"I'm no good for this anymore," she whispered. "Let's get out of here!"

We stood and the family spread out again, the mother looking relieved.

Now the door at the back of the cathedral was crowded with people coming in. Blocking our way. We waited a few seconds. Rachel still clutching my hand—only now she was squeezing it, hard, like she was about to panic.

Eventually we shoved our way through, spilling down the steps, out into the hot sun.

"Not a moment too soon," she whispered.

———————

We didn't speak until we got back to the Savannah. We'd been walking at a brisk pace and now we were sweating. Rachel still squeezing my hand.

We crossed over onto the grass, walking towards a bench beneath the samaan in front of the grandstand, shaded from the sun. The man, I noticed, was up there again, lying in the fork of the tree, thin black limbs spilling out.

We sat and Rachel untied her hat, shaking out her hair. She held it neatly in her lap.

"Met Eddoes yesterday in the band," she said as if in passing. "Actually I had Laurence introduce us. He tells me you three are now best of friends."

I was looking up into the tree, wondering if the man lived up there. If he ever came down. He had to at least eat, but from the looks of him it wasn't often.

I turned to Rachel.

"Wearing his magnificent costume," she continued. "His body-suit—can you imagine? I was limp at first. Perfect dishrag!"

"I told you he's good looking."

"Would you believe he wore his wings the entire afternoon? Two or three hours at least. Carrying them through the streets. Don't know how he managed it really—kept having to duck them forward to get them under the electrical wires. Minshall was in a flap, petrified he'd electrocute himself!"

"He's right. It's happened."

"Wasn't so pleased with me though. Sorry to say!"

"Eddoes?"

"Course not—Minshall," she laughed. "Later on, after he'd had some rum, he kept saying in his deep, dramatic voice—'Oh, he's gone off with his little French jamette!'"

"You're kidding."

"A-tall!"

I looked at her.

"How friendly *did* you two get?"

She paused, "We never even held hands, if that's what you mean. He's painfully shy."

I was pleased to hear it.

"You should keep it that way," I said. "You don't want to get involved with him. Not like that. It's more complicated than you think."

"Chut!" she smiled at me. "You know, he's already gone back. Told me he wanted to leave first thing this morning."

"Really? Should've waited till tomorrow. He could've come with us."

"That's what I suggested. But he seemed anxious to get back. He's been away nearly a month."

"If he's walking from here we'll get there first."

"Somebody offered him a lift, in a four-wheel-drive, far as Pinnacle Village."

"How's that?" I was surprised. "Never heard of a car going as far as Pinnacle, didn't think it was possible."

"Apparently it is," she shrugged her shoulders.

"Wonder who could've offered him a ride?"

"Think it was a couple of policemen."

"Forest rangers maybe? The police never go out there, unless they're planning to raid Hell Valley."

"You're joking."

"It's happened," I said. "Twice as a matter of fact. Once they even riddled the cocoahouse with their machineguns. Fortunately no one was hurt."

"I should say."

"Mother had one of her dreams the night before—an army of rats invading the cocoahouse—and in her dream she'd climbed into the cocoaloft with her daughters to escape them. So she was expecting those policemen, hiding up there with her two little girls when they arrived—she'd ordered the rest of the Earth People out to the fields. The policemen shot their guns off at ground level, just below their feet. And they kept it up until they heard one of the girls crying above. Then they left."

"Sounds dreadful!"

"No policeman would offer Eddoes a ride. They don't even talk to the Earth People. Except to order them around, hold them down and shave off their locks, cuff them up—"

I stopped, seeing Rachel's alarm. I regretted telling her so much.

"Of course," I said after a moment, "that was a couple years back. Still, I doubt any policeman would offer Eddoes a ride. Less things have changed dramatically."

"Maybe they're rangers then? In any case, whoever they are we should have gotten a ride too. Would've saved us the hike."

"That's my favorite part," I was happy to change the subject. "And it's important somehow—a slow transition, turning back the clock."

We sat there for a minute.

"The hike's only a couple of hours anyway," I said. "It'll be over before you know it. Then we'll be there. In Madamas!"

"What I need at the moment," she said.

———

When we got back to the hotel we found Laurence sitting on the green couch in the lobby. Waiting for us. He'd just breakfasted at the Hilton.

"No Eggs Benedict," he told us. "But they make a recognizable ham-and-rat-cheese omelet."

"Stop right there," Rachel said. "Less you want to return with me immediately."

She started to climb the stairs. But halfway up she stopped, looking back at us over her shoulder. Out from under her church hat.

"No need to wake me till dinner. I'm expecting something elaborate mind you. Least as good as the Hilton's breakfast. After all, you boys are taking me into the jungle tomorrow."

She disappeared at the landing, leaving Laurence and me sitting on the sofa.

But before we'd spoken a word between us a taxi pulled up in front of the hotel. Screeching to a stop, Alicia jumping out. Shoving her way through the hotel's door, running over, bending down to kiss us. Her cheek moist with a sheen of perspiration.

"On my way to the airport," she was half out of breath. "Where's Rachel?"

"Just went upstairs," I started to get up. "I'll go find her."

She held me down, "No time—I'll miss my flight as it is, if it's not delayed. Give her my love, and Shay-lee and Oony!"

With that she ran out and jumped into her cab again, slamming the door. The taxi taking off with another screech.

"It's over," Laurence said after a second. "Free-paper-bun!"

"Not quite. We still have a few days, Madamas to look forward to."

A minute later he asked, "Ready to go?"

Then I remembered—our drunken night in the Tiki Hut. My promise to go with him to visit his mother. Truth is I'd hoped to go over to Oony's, start getting ready for our trip, gathering together the stuff we'd need. I could even start packing up the jeep. But that would have to wait until this afternoon.

"OK," I said, and we went out into the bright sun.

We were waiting for a cab but a maxi-taxi came by first. Empty except for a man stretched out asleep on the back seat. The driver told us he was going up the hill, so Laurence and I climbed in. "Rocky Mountain High" playing on the radio. That's when it hit me that carnival really was over. Hardly seemed possible—jouvert morning seemed like last night.

During the ride Laurence and I talked some, mostly about our camping trip. Shay-lee and Oony were both working tomorrow, I told him.

"They should come with us," Laurence said. "Soften Rachel's monopoly."

"You kidding? Not those two in the bush. Even if they didn't have to work. Their idea of roughing it is a five-star hotel, room service."

"Really?"

"Besides," I was thinking of my talk earlier with Rachel, "they'd probably say it's too dangerous."

"Scorpions and mapapee snakes."

"Exactly."

We continued bouncing along, trying to blank the radio, "Blue Bayou."

There was something I needed to ask Laurence, but I couldn't come out with it. Even when the driver dropped us off—actually at the bottom of the hill—and we started climbing up the steep road, I couldn't bring myself to say it. Not until we finished our climb, sweating, winded, and Laurence went to flip up the horseshoe-shaped handle on the chain-link gate in front of his mother's house, did I put my hand on his shoulder and tell him to hang on for a second.

He looked back at me.

"Listen," I said, "before we go in there, you got to tell me why they sacked your father."

Laurence thought for a moment. He flipped the handle back down, turned around and led me across the street. Over to a rusted standpipe half-hidden by the weeds. Just beyond the pipe was the cliff, and down below that the Savannah, town. Stretched out in the distance below us like a ragged, sleeping potcake. Gray smoke rising out of the la basse, the garbage dump near the harbor. A couple of ships loaded with containers, sitting in the water down to their barnacle-line, anchored just beyond the entrance. You could see the tracks where their anchors had dragged through the mud.

Laurence turned the little wheel at the top of the pipe. It coughed twice, then the water came gushing. He caught some up in his hands, legs spread wide in front of the pipe, muscles tensed, leaning forward, drinking out of his cupped palms. He was wearing shorts and a white polo shirt, sneakers with his tennis socks, the little cotton balls hanging over his heels. When he finished drinking he wiped the water cupped in his palms across his face. Then he moved aside and I took a drink of the rusty water. I shut it down and sat beside him, our backs to the cliff, on a makeshift bench there beside the pipe, a plank supported by two cinderblocks.

The house was the same as I remembered it. Laurence had brought me home with him several times after school or football practice. A fairly large house for a woman now living alone. Clapboard, a single floor raised on groundsills a few feet above the grass, like most houses in the West Indies. But this one was neatly painted, white with red trim, red-and-white checkered curtains visible through the front windows. The yard obviously cared for, grass trimmed. There were even some orange flowers growing on either side of the concrete walkway—they looked like miniature carnations. Laurence's mother probably watered them twice a day.

She was a primary schoolteacher, well known and respected. For years she'd practically run the small Catholic school in Laventille. Which, though it gained her esteem elsewhere on the island, put her in a difficult position with her neighbors. To be openly Roman

Catholic in Laventille was to be excessively "social," like sending her son to the club for tennis lessons.

But there was something more significant than Sunday mass and tennis lessons to make her neighbors resentful. Laurence's mother wasn't simply an educated woman living in a poor community. For Laventille she was a highly overeducated woman, and for us an excess of book-learning was held as suspect. In addition to her teaching certificates—gotten slowly, through much adversity, from the University of the West Indies just down the hill—she was also a doctor of history, with a published thesis on the cultural effects of forced migration.

It had put Laurence in a difficult position growing up.

"They just sacked him," he said, and I turned to him, remembering what we were doing sitting there. "For a long time they didn't say why. I suppose because they couldn't, really, without incriminating themselves."

He paused, like it was my turn to add something. What could I say? I still had no idea what he was talking about. I leaned forward, elbows on my knees also.

"Name was Mario Dundonald. Nineteen. Actually West Indian—isn't there a Dundonald St somewhere near the harbor?—of West Indian background, I guess. And white—I don't think there're any black boys in the orphanage. Anyway, this Mario wasn't a boy any longer, not really. He'd grown up in the orphanage, but stayed on to train as a counselor. The orphanage directors kept him on, he was that well liked. They put him in charge of the dormitory—he continued to sleep with the boys. The directors assigned him to Daddy, put Daddy to oversee his training."

Laurence turned to look at me. Arms folded over his chest.

"So this Mario became sick. At first it looked like a bad case of the flu. But Mario refused to go to the infirmary—he remained in his bed in the dormitory. This went on for several days, and every day Daddy went to visit him. Eventually the nurse came by herself, examined Mario, and wanted to give him a blood test. Mario refused to let her do it. That same night two attendants arrived in the dormitory, and in the midst of all the boys fast asleep, they held him down and dragged him out. But Mario managed to get loose, going down the stairs. Attendants shouting down the dormitory, chasing behind him. He fled to Daddy's house. And when Mario was safely inside, Daddy shut the door in their faces."

Laurence turned to look at the ground, leaning forward with his elbows on his knees.

"Now, of course, Daddy took Mario to the hospital in town, and he was given the proper medicines. Now Daddy took charge, and Mario slept in his guest bedroom. Couple of weeks later, the orphanage sent notice that he was sacked."

Suddenly Laurence sat up again, looking at me.

"But listen here! A lot of those employees of the orphanage never wanted Daddy around—a black man, West Indian on top. None of those people were *ever* very pleased to have a nigger-buller walking round the place in a white coat!"

He took a breath, then continued.

"Daddy sued for slander—he brought all this down on himself, you understand?—and the orphanage countersued. Supposedly, when it went to trial, everything looked fine. Daddy stated adamantly he'd never abused his position as counselor, or his assignment as mentor to Mario, and there was no evidence to prove otherwise. Daddy even provided the results of his own AIDS test that he was negative. It even looked like the orphanage would have to give him his retirement pension. Either that or give him his job back! But William, I couldn't tell you because I wasn't there—I didn't find out about any of this till after—till a couple of weeks ago."

The pace of Laurence's speech had been speeding up. With each sentence. Now he made himself slow down. Like he was trying to understand what he was saying. Though I knew he'd been through it in his mind a hundred times. He leaned forward onto his knees.

"Thing is, towards the end of the hearing the judge asked Daddy point blank if he'd had sexual relations with one Mario Dundonald. Now Daddy went silent. He just sat there. Dumb. Refusing to answer. 'Well then,' the judge asked him, 'can't you at least deny that you're a practicing homosexual?' Daddy remained silent. The judge was ready to pass sentence—he would have too, if Daddy's lawyers didn't stop him. They demanded another hearing. Wanted to put an ailing Mario on the stands, let him give testimony. Of course, since then the poor boy's died. And Daddy's grief-stricken."

Laurence brushed a trickle of perspiration away from his temple. He sat up, arms folded over his chest. Breathing quickly. His chest rising, falling. Staring at the ground before him.

The silence, the heat, suddenly felt oppressive. Stifling. I needed to say something, but I had no idea what—I'd managed nothing more than to nod my head a few times during all this.

Eventually Laurence got up, drank some more water. Then I got up, and he led me across the street.

15

His mother wasn't home. Laurence knocked for a couple of minutes.

"Mum!" he called.

The woman in the house next door stuck her head out the window, "Mistress Boissière gone in teaching today you know!"

I breathed a sigh of relief. I think Laurence did also. I wasn't sure if he'd called ahead to tell his mother that he was coming. Maybe from New York? Now maybe he'd want to return later this afternoon, tonight? At least that was later.

But as soon as we turned around to leave we saw Laurence's mother coming through the gate, stack of books under her arm.

She kissed us both, like it was twelve years ago, and *we'd* just arrived from school. She unlocked the front door to let us in.

It was her lunch hour, she explained, more for my benefit. She told us she hadn't been sure, but she half-expected to see Laurence today.

"Ash Wednesday," she said, I noticed she had them on her forehead.

"Even prepared lunch for you boys just in case." Now she said it as though she'd been expecting me to come by also.

Laurence's mother spoke with the slight English accent, educated-sounding. Same as her son, though hers was softer. Still, behind the West Indian lilt, it was there—you could hear it in the way she pronounced the n in even. Chopping it off—eve-un, not eve-in.

Odd thing is she's never been to England. Never set foot there in her life.

She was dressed like a schoolteacher, I suppose, but not like the ones who'd taught Laurence and me. They'd been nuns and priests.

Loose flowered skirt that reached to just below her knees, leather sandals, aqua sleeveless knit jersey. A few gold bangles jangling on her wrists. Tall and slim, with an aqua kerchief tied around her shortish hair. Which seemed straightened, "relaxed," but maybe it was natural? Laurence had French blood, maybe on both sides? Maybe that's where she got her Catholicism?

In addition to her obvious intelligence, she was attractive and spirited, not a woman to take lightly.

I'd seen all the books. Still, they shocked me. Three times as many as I'd had in my own home growing up. They were cared for, these books, you could tell by the way they were arranged on the shelves.

The diningroom table showed the only disorder in the house, covered with papers and more books, an electric typewriter with a piece of paper still rolled into the carriage. One of those bulky old IBM office machines with the ball that jumps around. Maybe she was working on another academic book, I thought. Maybe Laurence's mother was writing a novel?

She collected everything up, quickly, shifting it all to a sideboard, including the big typewriter. It looked heavy, but she didn't strain in the slightest to pick it up. I caught the title of one of the books, *British Punitive Code*.

Now she started setting the table. Laurence was speaking of New York, telling her about his own teaching. A conversation I had no desire to partake in. Felt a little in the way.

Suddenly I found the tennis trophies, I'd been wondering where they'd gone. Moved from the window sills to a tall, glass-doored cabinet in the livingroom. I went over to take a look. Seventy-five or a hundred of them. All, like the books, carefully arranged. Cups or plaques with engraving, or little silver- or bronze-plated tennis players, standing on pedestals of dark wood or marble, some with their arms raised holding tiny rackets. Most of these trophies I'd never seen before—Laurence won them at Oxford. Now, as I looked closer, I noticed something else I was sure I'd never seen—that all of those miniature tennis players, standing proudly on their pedestals, despite that they were dunked in bronze or silver, were all clearly "white." You could tell by their features and the parts in their hair, bangs sweeping down over their foreheads. Not a black boy among them.

After a few minutes we were eating lunch. Laurence's mother didn't have much time before she had to get back to school. Fricassee chicken with rice, the rice pressed into the shape of small overturned bowls, leaf of shadow beni pressed into the middle. Stewed pigeonpeas on the side. Christophene steamed with butter. She told me, as expected, that it had been Laurence's favorite meal growing up. Portugals for dessert. His mother picked them from the tree growing almost sideways out of the hill in the backyard. We could see it through a window, laden with bright globes, from where we were sitting.

Laurence's father did not come up the whole time we ate. Probably to be expected. For one thing I was a stranger in the house, and I suppose the three of us knew that's why Laurence had brought me with him. But Laurence's mother would also have known that he'd explained something of the situation to me.

Not until we had a small pile of portugal skins in the bowl in the center of the table, did Laurence ask his mother what she was working on. What with the books and papers and the typewriter she'd cleared off the table?

It had occurred to me too—that if she'd expected us to come by, enough to prepare lunch in advance, why hadn't she cleared the stuff off the table?

She went on peeling the portugal in her hands. Bangles jangling. And she did not answer Laurence's question until she'd peeled it completely, reaching towards the bowl in the center of the table.

"Letter to the *Kent Gazette,*" she dumped her handful of peel into the bowl. "In explanation of Larry, understanding of Larry— not in his defense, mind you."

I could only think that it sounded like the title of a B-movie, awful sitcom—*Understanding Larry.* For a moment I couldn't even figure out who Larry was. Then I realized it was a diminutive of Laurence. Laurence was a junior, just as I was.

"A futile effort," she continued. "Foolish really. Nobody's going to listen to me, a black woman, primary schoolteacher living in her little village in the West Indies. Still."

She split her portugal, looking down at her hands. "I've tried to convince him to make some kind of statement in his own defense."

Now she looked up, directly at Laurence. "You've tried to convince him. But as you know, your father won't budge."

She paused, "What to do?"

She began to peg the portugal into her plate, but she did not look down at her hands. She continued looking at Laurence.

"So I am trying to understand him. Not to forgive or excuse," she repeated, "but to understand."

She glanced at me for a second, then turned her eyes back to Laurence.

"I am writing a letter to the *Kent Gazette,* analyzing the crime of Laurence de Boissière, Sr, perpetrated upon the young man, Mario Dundonald, not as some perverse abuse of power—and not as its corollary, either, some illicit form of impassioned love—but as a response conditioned in him by the history of his race."

III

16

We were alone, the three of us, climbing the winding road into Matelot. The air cool, wet, forest canopy high overhead so thick the sun could only squeeze its way through the gaps. Pillars of light, upward swirling eddies of insects. The occasional thick waterdrop landing with a loud *pak!* on the canvas top. Our little Suzuki coughing each time I downshifted from second into first. Touching the horn lightly at each sudden bend, on the off chance that somebody was coming the other way. Once I slowed down to cross a waterfall that washed directly over the blacktop. The sea flat, painfully blue, glittering each time we rounded a curve overlooking it. And tonight, according to that morning's *Guardian,* another gift—a full moon. Every likelihood a leatherback would come up on the beach to lay.

When we drove past Matelot, its half-dozen board-huts perched on the mountain high above a rocky cove, all the fishing boats were out, the village deserted. At the end of the road is the little Catholic church, its walled cemetery with a view of the sea. I parked in the grass lot on the other side, next to the priest's battered brown van. A Franciscan monk, his hair shorn, long brown cassock and leather sandals. He used the van to pick up parishioners from the surrounding villages for Sunday mass. But it didn't mean he was there. The monk also had a bicycle, which he pedaled all the way to town, his cassock flying in the breeze.

I got out and walked around to the back of the Suzuki, bending down and sliding the keys under the left rear tire.

"If a mapapee gets me everybody knows where the keys are."

They weren't listening. Crossing over to a spigot sticking straight out of the rock face, on the other side of the road, small blue-green pool beneath it. In order to get a drink you had to hop onto a boulder in the middle of the pool. The villagers did it with their buckets. Everybody in the area came here to collect water. Ice-cold, and I could hear Rachel, then Laurence shriek as they touched, then tasted it.

I was getting out our backpacks, each with a rolled sleepingbag tied across the top, cutlass tucked into the side. I lined them up against the lime-washed front wall of the church, next to the arched wooden door, its padlock bolted shut—the monk wasn't around. They looked nice like that, our backpacks. Sitting there in the sun. All roughly the same size and weight, except Rachel's, which was a few pounds lighter. Really there wasn't much we needed to bring with us. No tents—we'd sleep on the beach, in the open. Not much food either. We'd forage the forest for fruit, hopefully catch our own fish, crabs and crayfish from the river. If we got into trouble we could always ford the river and take the path winding through the bush to Pinnacle, buy tins of tuna and corned-beef hash at stout-faced Miss Bethel's parlor. But hopefully we wouldn't have to resort to that.

When I got across the road Laurence had wandered off to take a look at Matelot, Rachel sitting beside the pool with her feet soaking in the water, her sneakers tied together by their laces, slung over a branch above her head. She was smiling at me, leaning her head back into a patch of sun, catching her face and hair.

"What?" I asked.

"You're good at this, aren't you?"

"Nothing to be good at. Done it plenty times before."

But I did feel good, like I had things under control.

I stepped across onto the boulder, causing slight ripples in the pool, spreading out evenly around me, though the boulder seemed not to budge. I reached forward to cup the water, sucking in the shock as I felt the coldness on my palms, then my lips and throat. I swallowed a few mouthfuls. Hopped off the boulder shaking water from my numbed fingers. Standing there beside Rachel, looking down at her.

"Anyway," she said. "I feel protected. It's nice."

"I'm pleased. Thought I'd scared you yesterday. Put you off our little adventure."

"Not a chance!"

"Water isn't a bit chilly to be soaking your feet?"

"Actually warmish at the edges, where the sun hits it. You should try."

"After the hike. We'll all bathe in the river. Throw ourselves in and let it carry us out to sea. That's the reward for our labors."

Laurence was making his way up the steep road towards us. Smiling, his arms loaded with portugals, hugging them against his chest.

"Gift from a friendly villager," Laurence said. "Old lady insisted. Threatened to flog me with her cane if I didn't accept."

After the portugals we sat in the spotted shade for a few minutes. Only sound the water dripping out of the tap and down the rock face, swells rolling up in the cove far below, glassy tinkle of the smooth stones bouncing over each other as the water receded. Gull squawks.

"Right, gentlemen," Rachel said at last. "You may escort me into the bush."

We crossed the road, helping each other into our packs.

We were just about to start out when a little, peculiar-looking man appeared from around the side of the church. A white man, enormous gray handlebar mustaches. Wearing brown leather shorts held up by suspenders, over a white, long-sleeved, Shakespearean shirt—ruffles down the front and around his neck and wrists. Tall woolen socks and hiking boots.

He'd heard us talking.

"British, are you? Judging by the accents." He spoke with a pro-nounced British accent himself.

"We're Americans," I said. It was an odd claim to make.

"I see."

"We're camping on the beach for a few days."

"Well!"

He introduced himself as Dr Mippipopolous, actually a doctor of veterinary medicine. His area of expertise, livestock—swine to be precise. He'd been sent out by the Colonial Department, he told us, to instruct the Pinnacle villagers in their production and rear-ing. It was his own discovery that the animals flourished on coco-nut meat, and the palms from the abandoned estates were loaded with them. Free for the picking. In no time, the doctor estimated, the villagers would have a thriving industry on their hands. He'd been camping out himself, he said, for the past couple of months, in the monk's borrowed room behind the church. But every day he hiked into Pinnacle to check up on "all the young ones." Since arriving in the village the three pedigree sows he'd brought with him—gift of the "Queen Mum" to the natives, he told us—had each dropped splendid litters.

"Be sure and say hello when you get to Pinnacle!" he said.

After a second Laurence asked, "To whom?"

"Why, the young ones!"

"We'll be certain," Rachel said, and she led us towards the en-trance to the path on the other side of the cemetery. Hurrying away from Dr Mippipopolous.

———

For the first half-hour the path followed the contour of the cliffs, high above the sea. The ledge occasionally no more than a foot in width, with the sheer drop on the other side, and we weren't accustomed to the weight of our packs yet. It took your breath away. Both the stark beauty of the sea sparkling far below, and the thought of pitching over the side into it. We were climbing the whole time, in and out of sunlight, and though the air was cool, we were sweating.

Then the path turned inland, in a descent so gradual you hardly noticed, and we left the sea at our backs. Within minutes we found ourselves in deep rainforest. Mammoth mossy trunks reaching up around us, into the thicker layer of mist pressed against the canopy high overhead: bois canot, spiked boxwood, beech, cedar. Thick vines hanging down—we brushed them out of our faces. Pale green ferns sprouting from between the branches of the trees, from nooks and crannies in the boulders and rock walls. Carpets of damp lichens spotting the trunks. Thick curtains of Spanish moss draping down. The air still, misty, also pale green in color. Now we left the sun behind us too.

Occasionally one of us pointed out a bromeliad or orchid, the neon sprays of their blooms, purple or fire-orange or shocking pink. We no longer walked on solid ground, but over a thick, loose layer of leaf trash. Our sneakers slipping beneath us. The overwhelming smell of vegetable rot, together with the faintly smoky odor of the jungle. The world suddenly water-drenched, all edges softened. A film of water suddenly rolling down the bark of the enormous trunk beside us, bouncing over splotches of spongy moss. A sudden gush spilling, without warning, from the drooping bromeliad above our heads. If you looked closely you could see the tiny waterdrops at the apex of each individual leaf. Now and then the softened *puh!* of a thick drop falling to the leafy floor.

We hardly spoke. Only the soft padding of our sneakers over the leaves. If we wanted to point out something we simply pointed.

Like the time I touched Laurence's shoulder and nodded in the direction of a scorpion, making its way slowly up a barkless limb. Steel gray, long and fat as our thumbs. With the thick weave of its tail curling over its back, twitching, pointed barb stuck to the end like an oversized comma. Laurence raised his brows, moved in closer to watch. Usually, though, we kept on walking. Otherwise we'd feel the chill. Now our T-shirts were damp, but light on our backs, not saturated. Like we were walking through a cloud.

The path became harder to follow and sometimes we lost it. We'd have to stop and backtrack until we picked it up again, or better yet, spotted one of the rangers' markers. A red stripe above and white below, painted on prominent boulders and trunks. I had a compass in my pack just in case. I was walking up in front with my cutlass out, swinging at the occasional vine hanging before me. Laurence walking at the rear, occasionally held back by Rachel whose pace was slower. We kept tabs on each other, like deep-sea divers, there was a comfort in that, but no way to keep the solitary feeling of the forest from overtaking us.

We passed thick groves of banana-like balisier, bright red-and-yellow notched spears of their blooms shooting up. Legendary haven of mapapee snakes—thin, black, lightning quick—we kept our distance. Picking our way among giant, pale green ground-ferns, each separate frond the size of a mattress. Thick clumps of bamboo, enormous tufts of it, antediluvian in appearance. Some of the individual bamboo trunks as thick as your waist, reaching up a hundred feet. Suddenly creaking with a loud *cak! cak! cak!* followed by a flutter of tender moist leaves high above. It was almost as though you could see the bamboo growing before your eyes, supposedly a foot overnight.

All of this forest was second growth, and occasionally we passed moss-dripping cocoa trees, the deep purple bulbs of their pods stuck right to the stubby trunks. If they were soft and ripe we'd pick them, splitting them open with our fingers. Scraping out and sucking the sweet fuzzy white meat from the shiny black beans. Sometimes, spread high above the abandoned cocoa trees, a gigantic orange or yellow immortelle, its petals sifting slowly down, carpeting the forest floor, introduced as shade trees in the days of the cocoa estates. Pink poui. Purple jacaranda. A couple of times we stumbled across the rotting remains of a drying shed or storage hut. And if we searched them out, the inevitable trees nearby for us to fill our pockets with ripe cashews to be boiled later on, golden nuggets of nutmeg.

Any number of streams to hop over, the occasional winding river, plank bridges built by the rangers for us to cross, sometimes including a railing. Now we'd pause to lean over the railing, admiring the falls cascading down. A deafening roar of the white water. Great misty breaths rising up among the branches. With the rains last night there were lots of trees freshly down, particularly bamboo. If they were too thick across the path I cleared them away with my cutlass.

At one point an enormous cedar had come down, dense groves of balisier on either side of the path, the trunk difficult to circumvent. Just as hard to climb over. We took turns helping each other out of our packs, crawling on our bellies through a gap under the trunk, pulling our packs through to the other side.

Then, when we'd almost reached the point of having forgotten it for good, we turned a corner, stumbled down a sudden drop in the path, and burst into dazzling sun. We looked up, shutting our eyes for a minute, letting it warm our faces. As we continued the trees became wider spaced and smaller, they changed from cedar and bois canot to a few thin, straggly pines, then to almond and seagrape and casuarina. The ground beneath our sneakers became rocky again, then hard-packed dirt, then sand. In the distance, through a gap between two mangrove clumps, we saw the glittering, blue-black sea.

But it was still another twenty minutes before we trudged, sweating beneath the sun again, down towards the beach. By now our packs felt twice as heavy as when we'd started out. We found a shady spot beneath a huge, furry casuarina. Slight sea-breeze whistling through the needles high above.

We helped each other out of our packs. Setting them down on the carpet of crunchy brown needles, the acorn-like cones, sitting with our backs leaning against our packs. We'd filled our canteens with cold water from the spring in Matelot, and now Laurence had taken a drink of his and was handing it around. Still cool after the hike, with the faint tang of aluminum. Slight electric buzz along the fillings of your teeth as you drank.

It must have been four-thirty or five o'clock, and the sea looked like it was on fire.

We took off our sneakers and tied them by their laces hanging from our packs. Then, grunting, helped each other into them for the last, short spell, trudging through the loose sand. But when we got down to the hard, wet beach, it was easy going again. We walked along the water's edge, foamy swells lapping our ankles. Stepping over garlands of seaweed, tiny wet shrimp popping out along their lengths. Tiny crabs scuttling away. Spindly starfish beating up in the wet sand. After a hike of half a mile down the beach we came to the bocus of the river, where it was maybe thirty feet across, wider now after the rains than I remembered it.

We turned up and skirted the clump of mangrove, hiking along the hard-packed dirt of the riverbank for ten or fifteen minutes, till the ground turned rocky again, and we got to the place where the river narrows and seems, somehow, to shallow-up at the same time. Where you can cross over fairly easily.

We were excited, having made it almost to the end of our journey, and now we plunged into the river. Stumbling over mossy
stones through the deceptive hard-pulling current, the cold water
up to our waists in the middle. Bending forwards, trying to keep
our packs dry. Slowly climbing up over the rocks onto the bank at
the other side, Laurence giving Rachel a hand.

We'd arrived. Few more minutes downriver on this side, beneath a shady grove of almonds and seagrape, was the place we'd
make camp.

We spread our sleepingbags in a patch of sun to get the dampness
out. Hung our wet shorts and T-shirts from branches of the big
almond tree on the sunny side. Our pairs of sneakers slung over
the branches like a Christmas tree. Rachel wearing a purple bikini
bottom, Laurence and I our leftover carnival Speedos.

Rachel unpacked some stuff to make sandwiches. Everything
spread out on a piece of plywood wedged between the lower
branches of the almond tree which all the campers who came here
used as a table. Rat-cheese and crispy rolls of hops-bread, five dots
of red-and-orange-flecked peppersauce on each one. We were
starved. Must have eaten three or four sandwiches each. Dipping
our tin coffee mugs full of cool water from the river at our feet.

A little way downstream were the thick clumps of mangrove
on both sides of the bocus. But our kitchen jutted out partially
into the river, so you could look straight down it and out to sea.
The color of the water changing slowly from the greenish brown
of the river higher up, to blue-green, to bright aquamarine over
the white rocks and sand—where the sweet water mixes with salt,
welling up, appearing to become physically thicker, heavier—then
the sparkling blue-black of the deep water farther out. On our

other side we looked across the beach to the wide open sea. Above the beach a grove of spindly coconut palms, and almost immediately behind them the forest-covered rock face, shooting directly up. A wall, the cliffs impossible to climb, or pick your way through. By far the easiest way into the forest was to follow the bank of the river—or simply walk the river itself—winding through the rocky caverns. You could do it for hours, for miles, following the side streams where the river branched. Until the rock walls became too steep to climb, the forest too thick to penetrate, and cut you off.

But that afternoon, after our late lunch, we followed the riverbank only as far as the place we'd forded it earlier. Holding hands like overgrown kids we went trudging into the cold water again. Kicking it up, three of us together, and when we got to the waist-deep part in the middle, we threw ourselves in. Screaming with the shock of the cold water, still holding hands. But the pull of the river was so strong it separated us immediately. Now we were riding the current, fast, navigating our way among the boulders and the black staghorn-stumps protruding from both banks. Ducking our heads under trunks that'd fallen across the river, hanging on for a few seconds until the stream yanked us loose. Feeling the water temperature becoming warmer now, gliding past mangrove trees growing directly out of the water, their thick purple roots arching up. Riding the stream, right out to the deep sea. Where the pull suddenly halted—the water becoming turbulent, bubbling up around us—and then the current changed directions, dragging us across onto the shore. We were still screaming, still feeling like overgrown kids. It had probably lasted five minutes, at best, our ride, but it seemed to go on and on.

The sea current dragged us onto the opposite side of the river, back parallel to the beach we'd hiked across earlier. We swam for a few minutes, then rode the lazy swells into the beach. Now we climbed out and threw ourselves, panting, onto the still warm sand. The sun already dipping into the horizon before us.

Rachel stretched to give me a salty kiss.

We lay there on our backs, lazy swells rolling up to swash us with soft, foamy water. Watching the last of the sunset.

"I'm going back to collect firewood," I started getting to my feet. "While it's still light."

"You're a slave-driver," Laurence said. "Got it in your genes!"

"Disowned those long ago too."

I threw my arm over his shoulder, Rachel at his other side. We began trudging up the beach.

But before we reached the top we heard a distinctly incongruous low rumble, some kind of motor vehicle—though that, I told myself quickly, was impossible—coming from farther down the beach. Three of us turning in the direction of the noise. Already it was louder, and before we could properly take in what was happening, the jeep was on top of us.

Its motor suddenly cut dead, silent, rolling to a silent, menacing stop in the loose sand directly in front of us. Cutting us off. It was an English Land Rover, brand new and shining, lots of protective caging and chrome fenders, with the battery of lights across the top. Three uniformed policemen sitting inside.

All with the stiffly-starched, khaki shirt-jacks of their uniforms unbuttoned, drooping where the metal insignias were pinned to their collars and breast pockets, white marinos showing. All three with tightly trimmed mustaches and triangular wedges for sideburns. Only one wearing the brown beret, its thin black band cutting his coffee-colored forehead straight across, lobe on top drooping over the side. He was sitting in the passenger seat. His hand resting loosely on the rim of the windshield before him, bracelet of thin gold chain dangling from his thin, hairless, coffee-colored wrist. Glinting in the leftover light.

He was the one who spoke to us.

"Camping gainst jurisdiction on the public beach, you know. Hope all-you not intending to hang-out long."

We stood there for a few seconds, catching our breath.

"Since when?" I said. "People camp out here all the time."

He smiled. "We just looking out for trouble before it happen, you unnastand? Just acting in the public interest. Doing we job. All-you in the bush now. Long way from help if anyting happen."

"Thank your for your concern," Rachel said calmly. "We can take care of ourselves."

The officer had been looking at me. Now he turned to Rachel. Laurence was standing next to her, and he had his arm around her waist—as if to protect her.

The officer smiled again. "Right as rice," he said.

Then, after a pause, he continued.

"All-you stay-way from them bush-niggers, is what I come to inform. Unnastand? Them niggers is nasty. They ain't civil—ain't got no education, no manners!"

There was a long moment of silence.

"Only three niggers round here," Laurence said, "lacking civility."

The officer went on in a quieter tone, "All-you know what I talking bout." He was speaking to the three of us now. Looking slowly from face to face.

"Stay-way from them Earth People, unnastand? Them people is trouble. Specially when the foreigners come round."

We thought that was the end of it. But after another prolonged, tense silence, the officer continued. Now he spoke directly to Laurence.

"And listen here. You ain't the first smooth-talking nigger to wet he prick with a little white pussy. So watch you focking mout! And tell she cover up she bubbies. That gainst jurisdiction too!"

The driver started the engine. Jerked the Rover into gear, tires spinning up for a second. He completed the remaining half-circle around us, pulling the wheel hard against the loose sand to make it turn. Disappearing in the direction from which they'd come.

———

They left us stunned. Walking in a daze back to the place we forded the river, Laurence still holding on to Rachel. Now with her arms folded over her chest. Walking back to our side of the beach—the Madamas side—in a hurry.

One thing I did know for sure: they couldn't get their Rover onto our side.

In the remaining half-hour of light we threw ourselves into the business of making camp. That was our release. Laurence had his sneakers on, pulling firewood out of the bush. Piling it up a little way down the beach. In two piles. A larger one for fuel, the other would be the actual fire.

Rachel unpacked the rest of the stuff for our kitchen, there beneath the almond tree beside the river. The aluminum pot and frying pan and the tin plates and knives and forks. A few cans of baked beans and corned-beef hash, condensed milk, pigeonpeas, little bottles of instant coffee, salt, peppersauce. All neatly lined up along the edge of the table. A small bag of sugar and a sack of rice. Handful of limes. Rachel hung up the expendable food in a net bag away from ants. Then she carried our three sleepingbags down beside the bonfire Laurence was building, spread them out in a line before it, on the side of the sea.

I'd used my cutlass to cut off several fronds from a coconut palm that was bending over backwards, as if to touch its head to the sand, so I didn't have to climb it. Dragging the fronds across the beach towards our kitchen. I remembered building a shelter there beneath the almond tree, on the other side of our table, and now I spread the palm fronds across the same two extended limbs. On the side open to the sea, I built a breakwall with the taller fronds. Digging holes with my cutlass and burying the thick spathes of their stems beneath the sand, stomping it down, then knotting the leaves of the fronds to weave them together. I even stole a couple of planks from a pallet Laurence had broken up for the bonfire, which I laid crisscrossed, over the top of our shelter—they'd hold our piece of roof down if a wind came up suddenly with the rain.

By now it was pitch dark, and we lit the fire. The air completely still, water spilling up on to the beach in lazy swells. No mosquitoes though. No sandflies. On a windless night like this later on in the summer they'd roll out of the bushes in clouds at dusk, and the water would be the only refuge against them. Not tonight.

More rat-cheese sandwiches for dinner. Tin mugs of Lipton tea, Rachel squeezed a wedge of lime into each one, grated in a bit of nutmeg. For dessert I'd brought along a bag of marshmallows, toasted over the fire. Box of graham crackers and the bar of Cadbury chocolate.

Then the moon came up, huge and round, deeply-pocked, and suddenly the night seemed as bright as day. I was thinking of the huge leatherback that would come crawling out of the surf at any moment. Scanning the fluorescent line of foam where the water tumbled onto the beach lower down.

We heard a soft psst! behind our backs, and when we turned around we found Eddoes striding out of the bushes towards us. Also wearing his carnival Speedo, smiling, bearing gifts.

He knocked fists with Laurence.

I got up to hug him, but Rachel waited for him to bend down towards her, smiling now too. Amber glint of the fire in her eyes.

Eddoes sat at the other end of her sleepingbag, his legs crossed beneath him, spreading out his gifts in the space between them. Pulling them out of a cocoasack, like a magician, one after the other. More and more presents. A hand of sweet plantains, another of tiny bananas called sucrier-figs. A bunch of portugals tied together by their stems. More limes. Five artichoke-shaped sugarapples, pulled from the sack one by one. A piece of cloth with its corners knotted together—Eddoes untied them to reveal a bunch of purple governor's plums. He even pulled a melon from his sack.

There was another piece of cloth knotted around a small mound of weed, handful of joints already wrapped.

Rachel reached for one—it's what we'd all been needing for a couple of hours.

But when she held the flame of the matchstick to it her fingers were trembling, still spooked by those policemen. Her trembling so bad she couldn't manage to light the joint.

"Agh!" she whispered, handing it quickly to Eddoes.

He exhaled a lungful of smoke, then pressed the joint between her lips, and Rachel pulled with her eyes closed.

"Any moment she'll come crawling out the surf," I said, anything to break the tension. "Right up here beside us—do her dance in the sand and dig her nest!"

"Could be," Eddoes turned to study the sea for a second.

"Bound to happen."

"Tomorrow," he said. "When the wind come up lil bit. To-night too quiet."

"You think?" Laurence asked.

"Don't tink, I feel so. Is what the senses telling me." Eddoes touched the tips of his fingers lightly to his chest. "Tomorrow would be the night. You go meet the old lady of the sea sure nough."

"Don't listen to that guy," I said. "Fame swelling his head. Make him a carnival King he thinks he knows it all—even the focking turtles! Tonight's the night. And I refuse to allow anybody a minute's sleep. Relax up the vigil."

"Wha," Eddoes laughed. "Boy sounding serious. All-you got a work tonight!"

He was smiling, happy to be with us again. And we were pleased to have him back with us also.

But Eddoes "all-you" suddenly reminded us of those police-men—I could see it in Laurence and Rachel's faces—just when we'd managed to get our minds off of them for a minute.

Then I saw Rachel's hand trembling again, attempting to relight the joint. She handed it over and turned her face away, looking out to sea.

————

We smoked a lot. It was even a little aggressive, like carnival was still going on. Till we all got silly and giggly. All talking nonsense—all of us except Eddoes.

Just as he'd predicted our turtle never showed up. Though we made several trips down to the water's edge in search of her. Though every fifteen minutes one of us stood slowly on our sleepingbag, pointing, convinced she'd made her appearance. We kept our vigil up almost the entire night. Too nervy to sleep, even with the grass. Still too spooked.

But there was more to our talk than foolishness. And later that night we discovered two other things. Two more shocking things which came up in our conversation with Eddoes. First, that the policemen were not the only ones who didn't want us around.

Mother Earth—and this hit me with a real shock—did not want Eddoes or any of the other Earth People to mix with us. According to Eddoes she was still angry with him for running away to join the carnival. More than anything for playing mas in Minshall's band. For even associating with him, much less playing his King. She considered the band a pappyshow. And worse: it had been a mockery of everything sacred and true for the Earth People. The whole unfortunate business had been a boldfaced blasphemy.

"Maybe she go smooth over," Eddoes said. "But for now she vex like mapapee-self! And when I miscalculate to tell she I got friends coming in the bush to visit. Friends that want to meet Mother too—" Eddoes sucked his teeth loudly. "I tell you, she let loose a vengeance pon me natty head like a bomb. 'Is white focking people you bringing in the bush to meet me? white woman? better not! better don't not if you know what bad for you little black carcass! better focking not!'"

Eddoes flicked his fingers together in the air above his head, index finger clicking loudly against his thumb.

The other shocking piece of information Eddoes gave us that night, and of which he seemed utterly convinced, was that the three policemen newly arrived and stationed in Pinnacle were his friends.

Laurence and I shot a glance at each other. We didn't contradict him though, at least not yet. Neither did Rachel—how could we crack the shell of his innocence so harshly? Eddoes told us he'd ridden in from town with them in their fancy Rover. That hadn't pleased Mother much either. Cussing up a storm for that one too. But those three police officers, he said proudly, had seen him bust the trophy as King of the Bands. They had all been deeply impressed. Couldn't stop talking about his feat. Joking about his scandalous costume.

"Boy," Eddoes mimicked them for us, "you had all-them womans in the stands smelling salts! When them catch a glance at the bamboo, they! You had all-them womans feeling faint!"

Now Eddoes was laughing.

"Them boys is OK," he said. "Never mind they warriors of Rome. We even," and this seemed the most incredible thing he told us that night, "bunch a we even share a smoke on the road!"

We awoke late the following morning, the sun already high and bright overhead. Laurence got the fire going. I filled the kettle in the river and brought it back, hanging it on a limb above the flames. We drank our coffee sitting on our sleepingbags, warming our palms against the tin mugs, waking up slowly, admiring the sea. The tide was high and the wind had come up some, little whitecaps farther out. But in close by the beach the water was still flat and glistening. Family of five pelicans floating slowly past. Gulls dipping down.

Eddoes had gone back up to the valley to sleep for a few hours. He had to get up at sunrise, a few hours ago, to go with the rest of the Earth People out to the fields. They were harvesting cassava. But they'd stop work in the early afternoon to take their breakfast, he told us, and after that he was free for the rest of the day. He'd come back to take Rachel fishing, in the small carved canoe, an excursion the two of them planned last night. Eddoes was feeling more confident about Rachel, it was obvious, and I wasn't sure how I felt about it. Rachel wasn't exactly discouraging him either. Mother wouldn't approve of their fishing trip, but Eddoes told us he wasn't worried. After Breadfruit he was in charge of the canoe.

"And she go smooth over," he said. "You watch. We go bring she back a nice redfish!"

Laurence and I had felt a little left out, until I came up with an alternate plan for us. We'd follow the river up into the forest, a leisurely hike, searching the rocks and the caverns for crayfish. And we'd find out which of the two groups came back with dinner.

But that would be later on, and after our coffee we decided to hike into Pinnacle to take a look at the village, hopefully avoiding our three policemen.

"I simply refuse to let them spoil our trip," Rachel said. "It's too magnificent here, all this!"

The sea did look extraordinary, the day perfect.

"We're leaving tomorrow," Laurence said. "What can happen?"

"Let's get some coconut-bread from Miss Bethel," I said. "She bakes it fresh every morning. If we hurry it'll still be hot."

We pulled on our T-shirts, grabbing our sneakers as we went past the almond tree, waiting until we'd forged the river to put them on. Our T-shirts rolled up into our armpits to keep them dry.

Pinnacle was twice the size of Matelot, or so it seemed—there'd once been extensive copra and cocoa estates nearby—but of the two villages Pinnacle seemed to be in worse shape these days. Many of the houses appeared abandoned, rotting, their roofs caving in. Weeds growing up through the floorboards of the front steps and porches. Ferns sprouting at the eaves. Only one of the houses looked freshly painted, white with navy trim, a large gallery in front. And when we got closer we found out why—POLICE painted across a board in block letters, nailed above the front door. But the door was padlocked shut, wooden awnings closed down over the front windows. Best of all no Rover parked in front.

Not only didn't we run into our police officers that morning, for the moment at least, Pinnacle seemed deserted. Only a few half-starved potcakes lounging in the middle of the dirt road. As we approached they got slowly to their feet, stretching on their front legs, yawning. They wandered off, eyeing us sideways over their backs. Disappearing into the dark spaces beneath the houses.

When we got to Miss Bethel's parlor, also with its sign painted above the door, it was wide open. But no Miss Bethel inside. Her shelves, apparently, left unguarded. Including a tin tray next to the battered cash register with two freshly-baked loaves of coconut-bread. I looked around and squeezed one to make sure. Called out her name a few times. Then I knocked on the door behind the counter leading to the house at the back. Shouting her name again.

I was just about to suggest leaving some money and taking the bread when Miss Bethel appeared from inside the house. Leaning onto her cane, looking as stout-faced as I remembered her.

"What all-you want, eh?" she barked. "All this amount a racket!"

She was making more racket herself, beating her cane against the side of the counter. Three of us holding in our laughter.

We paid her for the bread and a few tins of sardines—in case both groups returned from our fishing trips empty handed. A couple cigarettes from the jar on the shelf behind her back for Laurence and me. Unscrewed and stingily meted out by Miss Bethel, 3½ cents each.

"For a diabless," Laurence said when we got outside, "she makes some nice bread."

We were breaking off chunks as we walked. Savoring our cigarettes.

After a few minutes the houses stopped, the dirt road opening up, and we came to a large shed, also ramshackle, there beside the rocky shore—the sacks of copra had once been stored here. Stretching out into the choppy water behind the shed, the rotting remains of a wharf where the transport ship had tied up.

A hundred yards farther down from the wharf is a small sandy cove, and that's where we found the villagers. Twenty or thirty of them, gathered there on the beach. Lots of shouting and laughter. As we approached we saw all the children, naked, splashing in the shallow water, screaming with delight. Among them all the "young ones"—Dr Mippipopolous's many piglets—swimming and frolicking happily in the water with them. And there, standing higher up on the beach, the doctor himself, surrounded by a group of attentive adults. Holding one of his piglets in his arms, feeding it with a nippled baby bottle. His piglet noisily sucking away. Several of the villagers—all of them men, the women down by the water with the children—also held squirming piglets in their arms. Awkwardly. Nursing them too.

When he saw us the doctor put his charge down on the sand and it ran off squealing towards the water. He came over.

"Great swimmers, as you can see," he smoothed back his huge mustaches, smiling, the proud father. "Very hygienic animals—extremely clean. Another of the myths wrongly ascribed to them!"

Unclear whether he meant the children or the piglets. In any case they were all having the time of their lives. Even the men, uncomfortable as they appeared nursing their piglets, seemed to be enjoying themselves. Something sentimental about the whole scene.

"Coconut water," Dr Mippipopolous held up his nippled bottle for us. "The young ones adore it. Even over their mothers' milk!"

He insisted on showing them to us, the mothers, and now we followed him back to the storage shed.

"They're in at luncheon at present," he said.

Soon as he shoved the door open the three of them came running, making enormous grunting noises—and the three of us nearly bolted in the opposite direction. These sows were the size of small trucks, minivans. But extremely docile, the doctor assured us, and this we soon witnessed for ourselves.

The three mothers came nosing up against the doctor's chest, licking at him like great, bald St Bernards. Nearly knocking him over. Actually hoisting the little doctor into the air for a second, the triumphant coach among his players. He fed them sugar cubes from his pocket. The mothers sucking away, noisily licking their lips.

The doctor returned to us.

"Here," he offered Rachel a handful of sugar cubes. "Wouldn't you like to make their acquaintance?"

"A-tall!" she took a step back.

"Or perhaps you'd prefer a sea-bath with them? They go for a dip every morning after lunch."

"I think not."

———

We wound up opening the tins of sardines for our own lunch. Eating them with the rest of the cheese on Crix crackers—most people don't realize the only way to eat sardines is with rat-cheese. But that turned out to be little more than an appetizer, because Eddoes showed up not long afterwards, carrying an iron pot of stewed melongen. Cooked with rice and sweet-potatoes. Together with a sack of freshly baked cassava bread.

"Present from Mother," he smiled.

I thought I'd misunderstood.

"Just as I was leaving to come down," he said, "Mother call me back, say, 'Make sure and carry lil breakfast for you white friends!'"

Apparently she'd awoken this morning with a change of heart. Just like that. And now Mother had warmed to us, overnight. Hard to believe, but I'd seen it before, on more than one occasion:

240

Mother was well known for her mood swings, her fits of temper and quiet benevolence. They were a symptom of her thyroid problems, chemically induced. But—as I suspected even before Eddoes offered his explanation—there was another reason. And for Mother it would have had far greater sway than her unbalanced chemical state: last night she'd had a dream. Mother's philosophy, the Earth People's entire way of life, had been shaped by her dreams and visions.

In her dream Mother had seen a white woman with bright red hair. She was the size of a giant—"size of Kong," Eddoes told us—and this white woman was standing on the backs of three man-sized rats. Crushing them beneath her feet.

They were the only animal Mother didn't like, a common feature of her dreams. Rats were unclean, they lived on garbage in the city—created by the white son through his "mutations"—they did not live in the forest with the rest of the animals.

"Mother say them black rats is the warriors of Rome," Eddoes told us. "Them three police. But now Mother feel like Rachel reach here to send them way. She dead sure. And Mother say how I must bring Rachel up to the valley to meet she."

Eddoes put the iron pot he was holding down on the sand, wrapped in a piece of sacking.

"Funny thing is," he continued, "I just bounce up one them boys from the village—he ask me for lil ganj—and Kojac tell me how them police gone back in Rome already. Or gone someplace. And I go and check the station and I see is true—door bolt-up tight, Ranger gone!"

We were relieved to hear it. All of it. Not simply that Mother had lifted her vendetta against us—that was one thing—but those policemen were gone. That was the best news of all. Of course

Mother's idea that Rachel had come here to magically banish them was another story, but what did it matter?

After lunch Eddoes left with her, climbing the steep trail up to the valley. They'd have to go up there in any case—whether Eddoes wanted to introduce Rachel to Mother or not—in order to get around to the cove on the other side, where the Earth People kept their canoe. Laurence and I washed up the lunch plates in the river, Mother's iron pot, and after we smoked a joint together. Then we started off on an excursion of our own.

———————

I dumped the remaining rolls of hops-bread, now rock-hard, into the river. Brought along the blue net bag in case we got lucky. I even thought to toss in a knotted, clear plastic bag with another joint and some matches. For later on.

Both of us stripped down to our Speedos again. We put back on our sneakers, and now we weren't attempting to keep them dry. We'd wear them to follow the river, lots of sharp stones along the bottom higher up, steep cliffs to climb over. We entered at the usual spot but this time we turned upriver, trudging through the fast-pulling current. The water ice-cold, and occasionally we'd lose our footing on the loose, moss-covered stones. Tumbling in. But when we stumbled to our feet again the sun was hot on our backs, tingling, in contrast to our numbed ankles and toes. It was hard going, walking against the stream like that, but we were taking our time. We had the whole afternoon before us. And the scenery was agonizingly beautiful.

After a while the river narrowed and we had to climb up over steeper, jagged rock walls, around huge boulders. Picking our way through dark, moss-dripping caverns. Sometimes we'd stop and sit on a flat boulder or a fallen trunk to rest for a while, looking back at the river tumbling its way down. There were waterfalls and we'd sit on a rock ledge with the water cascading against our backs and shoulders and necks. Now there was the thick forest canopy overhead, huge trees stretching out over the river. The sun making its way through in patches. A thin layer of mist floating a few inches above the flat, still-looking water. Vines and curtains of Spanish moss draping down around us. Pale green ground-ferns at the banks, huge as trees. Now there was a carpet of dead leaves on the river bottom, covering the stones and mud. The water a deep burnt-umber in the shadows beneath the trees. Copper colored where the sun hit it, floating with small gold disks. But washing over the rocks it was still translucent green.

We passed a spindly coconut palm, angling sharply out from the bank, high on a rock wall. Stretching its head into a patch of sunlight in the middle of the river—another impossible feat of physics. Loaded with clumps of green water-nuts.

Laurence decided we had to have some, and he climbed up the rock wall. Then, holding on to leafy ferns as though they were handles, he crawled across, towards the medusa ball of gray roots. Now he walked out across the trunk—out over the middle of the river—a gymnast on the balance bar, his arms outstretched at either side. Smooth muscles showing along them, along his calves and thighs as he took each cautious step, his bamsee beneath the white Speedo. Wet and clinging to his skin. His body seemed hairless, even under his arms, his chest wet and muscular and slipperylooking.

When he got to the head of the coconut palm he crouched down, knees splayed at sharp angles, and started twisting off the nuts. Letting them fall through the air to me waiting, fifteen feet below, standing in the middle of the river. My own arms outstretched ready to catch them. The first few I missed—almost got myself knocked unconscious instead—the nuts washing downriver, tumbling over the rocks, bouncing up high into the air.

Two of us laughing, cussing each other.

"On your right."

"Where?"

"Focking useless!"

"Fock you!"

Eventually I caught one. Held the nut by its knobby stem and tossed it over onto the grassy bank at the other side. Then another. Another. Until we had a small handsome pile. Laurence repeated his balancing act, stepping off the ball of roots, climbing back down the rock wall. We sat on a large flat boulder, in a patch of bright sun. Raising the nuts above our heads and then pounding them against the boulder between our splayed knees. Until they burst open, spray of water shooting out in every direction. Now we threw our heads back, holding the detonated nuts above our gaping mouths, trying to catch the water. Drinking far less coconut water than we sprayed over our faces and chests. Shaking out the last drops.

After we'd drained them we continued beating the nuts until a split opened up and we could tear them in half. A wafery sound. Snapping off a chip of the outer shell to use as a spoon, scraping up globs of the sweet, white, semitransparent jelly from the center of the kernel. Slurping it up. Then we tossed the split nuts into the river, watching them tumble down.

Until we'd exhausted our little pile.

We washed ourselves off lying on our backs in the shallow water, hanging on to a fallen trunk. Floating there, looking up though a gap in the trees at the sky above. Bright as glass. The clouds drifting past startlingly white, soft, three-dimensional. We continued our climb, taking up our search again. The entire afternoon we'd been looking for crayfish, overturning flat rocks, checking crevices along the ledges at the banks. Searching in the shallow water around the blackened stumps protruding from the rock walls. Among the purple mangrove banyans. And although every few minutes one of us was sure we'd found a crayfish, so far our sack remained empty. But we forged on.

Higher into the mountains and deeper into the forest we passed patches of anthuriums growing in stagnant, algae-floating pools. Their waxy spathes a deep red or milky white, spiky pale yellow stalks bending up out of the centers. Thick clumps of dasheen, also growing in the stagnant pools, their leaves also heart-shaped. The deepest of possible greens. Higher up along the banks we passed thick groves of balisier, their red-and-yellow notched spears. Orchids and bromeliads, drooping down moss-covered from the trees, brilliant sprays of their blooms.

I halted Laurence and pointed overhead at an enormous old iguana, making her way across the limb of a bois canot, stretched out over the river. She must have been four and a half feet long. Infinitely slow, patient. We watched her move her webbed feet, one after the other. So slowly she kept disappearing among the leaves, against the green-gray bark of the limb. We must have stood there staring for ten or fifteen minutes, until she reached the farthest extremity of the branch, in a clump of sun-edged, gently-rustling leaves, right out over the middle of the river. With her considerable weight the branch started to bow, then bob. Up and down. Slowly. Slowly gaining momentum. Until she dropped with a loud smack to the river below, and now she moved lightning quick, squirming across the surface of the water and up onto the bank. In a split second. Disappearing into the bush.

We continued our climb. Another hour. Until we reached a place where the river divided cleanly into two side-streams. Still we hadn't landed a crayfish. Doubtful we'd even seen one.

The truth is that neither of us knew much about catching crayfish, hadn't attempted this since we were boys.

"You're a blight," I said. "A scourge and a blight! We got to split up—see anything, shout."

"I'll send up a flare."

"Good."

We went off in separate directions, sloshing away in our sneakers. By now the water was hardly more than ankle-deep, occasionally reaching to our knees in the middle. Now the stream was sluggish. It should have been easier going but the rock ledges were steeper, more jagged, slippery with moss, more difficult to climb over. Sometimes the easiest way was to sit and turn around, crawling up like a crab, backwards. Bamsee suspended above the sharp stones. The blue net bag dragging from my wrist, snagging on protrusions of the rocks.

Only a few minutes after we'd split up I heard Laurence—bawling like a wild Warahoon Indian.

"Ay-ay-ay-ay-ay!"

I took off, sloshing in his direction.

"We got a cocktail party going on over here!" he shouted.

He was standing in the middle of a large flat boulder, on a muddy bank. Pointing down at his feet. The rock, and Laurence above it, seemed to be floating in a couple inches of water.

I sloshed over. Sure enough, all the way around the periphery of the flat boulder, you could see the long, faintly red antennae poking out, undulating in the crystal water, not much thicker than hair.

"Let's flip it!" I said.

"Never told you about my bad disk, did I?" Laurence put his hand on his lower back, massaging it.

"Don't play the ass!"

"Practically paralyzed at one point in my youth. Almost consigned to a wheelchair for life."

"Fock you!"

"Maybe I can assist a little, if I can get down there."

We crouched and cupped our hands under the lip. Then, heaving together, grunting out loud, we flipped it. Crawfish flapping loudly, all around our sneakers, beating up in the shallow water, stirring up little clouds of mud. I had the drawstring of the net bag open in a flash and we started tossing them in, one after the next. The captured crayfish flapping loudly against each other, knotting themselves up in the thin netting. We dug more out of the mud, pulled them out of crevices they'd scuttled into at the side of the overturned boulder. Half of them had scattered in different directions, and now we went chasing behind these, the crayfish walking backwards, across the mud floor when it settled, in a few inches of water. Sometimes they just sat there, in the clear water, waiting for us. As though they were blind, antennae undulating, tiny red legs moving along their sides, vibrating like a line of commas. Remaining in the same spot, and all you had to do was scoop them up.

When we'd caught as many as we could find Laurence and I sat together on a fallen trunk, catching our breath. The blue net bag at our feet, beating up, pulsing with life.

"Let's check the spoils," Laurence said, "shall we?"

"Hang on a sec."

I got up and carried the bag over to where the water was deeper, dragging it back and forth, washing off the mud. Then I brought it back and set it down on the flat boulder we'd overturned. We busied ourselves removing our crayfish, carefully untangling their delicate legs and antennae from the netting, pulling them free. Laying them on the flat boulder beside the bag, the crayfish still moving around, tiny pink fists slowly opening and closing, occasionally clapping up little wet squalls for a second or two. Thirteen in all, of varying size, from four or five inches from head to tail to six or seven inches for the largest. The biggest of them not pink like the others but a faint blue-gray color.

They looked so nice, lying there curled up back to back like that, wet and glistening.

I pulled out the water-beaded clear plastic bag from the bottom of the sack—its contents still dry, safe—laid it to one side.

Now we sat there on the fallen trunk for a while admiring our crayfish.

In a vaps I got up and went over between the trees. Pulling up a handful of soft moist fronds from a pale green fern.

"Read this in a novel," I said. "Or maybe it was a guide to trout fishing?"

"You white-boys read some slack shit!"

I was busy making a layer of leafy fronds at the bottom of the net bag, spread out on the rock in a blue ring, layer of four or five crayfish pressed back to back—they weren't kicking up now, wiry-feeling, half-dead—then another layer of ferns. Another layer of crayfish. When I was finished I pulled the bag's drawstring tight.

Laurence was watching me, smiling, shaking his head like I was nuts.

"What about a little medicinal herb?" he said. "After our hard work?"

"You do the honors."

I tossed him the water-beaded plastic bag. He ripped it open with his teeth, removing the joint gingerly with his long, delicate fingers, the box of matches, and lit up.

———————

Afterwards we just sat there a while longer. Side by side on the smooth trunk, our sneakers soaking in the warm, shallow water. It was late afternoon and the light was changing. Becoming more intense and softer at the same time. The edges of the leaves bright in the trees high overhead, shifting gently with the breeze. Dark, lichen-splotched trunks in shadow. Moss-dripping bromeliads. Leafy ferns stuck between the branches so pale they looked like faintly green clumps of mist. The sky visible in gaps of the canopy so brightly blue, clouds so intensely white. Far below the golden river sparkled.

I was trying hard to keep from looking at Laurence, sitting there on the trunk beside me. From turning my head. But I could feel him sitting there. The warmth rising from his bare skin, his smooth body, muscular chest rising and falling with each breath. We weren't touching except for a spot at our elbows. A breath of a touch. Thinnest skin to thinnest possible skin. It must have been unintended on Laurence's part, and it went unnoticed by him, this almost imperceptible grazing of our elbows. As it had started out for me. But suddenly I couldn't perceive anything else. My entire body seemed to emanate from this place of contact at our elbows. Everything began and everything ended there, in this minute place. Tingling. Burning icy-hot. Spreading out from this spot all over me. Ants crawling across the surface my skin—I was having trouble breathing—my head light, floating, up there among the brightly brimmed leaves.

"Let's get out of here," I said.

"What's the rush?"

"Come on!"

I grabbed up the net bag by its drawstring, slinging it over my shoulder. Sloshing away. Starting to pick my way down between the boulders, climbing down the rock walls, through the dripping caverns. Moving downriver. Laurence trailing behind. Moving quickly now, recklessly stumbling my way down, my sneakers slipping beneath me. Covering a lot of ground, at least in comparison to the upriver climb. After twenty minutes, when I reached a place where the water was deep enough, I stopped and turned around. Waiting for Laurence to catch up. Forcing myself to take a few slow, measured breaths.

I tied the drawstring around my wrist, two half-hitches, pulled it tight.

We waded over to the deepest part, both of us together, cold water reaching to the middle of our thighs.

"Think this's sufficient?" he asked.

"Just be careful," I winked. "Keep you bamsee up off the bottom!"

We threw ourselves in. Riding the current as we had yesterday afternoon. But since the water was shallower this time we rode the river on our backs—feet-first, protected by our sneakers—floating as best we could up close to the surface, up over the sharp rocks. Picking our way down—backwards, crab-wise—among the boulders. The fallen trunks. Staghorn-stumps protruding at both banks. The river slowly growing deeper, its pull stronger, and now we were riding fast again. Rushing past rock walls. Through the dark caverns.

At one point we flew over a sudden waterfall, dropping five feet through the air, hearts in our mouths for a second. Splashing down hard into a shallow pool, white water cascading over our heads. Our ride halted dead still for another spit second, the stream slowly picking up again, dragging us off. Gliding. Ripping between the rock walls.

We seemed to have climbed it for so long, this river—all afternoon—yet before we knew it we were passing the place where we forded it to get to camp. We rode past the clumps of mangrove on both sides of the bocus, their purple roots arching up. Right out to the deep water, the blue-black sea. Again the current stopped and switched directions, pulling us across to the opposite side of the beach, and we swam the lazy swells in and threw ourselves, panting, onto the warm sand. Rolling over onto our backs, lying there, our legs spread, foamy swells swashing over us.

"Incredible!" Laurence said between breaths. "Worth every minute of the climb."

"Every hour you mean!"

I was untying the drawstring of the bag from around my wrist—had to pull it loose with my teeth—my hand purple. Starting from the two thin, parallel white lines around my wrist. Like I was wearing a glove. I squeezed my fist shut and then open a few times. Our net bag covered in sand, its contents jumbled, a couple of the crayfish revived on the way down, flapping with a final effort.

The orange plate of the sun was just touching down against the black wall of the sea. Sky lit up a pale, orangey-pink behind it. Rosy three-dimensional clouds. In close by the beach the water was flat, bright red, sparkling.

We were still breathing hard, both of us. Laurence lying on his back, his smooth chest rising and falling, long legs parted, white toes protruding from the water, soft waves sloshing up over his white Speedo. I rolled over onto my elbow, looking at him. Boldly. A long minute. My entire body tingling again, icy-hot. And without thinking, without pausing for an instant, I stretched over and kissed his lips.

Suddenly I was above him, pressing my mouth down against his, hard, my lips opening.

Laurence shoved himself up onto his elbows, roughly, shoving me back. Our teeth knocking together. Then he got quickly to his feet, bending over with his hands resting on his knees, his head turned down, looking at the sand. Breathing hard. His chest expanding. Contracting.

I got up too. Slowly.

"Listen," he said, still not looking at me. "We known each other a long time. No love lost, you understand, but that just ain't my cup—"

"I know!" I cut him off. "Just wanted to find out." I took a couple of quick breaths. "I suppose I just needed to know for myself what it feels like."

"Fine! Let's forget it."

He straightened up and looked at me.

Now I watched his eyes drop to my waist, stop there a second, then turn up again. Suddenly the expression on his face changed. He looked angry. Disgusted with me.

"Focking buller!" he said.

I was angry too. Just as quickly. Panting. Disgusted with myself now. And I wanted to strike back—to wound him quickly, efficiently, as he had wounded me.

I said the first thing that came into my head.

"Just figured you had it in you genes!" I took a breath. "Like father like—"

This time it was Laurence who cut me off. With a back-handed swing across my mouth. Up and across. Like the cold slap of a seawave. Square in the face. My lower lip stinging. Burning.

We stared at each other, panting.

Laurence turned his back to me, starting slowly up the beach. Trudging through the loose sand. Towards the path alongside the river.

I stared behind him for a few seconds. Catching my breath. Then I began to feel something warm and wet, sticky, dripping down my chin, down over my chest. Flare of bright red in the corner of my eye. I looked down at the sand at my feet: one bright crimson drop. Then another. Landing and spreading out in the wet sand. Dispersing. One of those bright drops caught by the breeze and tossed onto the jumbled blue bag of our crayfish.

Then I saw something else. Also out of the corner of my eye. And I turned my head to look down directly at it. So shocked, in truth, that I almost tumbled over backwards. Almost let loose a bawl like a wild Warahoon Indian: pressing up out of the loosened draw-string of my Speedo, its blunt-nosed head like two purple cloves of garlic pressed tightly together, pointing up at me, trembling, my erect penis.

17

Back at camp they seemed to be having a party. Rachel had long since returned from her fishing trip, her cheeks red from the sun, glowing. Eddoes had taken the canoe back and climbed up to the valley to deliver a bucket-load of redfish to Mother. He'd left two more carved wooden buckets for us, both overflowing—not only with redfish, but with a couple of larger groupers and a turbot. Even a baby shark, its jagged tail hanging over the side. Five young boys from Pinnacle had seen us in the village this morning and they'd come to make friends. They helped gut and scale the fish and now they were helping us cook our dinner. On the bonfire, which the boys had gotten blazing again. Lots of noise—laughter, joking, horsing around—not many diversions for boys in Pinnacle.

I can't remember their names except for the eldest two. One had his head shaved like Laurence, he called himself Kojac. Fifteen or so. The other, about the same age but taller, more muscular, was Abdul. The youngest seven or eight years of age. All of them bare-backed, rail-thin, wearing frayed cutoffs.

They chopped long spears out of the bush, sharpened the tips, and then they laid the gutted fish on the sand. Pressed them down with the flats of their palms, opening the toothpick-lipped jaws, and they shoved the spears into their mouths, right through to their tails. Then they took the speared fish down to the water to wash off the sand. We held them above the flames, turning them like marshmallows, until they were scorched on all sides. The boys filleted the larger turbot, cut it up into chunks, together with the baby-shark. Pressing the chunks of fish onto the spears like shish-kebabs. Sometimes a piece would fall off into the flames, or they'd burn it, the boys cussing each other. Which we took part in too, especially Laurence. The boys, hearing his accent, called him English.

"English say he know bout turbot, but all them peoples does eat is cucumber-sandwich."

"And drink nough tea, not true, English?"

"The sole sustenance of an Englishman," Laurence said, "is tea and cucumber-sandwiches. The occasional avocado-with-prawns." He winked at me.

I was grateful for it. Earlier I'd been so distracted that I'd forgotten our net bag there on the beach. Walking back in a daze. Laurence didn't ask after our crayfish, and I certainly didn't bring them up. Rachel didn't question us about our fishing trip either. Or my split lip.

The boys had cut balisier leaves from the bush, which they laid side by side on the sand like a huge platter. Rachel squeezed lime over the cooked fish, sprinkling on pinches of salt and black-pepper. She'd set the big pot of rice down in the middle of the fire, flames curling up around it, boiling away. And when the rice was cooked she drained the pot and mixed in a can of pigeonpeas.

Abdul climbed a coconut palm higher up on the beach, hugging the trunk, his legs splayed frog-wise as he pulled himself up, cutlass clenched between his teeth. He cut down water-nuts. Then he descended and chipped the tops into points, punching them open, lining the nuts up in the sand before our growing platter of fish.

We'd been picking at pieces of the smoky fish the whole time, but now we got ourselves ready for some serious eating. Instead of our tin plates and knives and forks we used the balisier leaves, set down on the sand before us, pulling the fish apart with our fingers. Scooping the peas-n'-rice out of the pot with our hands. We ate to the last grain, last morsel of fish—the boys even sucked the charred heads and fins. All of us chewing the soft gristly cartilage of the baby-shark. Pausing only for a drink of coconut-water.

After our dinner we sat there for a few minutes, stunned. Even the boys were quiet for a while. Then we walked down together to the water and tossed in our balisier-plates, crouched down to wash off our hands. The boys hurled the empty coconuts out over the water. All of us standing there in the calm water up to our knees, warmish now that the tide was out. For a while it had been so dark we could hardly see each other except near the fire. Now we watched the moon rise up out of the water, huge and round and pockmarked. A light breeze and a slight chop farther out. The breeze cool, but only Laurence had put on his T-shirt. Rachel still in her purple bikini bottom—I'd overheard the boys more than once, joking about "she sweet bubbies." But either she hadn't heard or she couldn't be bothered.

Two of the younger ones disappeared as we stood at the water's edge—we assumed they'd gone back home to Pinnacle—but they appeared out of the bushes a few minutes later hugging armfuls of brown sapodillas to their chests. We broke them open, scraping the red-orange flesh from the insides of the papery skins with our teeth. Spitting out the shiny black seeds. Rachel split her sapodilla with a knife, scooping the flesh from the fragile shell with a teaspoon.

There was one joint remaining and now we smoked it. Sitting on our sleepingbags staring into the fire. Kojac demanded some but we wouldn't pass it to him.

"I got my own stash home you know. Plenty!"

"Then when you get back," Laurence said. "You can have a smoke."

"Isn't it time for you boys to be going home anyway?" Rachel asked. It must have been nine or ten o'clock.

"These childrens," Kojac said. "I does come and go how I please."

He was sitting over beside Rachel, stealing sideways glances at her "bubbies." He didn't appear bashful about it either.

"Wha!" one of the younger boys said. "You know he mummy go cut he tail soon as he reach home, same as we!"

"Worse," another said. "Cause you know Kojac already in the doghouse. He mummy beat he for riding round with them polices in the Rover. Catch he smoking ganj with them polices too!"

"Well," Rachel said after a minute. "Now I do think it's time for you boys to be getting home. You can come back and visit us tomorrow."

"Yes'm," one of them said, and eventually they all got up, wandering off together in the direction of the river.

But when they got to the bushes at the top of the beach, beside our kitchen where it was darker, the group split up. The three younger boys disappeared deeper into the bush walking towards the path. But the other two, Kojac and Abdul, moved off in the opposite direction. Skirting the seaoats and the tall grass. Moving quickly, quietly—they didn't want us to see—and I think only Laurence and I did. We looked at each other for a second, Laurence shrugging his shoulders.

We were exhausted from the long day, from the sun. Sitting there on our sleepingbags, hugging our knees, staring into the fire. Turning to look over our shoulders at the huge moon, its trail of soft white light floating on the water.

We heard a noise down the beach.

I got up—even reached for my cutlass, stuck in the sand beside me.

"Pssst!" the noise came again.

Eddoes appeared from out of the shadows, smiling, striding down the beach towards us. I crouched and stuck my cutlass back in the sand.

But he walked directly over and pulled it out, laying it flat on its side.

"Got to respect the Mother!" he winked at me.

Now Eddoes steupsed, looking around at Laurence and Rachel. "All-you go miss the old lady of the sea," he gestured over his shoulder. "Come!"

He led us down the beach. And after a couple of minutes we spotted her. Like a helmet-shaped, dark green boulder interrupting the open expanse of the beach. She'd just climbed out of the water, and now she was pulling herself up higher. But when we got twenty yards away Eddoes held us back. He didn't want us going too close yet.

"We go scare she back in the water," he whispered.

But we were near enough to see her huge, dull-green, almond-shaped eye. Close enough to hear her deep, watery breaths—like mist gushing through a blowhole in the rocks, or water blown out through a snorkel. She was pulling herself across the sand by working the pairs of her fore- and hind-flippers together, as though she were still in the water swimming. Her flippers scraping, tossing wet sand back behind her. With each strenuous pull she gained only a couple of inches at best. Often nothing at all. More effective was when she raised her tremendous weight up over the sand for a second, suspended on all four flippers together, and threw herself forward. Even then her gain was minimal. It took her half an hour to reach the top of the beach, where there was a thin line of dry, black seaweed. Loosely ruffled sand.

Then she stopped and we were sure she was going to lay. Still Eddoes held us back. Now she actually turned around and started moving directly towards us, her eyes glinting in the moonlight

—we backed up a few steps. Then she turned down towards the water and we thought we'd scared her off. That she wasn't going to lay after all. Our hearts pounding for a second. But she turned completely around again, heading up higher onto the beach, past the line of dry seaweed. She stopped for the second time and after a couple of minutes we saw her flapping her wide, pale green flippers up high in the air, a different kind of movement, tossing out loose sand behind her. Crisscrossed over her back. In the moonlight it looked like foam blowing off the crest of a boat's wake.

"Come," Eddoes whispered, smiling. "Once she make up she mind she don't change it."

We moved right up next to her, crouching beside her in the sand. Enormous—shockingly so—when you got this close: she seemed the size of a Volkswagen Beetle. At least the top, rounded part. Climbing up she'd seemed so impossibly encumbered by her own weight and bulk. Now, digging her hole, she moved with more dexterity. Sometimes appearing to stand right up on her hind-flippers out of the sand.

Her fore-flippers were narrower, pointed, smaller; and now she used her wide, more flexible hind-flippers to dig the hole. Alternating one to the other. She'd plant three flippers and with the remaining hind-flipper she'd reach back behind to cup out the sand. Not like a shovel or a spade, but like a human palm, pressing the inside edge in and curling her soft flipper around the sand, cupping out a flipper-full. Then, holding the flipper horizontally so the sand didn't tumble out, she raised it slowly and carefully out of the hole, rolling open the curl of her flipper. Tossing the flipper-full of sand behind her. Now she'd shift to the other hind-flipper, plant the remaining three, and repeat the entire intricate process on that side. One hind-flipper and then the other. One carefully cupped flipper-full of sand, then another.

Due to the shape of these hind-flippers—the notch near the middle of the outside edge—her hole came out square-shaped, with rounded corners. A foot and a half by a foot and a half, maybe a yard deep.

She had several old barnacles stuck to her back, pressed together in clumps of two or three—as large and thinly-edged as china tea-cups—yet when you touched them they felt as sharp as a knife's edge. Eddoes was crouching up near her head, actually stroking her flattened triangular crown. Not exactly safe—I'd heard stories of people losing their fingers like that, even their entire hand—but she seemed relaxed with Eddoes there beside her. He encouraged us to touch her also, and we pressed our fingers into the leathery, dark green plates of her back. Soft, thick, smoothly-sanded, like pressing your finger into the upturned heel of your foot. We felt the cool smoothness of her thin fore-flipper.

When her hole was complete she centered herself over it, and now she did seem to stand up out of the sand on her hind-flippers, her triangular head pointing up at the sky, at the bright moon. Green eyes glinting. She continued breathing heavily the whole time. You could see, hear the bulk of her great chest expanding and contracting each time. Enormous baffles. Each watery breath. Now she started to lay and we heard the eggs dropping softly into the bottom of the hole, like those heavy raindrops falling to the leafy floor of the forest. Two permanent tears of mucus had been forming at the outside corners of her eyes. They never fell, only became thicker and more elongated.

An effect, supposedly, of her eyes being exposed to the air for so long, of their drying out—not an indication of her emotional state—but you couldn't believe it. Somehow you couldn't separate those permanent tears from her profound agony. This tremendous risk she'd put herself under, for several hours. Making herself vulnerable to predators so much smaller and weaker—wild dogs, corbeaux, humans more than any other—dragging herself up into this world so foreign to her own, only to continue her clan. Those tears made the experience of our being here—of our being granted permission to witness this ancient, elaborate ritual—seem the more forbidden. All the more secret and extraordinary.

Now we moved around back behind her, peering into the dark hole, squinting to see the eggs falling slowly to the bottom. With all my careful preparations for the trip I'd forgotten the most important, most useful thing—a flashlight. But with the moon overhead we could see well enough to catch a glimpse of the soft, variably-shaped eggs dropping softly into the hole.

A little smaller than hen's eggs, and I remembered that when broken they tore rather than cracked. Their shells like a thin, fragile canvas. Some of the villagers ate them, very softly boiled—I'd tried them once myself as a child—years before I'd witnessed this ritual. Ripping the turtle egg open and shaking in salt and black-pepper, a dot of peppersauce. Then you'd raise it carefully to your mouth and suck the contents out of the soft shell.

120 to 160 in a nest, Eddoes told us quietly. At one point she stopped laying, seemed to struggle uncomfortably for a minute. Her entire body shaking in spasms. Eddoes moved around back beside us. He crouched down with his chest pressed into the sand, reaching his long arm into the hole, under her, gently freeing several eggs that had formed a blockage. Dropping them softly into the hole with the others.

To cover up her eggs she repeated the process of digging her hole, but in reverse. Cupping out a flipper-full of the sand behind her, holding it horizontally and moving it carefully over the eggs, uncurling her hind-flipper over the nest. Then she'd plant herself on her three alternate flippers and repeat the process on the other side. With one exception: now, after she'd covered her eggs with a few inches of sand, she'd press it down with the same hind-flipper. Each time she tossed on a flipper-full. Heavily. Recklessly. Standing right up in the air and pressing the sand down onto the eggs, with all her tremendous weight. So that each time you waited anxiously to hear those eggs burst beneath her. She stomped her nest down over and over, until she completely filled in the hole.

Now she performed what, for me, always seems the oddest part of the entire ritual. She moved around in the sand, over the place where she'd just dug her nest. Several exhausting full circles. Carving out wide, S-shaped turns of her trail in the sand. More than once turning in our direction, coming directly at us again. Two pale green, almond-shaped eyes lighting up for an instant. Again we stepped back as a group, laughing quietly now. She kept it up for another half-hour, her dance in the sand. So that when she'd finished—even though she'd buried her eggs just there at our feet—we had no idea where her nest was. Couldn't have found it if we tried.

Formerly the villagers, following her wide elaborate track up from the water's edge, used long rods to sound the nests. Pressing the rods deep into the sand and feeling for the place the rods gave way. But even the most practiced of them had difficulty.

She turned to face the sea again, and for the final half-hour of her labor, pulled herself back down towards the water. Again it felt ago-nizingly slow. But moving down the slope of the beach seemed a less strenuous task. Until, finally, she reached the water's edge. En-tering slowly, inch by inch. Dragging herself across the wet sand. Now when she pulled with her fore-flippers she tossed water up crisscrossed over her back. Soft swells washing over her hump.

Then it was as though the beach itself—the earth, the atmosphere, gravity—suddenly released the grip of its hands. Water welling up for a second over her helmet-shaped hump—you saw a flash of the pale green underside of a fore-flipper, slicing just below the surface—another second of the huge dark shadow pulling itself smoothly away, and she was gone. *Paf!* Dissolved into the dark depths.

The tide was out, still, and the breeze had dropped. The water before us smoothly rippled. Warm. We stood there for a few more minutes, soft waves brushing our shins, looking out in the direction she'd disappeared, down the trail of soft white light floating on the water, all the way to the horizon. The wide, pocked moon high overhead.

Eddoes turned and led us back to our sleepingbags, to our burntout fire.

He told us he was heading back up to the valley. He had to leave for the fields first thing in the morning. Harvesting cassava again.

But he promised to come back to see us after breakfast. Mother, he said, was happy to have met Rachel that afternoon. Rachel was just as she had appeared to her in her dream. And Mother wanted him to bring her up to the valley again tomorrow to say good-bye. Then, Eddoes told us, he'd escort us through the forest to Matelot. Give us a proper sendoff.

We knocked fists and he walked up towards our kitchen, disappearing into the bushes.

We were exhausted—I can assure you I was. And after getting the fire going Laurence and I zipped ourselves into our sleepingbags for the night. Rachel was down by the water again, crouching in the sand, looking away at the sea. Her hair pulled forward over one shoulder. Her back slippery-looking, soft, pale, bathed in moonlight. As I closed my eyes and drifted off.

———

But only a couple of minutes later, or so it seemed, I felt someone holding me by both shoulders, shaking me awake. Rachel crouched above me, serious look on her face. She pressed two cool fingers against my lips. Then she stood and moved off down the beach, in the direction our turtle had come up.

I unzipped my sleepingbag and started out behind her, hurrying to catch up. Walking along beside her for a minute. She took a quick step ahead and turned around in front of me, her arms crossed over her chest, wrapped around her, clutching her shoulders. Staring into my face.

"You must take me to him."

For a second it did not even register that she meant Eddoes.

"You must!"

I was still half asleep. Trying to take this in.

We stood there for a minute, staring at each other.

"Don't do it," I said.

"I have to."

"You can't. You have to stop it. Immediately."

She looked away. Her hair blowing in the breeze. Silent for a few seconds.

"Please don't be difficult, William. You know what I'm like when I get like this, simply can't hold myself back."

"You've got Laurence," I said. "Go with Laurence."

But even as I said it I knew I'd prefer to see her with Eddoes. I'd far prefer it. Regardless of the consequences. Suddenly I felt I'd do anything to keep her away from Laurence. Despite the danger.

"Laurence," she said after a moment, "has nothing to do with this!"

"No."

"If you don't take me to him, I'll find my way there on my own."

She would, I knew her well enough. But what would she actually do? Walk into the open shed at the back where the men slept, a dozen of them stretched out naked on the ground? Figure out which one was Eddoes, and get down on the ground beside him?

"Wait down the beach," I told her. "I'll bring him back." I paused. "Probably the others won't even realize he's gone."

Her back was already turned.

––––––––––

I'd climbed the trail up the rocky cliff to the valley a dozen times. But the last time was two years ago. And I'd never done it at night. Yet with the full moon I could see well enough. A steep climb, and after a few minutes I was sweating. Swatting at sandflies I'd stirred up out of the bushes. Climbing, barefoot, along the rock wall—I hadn't even thought to put on my sneakers—but the path beneath my feet was hard-packed dirt. Smooth. And now it turned inland. I made my way between the dark bushes. After a few minutes the path opened up between the trees, onto the flattened top of the grass-covered hillside in front of the old cocoahouse. It looked out over the sea, but in the direction of the rocky cove where they kept their canoe. Not towards the river and the beach where we were camped.

I walked across the grass, cropped short by an old billygoat tethered by a bunch of knotted ropes to a groundsill of the house. Busily pulling at the grass and chewing away, interrupting himself only for a second, turning to look at me over his back. His green-gray goatee bobbing up and down, wet with slobber, metallic eyes turned sideways in his skull—other-worldly, spooky-looking—he put his head down and went on pulling, grinding.

I made out the faded black letters painted across the front boards of the house, on either side of the doorless frame:

HELL VALLEY   THE DEVIL LIVE HERE

A tall avocado-pear tree pressed against this side of the house. A dark shadow, leaves shifting in the breeze. Olive-colored lobes dangling. I hurried across the grass, skirting the house by ten or fifteen feet, ducking through some low bushes on the other side— pigeonpeas I thought, but I was moving too fast to tell—then I came out at the back, between the two sheds. One for storing ground provisions, the other—I could tell by the stench—for drying fish.

Attached to the back of the cocoahouse is what, in the estate days, had been called an extended roof. An open shed, without walls—the beans would have been spread on racks with the roof split down the middle, its two sides on metal wheels and runners. The roof opened up during daylight hours to let in the sun, closed again at night to protect the beans from dew, a sudden summer squall. But this roof had rusted up in the shut position years ago. It was where the men slept now. Ten or fifteen of them, deeply black figures against the gray earth, three-dimensional shadows.

I had no idea which one could be Eddoes. *What the fock?* I slipped around to the side. Crouching over one of the sleeping shadows— he seemed about the right size—I reached out and gently touched his shoulder.

Eddoes opened his eyes, lying there on his back, staring up into my face. I waited for a flash of recognition, turned quickly and slouched away into the dark. Hurrying around the other side of the house, ducking under the limb of a dark tree—stumbling straight into the focking goat. He turned his head to look at me, still chewing, his green-gray goatee bobbing, dripping with slobber.

I kicked him out of my way. Hurrying over towards the entrance of the path. Eddoes there beside me in a second. He'd put back on his Speedo, pale white in the moonlight.

"Wha?" he whispered.

"Rachel needs to see you is all."

I didn't even pause to see how this registered. Only wanting to get back down onto the beach. But after a few steps I stopped and moved aside, let Eddoes pass me up—he'd be quicker.

Now I followed behind his white Speedo.

In no time we were back down, just about to walk out of the bushes beside the kitchen. I reached forward and held on to his shoulder, and he turned in the dark to face me.

"Over by where the turtle came up," I said.

He started down the beach.

I watched behind him for a few seconds, turned, and hurried towards my sleepingbag. Zipped myself in.

———————

When I awoke it was late morning, but the sun wasn't shining in my face. Hidden behind a wall of gray clouds. Laurence still asleep.

I looked over; Rachel wasn't back.

I lay there for a minute, then I jumped up and started down the beach.

After a few minutes I stopped, scanning the remaining half mile of beach. As far as the place where the rock cliffs and mangrove cut it off. Deserted. Then I noticed something directly beneath my feet—the smoothness of the sand disturbed, messed-up. I looked around. But I stood staring for several seconds before I realized what it was: writing. Big block letters. Stretching almost from the water's edge, all the way up to the thin black weedline. Scraped into the smooth sand with the heel of somebody's foot, or a stone. I turned my back to the water, looking up, slowly making out the letters:

FOCK
NIGA

A few yards down the beach I saw the elaborate trail where our turtle had crawled back down to the water, and another few yards beyond that, the smoothness of the sand disturbed again. More writing. I hurried over, stepping across our turtle's tracks, and turned around:

WITE
CUNT

I stood there for another minute. Staring. Then I raised my eyes higher, looking up the trail of our turtle's track, just beyond the weedline—and I found Rachel, her smooth shoulders, her pale back with the seaoats shifting in the dull light a few yards behind her. Hair blowing in the breeze. Crouching in the sand, looking down, so I couldn't see her face. I hurried up towards her, through the loose sand, suddenly stepping on something. Hard, but not exactly. Slimy—wet.

I raised my foot, turning up the sole: the flattened shell of a turtle egg. I peeled it off. Now I looked around and saw that the eggs were smashed, all around me, all over the sand—a hundred of them, all torn, ripped open, their shiny contents spilled out in faintly yellow-red star-shaped splotches—as though they'd been thrown down hard against the sand. Splattered.

Over to one side I saw the wide, deep hole where the nest had been dug up.

Then Rachel turned to look at me, and I saw that her face was red—splotchy and messed up like the sand at my feet—wet with tears. Red curls plastered to one cheek, along the side of her neck. Sobbing.

"Who?" I asked.

"Them," she gestured down the beach.

I looked over but couldn't find anyone. Turned to Rachel again.

"Those horrid boys!" she sobbed. "Kojac. And Abdul."

Breeze whistling through the seaoats for a second.

"Where's Eddoes?"

"He went back up. To the valley. I sent him back."

"When was that?"

"Only a few minutes ago. There's a path down there, through the bush." She gestured over her shoulder. "He left and I started back to camp. On my way I stumbled over this!"

I surveyed the splotches all around us, then turned to look down the beach again. Now, over beside the edge of the bushes, I saw two dark figures. Two shadows, crouching. They saw me too. Disappearing higher into the trees. As they went I saw a flash of the cutlass one of them carried in his hand—a cutlass probably stolen from us.

I crouched down beside Rachel and held her against me. Wet, shaking. Her skin cold. Clammy. Suddenly small and fragile in my arms.

"Go on back to Laurence," I told her. "You don't want to be around this mess!"

I raised her to her feet, holding her against me. Rachel pressing the side of her face against my neck. Cold and wet. Her hair wet. Shoulders trembling beneath my hands.

"It's OK," I whispered. "Go on back."

I held her for another second.

"Let me see if I can catch those little fockers!"

Lying on the sand behind Rachel I saw a long, charred spear— one of the ones we'd used to cook the fish, which the boys had used again to sound the eggs. I let go of Rachel and grabbed it up.

"Go on," I told her gently, and I watched her turn and start down towards the water.

I watched her for a couple of minutes. Saw her stop when she got to the writing, turn to look up at it, deciphering the letters. She turned and continued on.

I took off running down the beach. Through the loose dry sand. Towards the place the boys had disappeared.

But when I got there I couldn't figure out where it was. The bush thick—seemingly impenetrable—I couldn't find a way in. I stood staring for several seconds, breathing hard. Then I found a gap between two half-dead, gray casuarina trunks—and in the dried needles at the base of one of them a small white clump: four unbroken eggs. I took off between the two casuarinas. Climbing through thick bush, past spindly pines, the ground hard rock, sharp against my feet. It seemed hopeless—I'd never find them in this bush. I threw the stick aside, whipping for an instant through the air. And pushed on, moving recklessly now, blindly, feeling my way between the trees. Over thorny bushes—agave, poisonwood, prickly-pear. Scratching up my legs and chest. Holding on to branches with both hands and pulling my way through. Then the ground, the hard rock floor beneath my feet seemed to slope up sharply. And I was climbing in the dark. Grabbing at branches and pulling myself higher.

Suddenly the trees opened up—like a thick blue-velvet curtain— and in a gap of the forest I found a high rock mound. A cliff, a small precipice, with a flattened plateau at the top. Sticking straight up out of the forest. Up above the tops of the short pines, shaggy heads of palmetto palms. I stood there, breathing hard. Sweat rolling down my chest, my forehead, burning my eyes. Blinking. Staring up at the apparition before me: there, abandoned at the top of the small mound, just at the edge of the precipice, the policemen's Rover.

I stood beside it for a few seconds, holding on to the bar of one of the rearview mirrors. Catching my breath. Wiping sweat from my brow with the back of my hand.

Stretching behind the rear tires I made out two fresh tracks—flattened weeds, and farther along, flattened bushes, knocked-over spindly pines—where the Rover had come through the forest. Parked here at the edge of this short cliff with its headlights pointing straight at the beach. At the blue-gray sea—a focking lookout tower.

I paused for another second. Then I climbed up and slid into the driver's seat, still holding on to the bar of the rearview mirror. Black vinyl sticking to my wet back. Cold. I looked down and saw the ignition keys, jingling at the base of the steering wheel. Scattered on the floor on the passenger's side, leftover cellophane packages of Cheetos, Corncurls, empty Coke cans. Crumpled Camels packs. Ashtray overflowing beside my knee.

Now I put my two hands on the steering wheel and held it, slightly spongy, wrapped in the same black vinyl. And looked around. Out across the horizon. Out over the dark green and yellow bushes and the shaggy treetops below, the sea spread out beyond the beach like an old blanket. A filthy, green-gray, shag-carpet. Chopped up. To my far right I saw the clump of dark mangrove on this side of the bocus of the river. I let my eyes slowly follow the broad white band of the beach, until they came to our campfire, smoking, red and yellow flames licking up. Laurence sitting on his sleepingbag, drinking a mug of coffee—I could even see the dull flash of the tin mug in his hands. Clear as day. Rachel sitting on her own sleepingbag, a dark-green rectangle set down in the sand, her arms wrapped around her knees, hugging them against her chest.

My eyes continued along the line of the beach, looking through the bright green glass of the windshield now, coming to rest just in front of me—on the area of messed-up sand, all the splotches of the splattered turtle eggs. Tiny wet-looking dimples in the sand. As though—if not for the windshield in front of me—I could reach out and touch them. Farther down, beyond the mess, spaced almost symmetrically, stretching down to the water's edge:

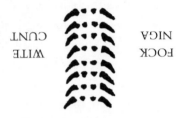

I reached and turned the ignition key—the Rover still in gear, lurching forward. Almost bounding over the cliff. My ribs jamming into the bottom of the steering wheel, back of my neck rebounding against the headrest. Stinging. I took a deep breath. Placed my foot carefully on the clutch, pressed it smoothly to the floor. The sound of a spring retracting somewhere beneath the hood. I turned the key a second time. Slowly. A moment of the hoarsely grinding crank. The Rover purring beneath me.

I listened for a few seconds. Suddenly I heard shouting, several voices. Scrambling in the forest behind me. I turned the key again: the Rover sputtered and went silent.

Few seconds of quiet, then more shouting—hard to say which direction it was coming from.

"Hold he, na!"

"Foking bush-nigger! he gone!"

"Hold he, man!"

"I tell you he get loose!"

Those policemen's voices. That much I could tell: it wasn't Kojac and Abdul out there now. More scrambling through the bush.

I jumped down from the Rover and stood, holding on to the rearview mirror, listening. Nothing. Only the pounding of my own heart. I started through the trees, moving in the direction I'd heard the shouting. Best as I could tell. Deeper into the forest, tearing my way through. But after a few minutes the trees opened up suddenly, and through a gap I found the sea again, choppy and muddy green—I was sure I'd been going in the opposite direction.

I bust out of the tall weeds, onto the loose sand. At both sides the beach was deserted. No one in sight. Foremost on my mind now was Rachel. I turned down the beach, hurrying towards camp.

———————

When I got back she was sitting there by herself on her sleepingbag. Arms still hugging her knees. Staring into the fire.

"Where's Laurence?"

She didn't answer for a few seconds. But when she turned her face to look up at me, I could see that she was better. No longer crying. Her face no longer red and splotchy.

She simply looked tired. And for the first time since I'd known her—drawn. Old.

"He went to Pinnacle. For coconut-bread."

I stared at her for a second, "*What?*"

"I sent him. Told him I wanted to be by myself for a while."

"You mean he left you here alone?"

Rachel actually smiled. Shaking her head.

"William, they're a couple of foolish boys. Destructive adolescents, punk kids. Nothing more."

I took a deep breath.

"It's just that we need to pack up and get going!"

She continued smiling. Calmly. Still shaking her head.

"William, we're not leaving till this afternoon."

I had the feeling of backing myself into a corner. I looked away at the sea, the bruised gray wall of a sky behind it.

"It's going to rain," I said slowly. "And we have to get out from under it. Otherwise we'll be stuck here. Who knows how long."

I'd pulled it out of the air, but it made sense. We did need to get going, and in a hurry. Regardless of what was going on with those policemen, their abandoned Rover, Kojac and Abdul and everybody else in this focking place. If it started to come down we could find ourselves in serious trouble. This was the beginning of the rainy season and it could continue for days. We could end up stuck here for days.

"I'm not leaving before we see Eddoes," she said.

I turned to look at her. Staring into the fire, her arms wrapped around her shins, hugging them against her chest. Her flattened white kneecaps. Hair falling forward around them. And I realized none of us would be leaving for a while.

I made us coffee. We sat on our sleepingbags drinking it. Soon after Laurence returned. Plonking himself down, heavily, breathing hard.

"Miss Bethel out of bread?" Rachel asked.

"I didn't get any. Didn't even make it to the old hag's parlor. Some kind of row going on at the police station. Big commotion. All the villagers shouting, carrying on. Complete commesse!"

He paused, "I thought it prudent to get my backside out of there as quickly as possible."

I looked over, "What's it about?"

"Your guess's as good as mine."

Laurence reached for a branch and started poking it into the fire, sparks jumping.

"Focking assholes playing some kind of game with their Rover," he said. "Kept revving it up, throwing in the clutch, jerking it forward. Revving it and jerking it forward again. From a distance, looked like half the village hanging on to the back."

"They had their Rover with them?"

He looked at me. "Yeah. What of it?"

"How you mean?"

Laurence raised his eyebrows. "Those policemen don't go anywhere without their vehicle. Or haven't you noticed? It's their focking name tag."

He turned and went on poking the fire, stirring up sparks. Rachel and me watching. Several minutes of silence. Only the fire crackling.

"Listen," I said. "Let's pack up. Soon as Eddoes comes we can take off. Hopefully before the sky breaks loose."

———

But as soon as we'd finished, just as Rachel had rolled up her sleepingbag, tied it neatly across the top of her pack, we felt the first raindrops. First few thick pellets.

I turned around. Out at sea it was coming down in sheets.

We hurried up towards the kitchen, dragging our backpacks across the sand behind us. Three of us huddling together, sitting on our packs, beneath my piece of roof. Watching the white wall of rain brush swiftly over the sea towards us. A line of blue-gray water boiling up beneath it. More and more pellets pelting the flimsy cover of coconut fronds above our heads. We'd dressed— first time since we'd arrived—in T-shirts and jeans. I was wearing a pair borrowed from Laurence. And we'd put back on our sneakers. Even though we'd have to take them off again, along with our jeans, to ford the river.

The wind picking up, already whistling through the trees, rain pelting harder—so it was a good thing we'd dressed, still fairly warm, fairly dry, huddled beneath my piece of roof.

It was holding up. Even my breakwall, standing solid against the wind—at least I'd had the foresight to build it.

But just as that thought passed through my mind, we watched the white wall brush across the beach and over our heads. Like the shadow of a cloud. Sweeping swiftly across. With the rain came more wind, screaming, vibrating through the trees—*voof! voof! voof!*—and suddenly it picked up our entire shelter, in one piece, tossing it like a folded paperplate into the trees behind us. Rain pelting our heads now, our faces—so hard it was painful—our foreheads and cheeks stinging, holding on to each other as if the wind could take *us* with it at any moment. Soaked to our skins in a second—our backpacks with our sleepingbags tied across them instantly waterlogged—huge sponges, heavy as blocks of wood.

"What'll we do?" Rachel shouted.

"Here," I shouted into the wind, each word a blast of water. "Over here!"

I crawled around the side of the almond trunk, squeezing myself under the plywood table. The others following close behind. Three of us huddled beneath the table, our arms wrapped around each other, tops of our heads pressed against the piece of plywood, rain pelting it as hard as rifle shot half an inch away. The wind screaming through the trees like an ambulance siren, vibrating, whipping our hair, blasting our faces with sand, pellets of rain, our eyes shut tight.

We must have sat for half an hour like that—shivering, clutching each other.

Then, just as suddenly as it had overtaken us, the squall swept swiftly away. Disappearing behind the forested cliffs at our backs. Suddenly the wind halted, then the rain, and within minutes the sun was shining. For the first time that morning. The sea perfectly flat—pristine, glistening.

We crawled, one by one, out of our hovel. Sloshing to our feet in our waterlogged sneakers. Shaking water from our hands, wiping it off our faces, pulling our saturated T-shirts up over our heads and wringing them out.

Suddenly the sun was hot, hard, stinging our faces and backs.

It must have been one or two o'clock. I looked around—perfectly clear sky. Cobalt blue. Not a stroke of white.

Long as we got out of there by five, I realized, we'd have plenty of time to make the hike to Matelot. And with Eddoes to guide us through the forest it would be even quicker.

Now I saw there was no reason to hurry at all. On the contrary, we'd been lucky the rain caught us, fortunate to have stayed put on the beach—weathering the storm here as opposed to facing it in the middle of the forest, trees coming down around us, quite possibly losing our way. The sky cloudless now, no threat of storm remaining. We would actually be better off sitting tight for another hour or two, before we started out. Give the forest floor a chance to soak up the downpour.

We stripped to our Speedos again, wringing out our clothes and hanging them up, our knotted sneakers from branches of the almond. We unrolled our sopping sleepingbags on the hard sand lower down, unzipped them and spread them out beneath the blazing sun. Pulled the stuff out of our packs, piece by piece, everything waterlogged, dripping, spreading it all out on the sand. Then we hung our packs up among our already drying clothes, the almond a Christmas tree again.

Laurence had attempted to get the fire going, but eventually he gave up. We opened the two remaining cans of corned-beef hash for lunch, eating it cold with the last crumbled Crix crackers. Rachel carrying our plates up to the river to wash them off.

Our sleepingbags were already dry on the one side, and Laurence and I flipped them over.

"Going for a stroll down the beach," I told him. "Back in a minute."

I started down with a vaps. But after a few steps I turned around and went back up to the almond tree to retrieve my sneakers. Passing Rachel on the way, carrying our tin plates back down. Smiling at me.

All of us relieved, relaxed, having made it through the storm. Now with the sky so brilliantly clear. The scenery magnificent again. Little more for us to do than to savor our last few minutes in Madamas.

Soon as Eddoes came down from the valley—any time now— we'd repack our things and start off. An easy hike to Matelot. Leisurely drive back to town. We'd probably get to Oony's before dark. She'd be waiting for us with Shay-lee. We'd unpack the jeep, shower, then we'd all go together to Apsara's for dinner.

I wasn't exactly sure why I was heading down the beach. What I hoped to find down there. Maybe some evidence that I'd actually seen the Rover, abandoned there in the bush. That I wasn't going crazy—to recognize the flattened tracks where it'd come through the forest would be enough.

Why those policemen left it there I still had no idea. How they could have gotten it back to the village in such a hurry I didn't know either. But I wasn't much bothered by any of that: by now I'd comfortably resigned myself to the fact that I no longer knew much about the geography of this place. I was a stranger here.

Madamas had transformed itself completely in the two years of my absence.

The storm had erased all trace of the writing from the beach. Hard-packed sand now, the surface covered in goose-pimples left by the rain. Crispy. Pleasant against the soles of my feet. Even the wide trail left by our turtle going down to the water had disappeared. The line of dried black seaweed at the top of the beach blown away. The flimsy shells of the splattered eggs, all gone. Carried away. Every last one of them. The beach white, smooth, unblemished.

Only when I picked out the two half-dead casuarina trunks could I be sure I'd found the entrance. I started to put on my sneakers. Then I paused for a second: just beyond the two gray trunks, now I made out a seemingly well-worn path. Curving up into the bush, then through the forest deeper in. How I'd missed it this morning I hadn't a clue.

I started along it carrying my sneakers again. The path hard-packed sand, then dirt, smooth against my feet. Winding through the bush, between the palmetto palms and spindly pines, and then it started to climb. A minute later the trees opened up and I recognized the small rock mound where the Rover had been parked—only now I approached it from the side. The flattened plateau at the top of the mound—those policemen's lookout.

I walked out across it. Deciphering the two narrow, flattened tracks stretching from the edge of the cliff, back into the bushes. Less visible now following the rain, but clear enough. Knocked-over spindly pines farther along. Flattened bushes.

All right, I thought, and I turned to leave.

Then something caught my eye, over among the weeds. Beside the low bushes. Next to where the Rover had been parked, just beside one of the tire tracks—like two small orange sticks, sitting on top of a small pile of jet-black steelwool, wet and gleaming.

I walked over. Bent down to examine it. Picked up one of the orange sticks—a plastic Gillette disposable razor. The steelwool—a pile of human hair. Severed locks.

———

I needed to get Laurence aside. Alone. Tell him what I'd seen. Not that I hoped he could make sense of it—anymore than I could—but at least he could help me break the news to Rachel. Gently. Calmly. And then the two of us could convince her the only thing for us to do was to get going. Before our presence around here caused any more problems—for Eddoes and everybody else. If those severed dreadlocks belonged to him.

By the time I'd gotten back they'd already repacked—our sleeping-bags dry now along with everything else—rolled up and tied neatly across our packs. They'd dressed again, and now I pulled back on Laurence's borrowed jeans and my T-shirt and sneakers. With nothing else to do he'd managed to get the fire going. Even though the sun was bright, the afternoon warm now. Three of us sitting there on the hard sand, leaning against our packs, ready to leave. Waiting for Eddoes to show up and escort us through the forest.

But before I'd managed to get Laurence aside we heard what we'd been fearing most for three days. Since we'd arrived at Madamas: the low rumble of a motor vehicle. Distinct but distant—difficult to tell exactly which direction it was coming from. It stopped abruptly. Dead silence. We looked at each other.

Five minutes later our three police officers came trudging out of the bushes up near our kitchen—I'd expected them to come from the opposite direction, from down the beach. Their pressed khaki pants wet to midthigh after forging the river, tall black lace-up boots with the pantlegs tucked in all sopping, caked in sand. Still with their starched shirt-jacks unbuttoned, flapping at their sides, marinos showing.

They walked towards us, then the one with the beret said something to the other two, and they turned around and went back up to the kitchen. We could see them standing half-hidden among the trees, the tall grass, sharing a cigarette.

The officer with the beret came down and crouched before us, kneeling on one knee in the hard sand.

"Afternoon," he said quietly, and I knew we were in trouble.

He looked slowly from face to face. Then cleared his throat.

"Been a beating in the village," he said.

Now he pulled his beret off and held it folded against his thigh. And I was shocked to discover that his head was completely bald beneath it. Triangular wedges of sideburns like they'd been pasted on. Tan line running straight across his forehead where the cap cut it, the top half of his brow and his scalp like an overturned milky-brown bowl, going right around, smooth and glistening in the sun.

"But the boy OK," he said. "He strong, you unnastand? Go be right as rice soon enough."

He wiped the beret across his two-toned forehead.

"He back home with he mother, she futsing over he!"

He paused, "Them villagers in Pinnacle, you unnastand, they ain't used to no white people coming round the place. White woman!" He turned his head to spit into the fire. "And listen here: ain't nobody round these parts accustomed to no white woman bulling none a them bush-niggers, neither! Not out in the open, front everybody. Nobody round these parts never hear a noting like that before!"

He wiped the beret across his brow again. Shifting his crouch to the other knee.

"That go gainst the ways of tings round here, the natural order, you unnastand? Them boys, Abdul and Kojac, they get all excited, start to shooting off they focking mouth. Next thing you know everybody all worked-up. Vex. Hot-up with theyself. Want to hold and beat the boy. Buss he face. And ain't noting nobody could do to stop them neither. Not even the officers of the law."

"Just who are you referring to?" Rachel interrupted suddenly. "Which boy?"

He paused. Looked straight at her.

"Call he Eddoes. The carnival King. All-you friend."

Few more seconds of silence.

"But just as I saying, he go be all right. He strong. Them bush-niggers used to plenty sufferation. They skin hard. Back hard. Ain't no cause for worry to no white woman. Nor none a the rest a you foreigners neither." He spit again, sharp sizzle in the fire. "Onliest ting I got to advise—onliest ting I come here to inform, as an officer of the law—is for you people to carry yourself. Go on back to wherever you come from, England or America or wherever the fock it is!"

With that he stood, putting back on his beret. Lined up across his forehead again. He turned his back to us. Trudging in his water-logged, sand-caked boots back up the beach.

18

We sat leaning against our packs, staring into the fire, watching it smolder, slowly burn itself out. Nobody had spoken a word since the policemen left.

"I'm going up," Rachel said. She seemed to be speaking to both of us, but she was looking at me.

"Come if you like."

I got to my feet, following her.

Rachel led me into the bush, up the steep path, like she'd been climbing it all her life. When we walked out between the trees, onto the patch of grass in front of the house, the billygoat still grinding away, she continued walking. Straight towards the front stoop. Then, halfway across the grass, she stopped and turned around.

Rachel crossed her arms in front of her and pulled her T-shirt up over her head.

"Here," she handed it to me.

She bent down and pulled off her sneakers, dumping them into my arms. Reached and pulled off her jeans, the purple bikini bottom, all dumped into my arms.

By the time she turned around again Mother had appeared in the darkened doorway. Naked too, staring out at us. Her face blank—at least there was nothing I could read in it. Pain or anger or anything else. Her face seemed to me as blank and wide open as the sky above my head. She leaned against the empty doorframe. One hand holding the wrist of the other. The swelling at the side of her neck even larger than I remembered it.

Rachel walked up the three steps of the front stoop, straight past her, disappearing into the darkness. Mother didn't flinch, as though she hadn't seen Rachel walking past. Now she stared at me for a few more blank seconds, still holding her wrist. Then she turned into the house behind Rachel.

I stood there with the bundle of clothes in my arms. Not knowing what to do with myself. Eventually I turned and walked back over to the entrance of the path, setting the stuff down on the grass. Crouching there and looking down over the cliff, at the cove with the canoe pulled up onto the rocky shelf. I could even make out the safety line tied to a mangrove limb. Open sea stretching out beyond the canoe. Flat and glistening. Glassy tinkle of the smooth stones bouncing over each other each time the water receded. Washed up. Receded.

"They shaved his head," Rachel spoke quietly, almost distractedly. "Those policemen."

She was bent over pulling on her jeans, stepping back into her sneakers. She'd been crying, I knew, but now she seemed OK. Much better, anyway, than I expected.

"He looks like Laurence," she said. "So beautiful, lying there asleep like that, even as misshapen as his face is with all the pounding. His entire body. He is still so beautiful."

Suddenly her expression changed—as though a screen, a curtain had been pulled away from in front of it.

"All but his wrist!" her voice shaking. "Somebody'd bandaged them, but one bandage had pulled up so I could see. I couldn't look away, William. Couldn't turn my head. The skin chaffed right down to the bare white bones." She swallowed. "They handcuffed him to the rollbar of the jeep, according to Mother, and dragged him behind. And William," she looked up at me, "that was a kindness compared to what the villagers did."

"But he'll be all right," I said quickly. "He's strong. He's going to be all right!"

She paused, "Right as rice. Right as any of us."

Rachel walked past me, and I followed her into the bush. Back down to the beach.

19

Laurence left on the same flight as Rachel, to London, early the following morning. Three hours before my own flight departed for New York. Rachel had a connection onto Paris, then Nice, and I don't know if Laurence had decided, at the last minute, to change his flight and go to London because he wanted to see his father, or if he had another reason. Maybe he wanted to accompany Rachel? He never told me. And I was disappointed to learn I'd be flying back alone. But we were all relieved to be going someplace.

We'd managed, the previous afternoon, to get to Oony's just after dark, where we found her waiting for us with Shay-lee. Over a dozen little tin plates at Apsara's we tried, in whichever way we could, to explain what happened. Though we were still unclear about the details ourselves. Rachel, presumably, knew more, but she hardly opened her mouth. Hardly ate. She slept in Oony's spare room, Laurence and I on lounge chairs in the screened-in gallery. And Shay-lee woke us at dawn, already dressed in her Bee-wee uniform.

I'd gone into the departure lounge to see them off. Three of us hugging together for a second, then they turned and walked through the glass doors and that was that. End of story. Thank God. Suddenly I found myself sitting in an otherwise empty departure lounge with three hours' wait on my hands. So that I was relieved, considerably, to see the little old man arrive with his HiLo supermarket cart loaded with newpapers, whistling, pushing it over to his stand in the corner. I gave him a few minutes to get his papers arranged, everything set up, then I went over and bought a copy of the day's *Guardian*. The old man still whistling as he handed it to me. I didn't even take in the headline until I got back to my seat:

Carnival King Rapes British Tourist, Held and Beaten by Pinnacle Villagers

First Officer Barclay Pierre, recently stationed with two assistant policemen in the northern coastal village of Pinnacle, in the parish of St Johns, reported yesterday evening to his superiors and later to assembled members of the press including this Guardian *reporter, the events surrounding the beating of one Edward Baptiste, member of the notorious Earth People's clan, and better known to them as "Eddoes." Baptiste, however, is best known to the island at large for his recent successes on the Savannah mainstage, as only seven nights ago he represented Pete Minshall's River in the Dimanche Gras competition, where he was crowned King of the Bands.*

According to Officer Pierre, during the festival Baptiste befriended a group of British visitors, two males and one female, who had come to the island to celebrate the carnival. They are now safely returned to their homes in England and for their protection the officer has not surrendered their names.

As early as Ash Wednesday morning Baptiste is said to have quit town in order to return to his Earth People's clan. But he had instructed his British friends how to make their way on their own from Matelot, hiking through the rainforest to Madamas, a deserted beach where the tourists planned to camp for a few days. The beach is located not far from Pinnacle Village, and just beneath the cliffs of "Hell Valley," as it is known to the Earth People, the abandoned cocoa estate where the clan has squatted these past several years. Officer Pierre met the British group on Thursday afternoon, just after their arrival at Madamas, and he warned them at that time that camping was against jurisdiction on the public beach, and to keep their distance from the Earth People. He cautioned the foreigners that the clan was dangerous, known trouble makers, and possibly violent. Nevertheless that same evening Baptiste was reunited with his white friends. According to

Officer Pierre, it is also probable that at this time he gave them a quantity of cannabis, known to be cultivated copiously by the clan. Readers will further bear in mind that through all of his interactions with them Baptiste went stark naked, as is customary for the Earth People.

The following afternoon a group of young boys from Pinnacle came down to the beach to make friends with the British group, helping them cook their dinner over the campfire. Thereafter the boys returned home. Fortunately, however, the two eldest boys (going by the names of "Kojac" and "Abdul," according to Officer Pierre), wandered down the beach on their own. Not long after Baptiste arrived himself at Madamas to show the foreigners a leatherback that had crawled up on to the beach to lay. They all watched the turtle lay her eggs, after which the group returned to their camp, probably to take more cannabis. But sometime later that night Baptiste and the white woman apparently went off down the beach together. It is at this time that Baptiste is said to have held the woman and to have forced himself upon her.

The two young boys, Kojac and Abdul, hearing the woman's cries for help, and seeing the ensuing struggle, ran to Pinnacle and returned with several men from the village. These men held Baptiste, still there on the beach with the white woman. She escaped in the fray, fleeing to her friends at camp.

The men beat Baptiste, dragging him back to the village.

At this point, in the early hours of Saturday morning, Officer Pierre and his assistants were awakened by the row taking place not far from their own doorstep. But by the time they were able to pull the enraged villagers off Baptiste they'd beaten him soundly, shaved his head of its dreadlocks, and performed other acts of ridicule upon him. The policemen, under assault themselves by the vexed villagers, carried Baptiste, now unconscious, into the station. *Officer Pierre then went in search of Dr Mippipopolous, a British veterinary surgeon sent to Pinnacle by the Colonial Department (he had come to instruct the villagers in the production of pedigree "Cheshire" swine, in what is hoped will soon become a lucrative industry for them). Fortunately the doctor had his medical bag. He examined Baptiste and cleaned and dressed his wounds. Afterwards the policemen delivered Baptiste themselves to his mother in the valley. According to Officer Pierre, by the time he was handed over to "Mother Earth," as she is known to her clan, Baptiste had fully regained consciousness. It was his mother who then administered a "bush" tea as a sedative.*

A further statement was obtained yesterday evening by this reporter from Dr Mippipopolous (via Fr Agustini's ham radio at St Maggy's church in Matelot). Dr Mippipopolous reiterated Officer Pierre's assessment that, though soundly beaten, Baptiste will recover before long. "As for the operation itself," he said, "it is practically bloodless." According to the doctor, he had instructed the villagers in the surgery himself, on no less than a dozen of the young hogs, as it is the standard procedure to prevent the meat from souring in later adulthood. "A 2–3-cm incision is all that is required, through which the testis and attached vessels can be passed and pulled free. For the practiced villagers, amateur surgeons themselves, it could have taken them no longer than a couple of minutes."

In his statement to the press Officer Pierre expressed his deep regret over the incident. He remarked that due to the precarious position he now finds himself in with the Earth People, known for their violent history, in addition to the villagers, he has petitioned his superiors for relocation to another district. He recommends that the station at Pinnacle be closed permanently. "To sum things up," Officer Pierre remarked, "I have every confidence that my transfer will be granted, and we can all put this mishap behind us as soon as possible."

I emptied myself into my teaching. I had no choice, really, at least for the first few days, since I'd scheduled double makeup sessions for all my classes. And when class was done I took the kids out for pizza and beer. Even though I was exhausted. Even though I was dead broke. On my way to school in the early morning, when the train burst suddenly from underground so that the light that came screaming through the window was no longer artificial, and I looked, it was spring out there. Not rainy season. I could hardly ignore it.

When I'd arrived home in New York there was a letter waiting for me in my box. From Worthington Press—Ashling's father, my editor. I held the envelope in my teeth to rip it open. Climbing the stairs, duffelbag slung over my shoulder, suddenly excited, sure that it was a check: *We are sorry to inform you that due to the present general slump in British publishing, we are having to reduce our list by a number of titles. Unfortunately, your novel . . .*

Yet as I stood there beneath the dull yellow light, staring down at the letter in my hand, I was surprised to discover that I wasn't upset. On the contrary, I felt a kind of relief. Release. The whole thing, I knew from the start, had been a scam. I wasn't a novelist, I was a schoolteacher. I'd better get used to saying it again.

Three or four nights after my return I was lying in bed in my robe dutifully marking papers when the phone rang. I got up to answer it: Rachel, at Kennedy Airport. Just come through customs.

"You're all right?" I asked.

"I need to stay with you for a few days. It's not a problem?"

"Course not." Somehow, vaguely, I'd been expecting it.

"Truth is," I told her, "I've been worried about you."

"I'm fine. I will be. After a few days."

There was a pause, and I thought she'd hung up.

"Where is it?" she asked.

"My apartment?"

"You never told me."

I gave her the address. Put the phone down and got on some clothes. Then I tidied up as best I could, went down to wait for her in the street. A few minutes later a cab pulled up and Rachel got out. Wearing a khaki-colored raincoat and holding a small suitcase.

We hugged.

She let out a breath, "Flight seemed to take forever!"

"Come on," I took her suitcase from her. Held my arm around her going up the stairs.

"Hungry?" I asked coming through the door.

"Famished!"

It was a good sign.

"I'll call for something."

Rachel sat on my bed, smiling. "Not much of an apartment, William."

I saw her notice the dilapidated tennis racket I had hanging on the wall. Though she didn't comment.

"You haven't seen the view from the fire escape," I said.

"You'll show me tomorrow. First you need to feed me and put me to sleep. After that I promise not to be a burden."

"A-tall!" I sat on the bed beside her. "Always said I wanted to live together. Now's my chance. I couldn't be more pleased."

"I'll remind you of that in a few days." She turned to me, "Can you believe it? All my life I've needed people around. Constantly. Now I have to be alone. Few days and I'll be ready."

We sat there for several minutes. Only the soft rumble of cars in the streets down below. Gentle thump of tires over a manhole someplace.

"There something you don't know, William."

She paused. Again I had the feeling of the dream repeating itself.

"Mother told me," she continued. "Something terrible those villagers did to Eddoes. Something unimaginable."

I cleared my throat. "There was an article in the *Guardian*. Same morning we left. Those focking policemen had it printed to clear themselves."

"Jesus."

"It was all there."

Now she was crying, softly. I put my arms around her and held her to me, her trembling shoulders.

"I can't help feeling it's all . . . I'm devastated, William. It's just unbearable!"

"Shuuu," I whispered. "Shuuu."

————————

We slept together in my single bed, like the Bob Marley song, except it wasn't the Bob Marley song, and we slept buried under blankets. Rachel wearing one of my T-shirts. The next morning, when I awoke, we were still holding each other. I got up quietly and showered and dressed, and when I left Rachel was still fast asleep. I got back in the early evening. The apartment a shambles, Rachel's stuff spread all over, and mine. But there was a bouquet of flowers sitting in the middle of my desk, arranged in a jug of water. Rachel sitting on my bed wearing a plaid skirt and black tights, one of my thick wool sweaters, her hair pulled back. Compact-looking. Older, but not in the same tired, worn-down sort of way.

She'd spent the day walking, she said.

I grabbed my cigarettes and we climbed onto my chair and out the window, up a flight of steps to the top of the fire escape. The lights were just coming on, reflecting off my swatch of the East River. A fishing boat chugging slowly upstream, surrounded by a flock of noisy gulls. From there you could see the lights all the way up to the buildings uptown. We watched them slowly coming on. The western sky changing from faint pink to deep purple. It was the kind of view, if you had it through your living room window, you'd pay a million dollars for.

I smoked a couple of cigarettes. Then we went down and had dinner at the place in Chinatown with the ducks hanging in the greasy window, and the live chicken that tells fortunes. Fairer days was what she told us. And how could it be otherwise?

———

That's how we spent our time. When I got back from class we walked the streets together, Rachel's hand resting lightly in the crook of my arm.

One of those days, when we got back to the apartment, I found my answering machine blinking. Rachel standing behind me as I pressed the button.

It was Laurence, calling from London, with me jumping slightly at the sound of his voice: "Back in town early next week. Encouraging turn in Daddy's story. Let's get together for a drink, I'll fill you in—and we got to get those rackets out someday soon." He paused, "By the by, where's that cousin of yours? Called a couple of times and she's not at home. I'm a bit worried." He hung up.

We stood there for a few seconds. Then Rachel took a step forward and put her arms around me, from behind, pressing the side of her face against my back.

———

Our last morning together, a Saturday, she opened her eyes, actually smiling. We turned onto our sides, shifting beneath the heavy blankets, facing each other.

"What can we do that's special?" she asked. "It must be something extravagant."

"We can have breakfast at the All-American Diner."

"Perfect," she said.

Afterwards we started up Broadway, keeping to the sunny side. And we just kept walking. Two or three hours. All the way up the middle of lower Manhattan. Through Union Square, Madison Square, Times Square. Past Columbus Circle, and his statue, and the shining aluminum globe. All the way up to 59th St, bottom of Central Park, where we got sodas from a vendor and went to sit on the grass by the pond to drink them.

We still had a couple of hours and on Rachel's coaxing we got into one of those horse-drawn carriages for the tourists, lined up in front of Grand Army Plaza, in the southeast corner of the park. One of those carriages where you sit on the back, riding backwards. It took some getting used to, those stately English elms with their bright new leaves, receding into view. Like watching a film in reverse. Rachel settled back comfortably against my arm. Kids on rollerblades. Nannies on skates, their skirts blowing in the breeze. The horse's metal shoes clopping softly over the blacktop.

Our coachman slowed to a stop at a crossing. He pulled away smoothly again and Rachel pressed harder against me. She looked up.

"Oh, William," she said, "we could have been so good together."

Her eyes were the same color as the leaves gliding past. I wanted to let myself go, fall into them. It would have been so easy.

"Yes." I said. "Isn't it happy to think so?"

Acknowledgments

With thanks for his genius, inspiration, and friendship to Peter Minshall; I am indebted to Roland Littlewood and his *Pathology and Identity, The Work of Mother Earth in Trinidad* (this is not the book I'd have written for you or for Mother Earth, but perhaps one day I'll get to that one); to several novels in the carnival tradition, especially Earl Lovelace's *The Dragon Can't Dance,* Sam Selvon's *Moses Migrating,* Wilson Harris's *Trilogy,* and Laurence Scott's *Night Calypso;* to Peter Mason's *Bachanal! The Carnival Culture of Trinidad,* a handy reference; and to David Rudder. I thank my brother and sister, Brian and Janine, for unwavering support in all things; for friendship and encouragement my endless thanks go to Nicole Matos, Laura Mullen, Caryl Phillips, Cristina Garcia, Richard Patteson, Brad Morrow, and to Derek Walcott; to everyone at Grove/Atlantic, especially Judy Hottensen, Elisabeth Schmitz, Morgan Entrekin, and Dara Hyde; to all at Faber & Faber, especially Walter Donahue and Lee Brackstone; to Timo Ernamo; to Jorge Herralde; to Kim Witherspoon and all her associates; to Henriette Hubacher and Isabel Monteagudo; to three brilliant translators, Bernard Hoepffner, Anni Sumari, and Jesus Zulaika; and in memory of George Plimpton, blowing his bugle to gather us around. For the cover image of *The Sacred and the Profane,* King of the 1982 Carnival band Papillon, I am indebted to Kathryn Chan, photographer Noel Norton, masman Peter Samuel, and designer Peter Minshall. Plenty plenty love and thanks to all my friends, especially Merlene Samlalsingh, Lorraine and Ruth O'Connor, Rosemary Hezekiah, Meiling, Carol & Mark, Jack & Ana.

Author photograph: José Furio

Robert Antoni's first novel, *Divina Trace,* won the Commonwealth Writers Prize for Best New Book and is recognized as a landmark in Caribbean literature. He is the author of another novel, *Blessed Is the Fruit,* and the acclaimed story collection *My Grandmother's Erotic Folktales*. Antoni holds a master's degree from Johns Hopkins University and a doctorate from the Iowa Writers' Workshop, and divides his time between New York City, the Caribbean, and Barcelona.

www.robertantoni.com